NEW BEGINNINGS

E.R. nurse Leila Matthews's whole life turned upon one single sentence: "Brody, I'm pregnant." What she thought would be the happiest day of her life became a nightmare as she was abandoned by the father of her soon-to-be-born child. If her friend Jaxon wasn't there to pick up the pieces, she couldn't have coped. Then what had started out as a deep and abiding friendship became a soul-searing love.

Yet, while Jaxon is the man of her dreams, Leila doesn't want her child to grow up not knowing its father. The situation, a triangle involving tortured pasts and unstoppable passion, will test everyone involved. Both suitors will seek forgiveness for terrible mistakes, and Leila will soon be pulled between two powerful men: a handsome CEO who owns all he surveys, and an ex-soldier whose M.C. teeters on the brink of the unforgivable. Leila must choose the man who is perfect for her future…and for the future of her child.

PRAISE FOR *PUSHED,*
BOOK ONE IN THE *TORN* SERIES

"The chemistry between Brody and Lei is off the charts."
—L. Wilder, Author of *Combust*

"A.F. Crowell writes a sassy and intriguing story of lust, love, and heartbreak that will leave readers begging for more!"
—*USA Today* Bestselling Author Author J.C. Valentine

PULLED

BOOK TWO IN THE TORN SERIES

A. F. Crowell

www.BOROUGHSPUBLISHINGGROUP.com

PUBLISHER'S NOTE: This is a work of fiction. Names, characters, places and incidents either are the product of the author's imagination or are used fictitiously. Any resemblance to actual events, locales, business establishments or persons, living or dead, is coincidental. Boroughs Publishing Group does not have any control over and does not assume responsibility for author or third-party websites, blogs or critiques or their content.

PULLED
Copyright © 2015 A.F. Crowell

ISBN 978-1-942886-85-3

To Mark

For all the uncooked dinners, late nights on the computer and all the time I spent away from you and the boys. Thank you for supporting and encouraging me on this newfound dream.

I love you. Irrevocably. Then. Now. Always.

ACKNOWLEDGMENTS

There are so many people that have supported, encouraged, inspired and helped me during writing **Pulled**. I couldn't fit everyone in here, but there are a special few I have to acknowledge.

My husband Mark, I love you babe.

My boys James and Chase, guys Momma loves you to the moon and back. 555

My mom, she's my biggest supporter, loudest cheerleader and best friend, there are no words. I love you Momma!!!!

Emmaly, you really are the best. I love you girl. I am beyond grateful and blessed to have found you. You have become my BFF, partner in crime and the second voice in my head.

My PAs, Thai and Sierra. Wow, you guys really put up with a lot. I'm so forgetful and y'all having my back means the world. It's always an adventure and I'm glad to ride the rollercoaster with y'all beside me.

My street team, Sexy Little Sparks. From the bottom of my heart, I thank you.

Michelle, my publisher, editor and noodler. I am grateful to have you in my corner and trust you implicitly. Thank you!

TABLE OF CONTENTS

PULLED

Chapter One

~Leila~

Did you ever have a life-flashes-before-your-eyes moment? I was living one right now. The past three months played through my brain like an HBO special as I made my way to the lobby doors. I glanced back, once. Praying.

Praying was what I was doing when I met Brody Davis. I'd been pacing and praying my cop brother, Drew, would recover from the gunshot wound that threatened his life. Until that night, Drew had done an excellent job making sure I had never pinged his friend Brody's radar, but when Brody showed up at the hospital, all bets were off. Before I knew I was falling, Brody had invaded my life.

Now I was fleeing. The doorman of Brody's New York apartment building opened the door and asked if I needed a car brought around or a cab called. I thanked him, but told him I was waiting for someone.

I didn't have to wait long; Jaxon—my friend? my kinda sort of knight? *Can a biker be a knight?*—pulled up in a Lincoln Town Car, seconds after I came outside. Dressed in his form-fitting tuxedo, he waved off the driver and personally helped me in the backseat, then slid in beside me.

I kept praying, begging the fates to bring Brody to his senses. Didn't work. I looked back at the lobby as we pulled away to see Brody standing in the doorway. He saw me look back, but didn't try to stop me or to get my attention. That was the last time I would look back for him, I told myself. I had to start looking forward.

Alone.

"Leila, what the hell happened? What did he do to you?" Jaxon handed me a box of Kleenex.

"It's a long, story that I promise to tell you, but, please, not right now." *How do I explain that the man that swore he loves me more than anything just walked away when he found out I'm pregnant with his child?* "First, I need to find a flight back to Charleston. Then I need to get something to eat. After that I will give you all of the gut-wrenching details." *Maybe.* I blew my nose. The driver reached a small trash can back through the sliding privacy window.

"You can ride home with me." Jaxon brushed escaped tendrils of hair out of my eye. "I'm borrowin' the Semper Fi Fund company jet. You can crash with me tonight and then we'll fly home in the morning."

"Better I take a regular flight, dontcha think? Less complicated."

"Stop. You're flyin' with me. Besides, I'd be bored as shit on that thing by myself, so you'd be doing me a favor. Now, what do you like to eat? I'm staying at the Surrey, so we can get room service if ya want."

"Room service would be good," I mumbled.

Crap. Back to the same hotel as the Charity Ball Brody and I attended earlier this evening. I hadn't known Jaxon was going to be there, but boy was I glad he had been. I wasn't a *save me* kind of woman, but tonight, I didn't mind being rescued one bit. We drove a couple more blocks and pulled up to the hotel. "Ugh, I hope we don't run into anyone from the dinner. How embarrassing would that be?"

"Seriously, Leila, stop. You're fine. I don't give two shits what those snobby-ass fuckers think of me and neither should you." He opened the door and hopped out, grabbing my duffle as he went. He slung it over his shoulder before handing me out of the car.

"Thanks man." He tipped the driver and spun back around to me. "Ready?"

"I guess so." I tried not to sound so defeated but I was. Not thirty minutes earlier I had told the man I loved I was pregnant with his child and he flipped the fuck out on me. *Seriously, who does that does shit?*

Jaxon lead us through the lobby in the opposite direction of the ballroom to a bank of elevators. We went up to the fifteenth floor where he was staying in a suite with a separate bedroom. Thank you, God. I guessed the living room had a fold out couch, where I could stretch out and maybe get some rest.

Jaxon handed the room service menu to me. "Why don't you find something to eat? I'll put your bags down in the bedroom and change real quick."

"Okay." I cracked open the binder. "Hey," I called after him. "This menu doesn't have any prices, how am I supposed to order?"

"Just get whatever you want and don't worry about it. I got this," he hollered out from the bedroom.

I looked at Café Boulud's menu and as soon as I saw the lobster fettuccine I knew what I was having. "Jaxon, would you like something?"

"Nah, I'm good. I had dinner downstairs after you left." He came back out to the sitting area wearing a T-shirt with the sleeves cut off and a pair of basketball shorts. His hair, no longer tied back, was falling in his face. The sleeveless shirt showed off his massive biceps and tats. Most of the tattoos were black tribals with amazing shading; also, he had the USMC eagle, globe and anchor etched onto the top of his arm.

He sat down on the left side of the couch with his right leg stretched across the cushions. He grabbed the remote and turned on the large flat screen. Initially, I couldn't've cared less; the TV was welcome white noise drowning out the commotion in my brain. Then I heard commentators talking about football and immediately they caught my attention as they discussed the latest suspensions and injury report.

"Hey, can you turn that up?" I sat down at the other end of the couch.

"Sorry, I think I heard you ask me to turn it up." He bent his right leg in a little giving me enough room to sit cross-legged in my corner.

"Yeah, as in the volume. Make it louder, you follow?"

He turned the volume up slightly. "Sorry, it's not every day I hear a woman ask for *SportsCenter* to be turned up and not off."

"What can I say, I love football."

"I knew there was a reason I liked hangin' out with you." He turned his attention back to the video clip of a quarterback dislocating his ankle. "Ow, fuck. That's gotta hurt," he said as he grimaced.

"Can I use the phone to call down for the food?" My stomach grumbled. I was grateful it was hungry and not nauseous. God only knew how long that would last.

"Whatcha want? I'll call for you." He got up and walked to the desk.

I gave him my order and then tuned back in to ESPN. I leaned my head back and rested it on the top of the couch. Before I knew it, there was a knock at the door. I jumped up, but Jaxon caught my arm and answered the door. Part of me thought it might be Brody, coming to take me home. Would I have gone? Moot point. Jaxon opened the door for the attendant with the food.

Jaxon must have known what I was thinking, because he brought me the box of tissues. He sat close on the couch and pulled me into a hug. Which, honestly, was probably the worst thing he could have done, because his compassion was the last brick in my teetering wall. Tears welled, fell and flowed. I bawled my eyes out until I struggled to breathe and my body shook.

"I'm...mmm sorry," I babbled. "I don't know why I thought it would be Brody. I just hoped he'd change his mind." Knowing I needed to unburden myself—I wasn't a hold it in kind of woman—I shared the whole awful story with a now livid Jaxon.

"So let me get this shit straight, forget for a moment about that whore of an ex-girlfriend that he danced with at the ball. You get back to his place, tell him you're fuckin' pregnant and not only does he yell at you, he suggests you have an abortion *and* throws a fuckin' bottle past your head?" Jaxon's jaw muscle was working overtime while his fists open and closed in time to the cadence of his jaw muscle.

"Please," I sobbed. "I can't deal with you flipping out too. Please calm down." Like someone flipped a switch, I watched all the hostility leave his face.

"I'm sorry baby girl, you're right. You don't need this right now. I'll deal with that shit later." He walked to the granite counter, grabbed the food and brought it to me. "Let's get you fed and then you can climb in bed and get some sleep."

He sat the food on the coffee table in front of me and handed me the fork. As I took the fork from his hand, mine stilled. "Thanks Jaxon. Thanks for coming to get me and not rubbing it in my face. I know you don't like him—"

"He's a piece 'a shit, but you love him. I get it. I'll do my best to keep my two fuckin' cents to myself. For now," he said ominously.

Being pregnant cancelled out the usual I-can't-eat-'cause-I'm-upset thing. Two forkfuls and I was working it like a truck driver at an all-night diner. After I finished eating I went to the bathroom, washed my face, brushed my teeth, then walked into the bedroom. Jaxon was pulling a pillow off the plush king-size bed.

"What are you doing?" I stopped in the doorway of the bathroom.

"I only need one pillow and there's a blanket in the closet. You take the bed and I'll sleep on the fold-out in the couch." He turned and headed out to the living room.

"No, this is your suite, I'll take the fold-out. You were nice enough to pick me up, let me stay here and you're flying me home tomorrow. Taking your bed is just way too much." I grabbed my phone from my purse and started out the door when a huge, calloused hand grabbed my arm stopping me dead in my tracks, almost giving me whiplash.

"Listen here princess, I'm not letting you sleep on the couch. First of all, you're my guest and secondly, you're fuckin' pregnant. Get in the damn bed or I'll put your ass in the bed." He was as serious as a heart attack because I hesitated a second too long. He dropped the pillow, scooped me up and cradled me against his chest, then tossed me, yes, actually tossed like a sack of potatoes, onto the bed.

I bounced with a little squeal. "Okay, okay. I'll sleep in here on one condition. We share the bed. We both know those fold-outs are small. The bars will dig into your back all night, and your legs are gonna hang off."

"I'll be fine—" It was my turn to cut him off.

"No. I'll just go to the lobby and get my own room. I think I have enough money on my Amex to cover one night." I got out of the bed like I was going to get my stuff and go. Total bluff by the way, but he bought it.

"Fuck…Fine," he groaned. "You win, we'll both sleep in here," he acquiesced. He grabbed the pillow off the floor.

"Geez, for a man who pursued me relentlessly for weeks, you sure don't want any part of me now," I tried to make a joke.

"Aw, come on. You know it's not like that Lei." He plopped down on the left hand side of the bed. "I'm just tryin' to be a gentleman here. I don't do it often, so don't go getting used to it. And, sure as shit, don't tell anyone."

I smiled, pulled the white, soft down comforter back and climbed into bed. I threw two of the four pillows that were on my side onto the floor. Jaxon got up, went to the bathroom and shut the door. I fluffed one of the pillows under my head and wrapped my arms around the one I had tucked in front of me. I faced away from Jaxon's side of the bed and noticed the clock read 11:48 p.m. As I lay there watching the minutes roll by, I wondered what Brody was doing.

Was he still at the bar?

Was he drunk?

Was he okay?

The bathroom door opened, letting the light dance off the far wall for a brief moment. Jaxon settled down into the bed and said good night.

You know when you're so close to sleep that you can't even talk, but you can still hear and understand, yet the words just can't seem to find their way out? Well, that was me. I wanted to be able to say good night, but the words were trapped in my head. Because, for a change, my mouth went to sleep first.

*****

~Jaxon~

I climbed into bed and told her good night, even though all I got back was a mumbling mess of noises that may have been a good night. Instead, it sounded like she had marbles in her mouth. She was exhausted and emotionally worn the fuck out. What kinda fuckin' prick yells at his pregnant girlfriend? I wanted to snap his fuckin' neck.

Jesus, listening to her cry damn near broke me and I'm not dating her or having a fuckin' kid with her. What a fuckin' douchebag. I couldn't wait to see him once we were home. He was gonna be shitting his teeth out his ass when I was done with him.

God, I wanted to curl up behind her and hold her soft, warm body against me all night, but I couldn't. I promised her weeks ago, only friends. She didn't need to complicate her life with me right now. She had her damn hands full with pretty boy.

Laying there flat on my back, arms crossed behind my head, I stared at the ceiling, trying to fall asleep, but my mind had other plans. Hours later sleep finally came.

I woke to my face full of coppery red curls and a small body tucked into my side. This took me by surprise, because I forgot where I was for a split second. As I blinked my eyes open, I tilted my head down and saw her. She had her head resting on my chest, hand on my stomach, her leg over my thigh and my hand was snaked around her back resting on her hip. I wanted to lie there like that for days, just holding her, watching her dream and listening to her breathe. In that moment, she wasn't crying or hurting. She wasn't remembering the rejection and betrayal. She was at peace. When she woke it would all come crashing down around her again, but from here on out I vowed I would be there to try and help her pick up the pieces. *If she let me.*

She started to stir and she made the cutest noise. "Mmm Bro—" She stopped before she called out his whole name. She shot straight up in the bed and tensed. "Oh my God, Jax, I'm sorry. I didn't mean…I thought…shit. I didn't mean to almost call you him. I just…I guess I'm used to waking up with him…like this."

"Stop apologizing, it's all right, I get it, but I'm not sorry you curled up with me. I'm glad I got to hold you and comfort you. You needed it."

She relaxed a little, then climbed down from the bed, went to the bathroom and closed the door behind her. I knew she was probably sitting in there crying, so I decided to take her mind off of it for a little while.

"Aye, yo. We gotta get movin' princess. Plane's taking off in an hour and fifteen. So we need to leave like now." I grabbed my pack and shoved my clothes in. My tux hung in the closet so I pulled it out and threw it on the bed. I heard the toilet flush, then she came out.

"Will we have time to stop for a bite to eat? I'm actually hungry." She sounded shocked as she put her toothbrush in her duffle bag and tied her hair back again.

"You're surprised you're hungry? I thought women were hungry the entire pregnancy."

"I wish. I haven't been able to stop throwing up," she said, scrunching up her nose.

"We can pick up something on the way." I didn't do late. I was always on time.

"Do you mind if I take a quick shower?"

"'Course you can. I took mine last night, so it's all yours. I just gotta piss first." I walked past her into the bathroom.

We finished getting ready, then met the car service downstairs. We stopped at the Carnegie Deli for takeout and made it to the hanger with fifteen minutes to spare. We boarded the fourteen-passenger jet and ate our sandwiches in comfortable silence.

*****

~Leila~

Once we got home, I drove out to Johns Island, praying the entire way. One minute I prayed Brody would still be in New York. The next I prayed he would be there, waiting for me, ready to tell me what a fucking moron he had been.

I knocked on the door and Jane answered. I could see the pity in her eyes. She knew. I felt the tears welling up in my eyes, but I swallowed, blinked them back and went inside with her.

"Ruger is just out back. Come on. Let's go to the kitchen. Are you hungry? Can I make you some lunch?"

"No thanks Jane. I'm not hungry. I don't really have an appetite at the moment. I just want to get Ruger and get out of here before he gets home," I said, looking around for my Shepherd. "You don't know when Brody is getting in do you? Because I don't want him to find me here. He was mad enough last night. I just want to grab my stuff and my dog, then I will leave him alone, like he wants."

"Sweetie, I understand y'all are havin' some issues right now, but just please give him some time to come around. He will. He just needs time."

"Jane, I love you to death, but I don't have time to wait for him to pull his head out of his ass. I have a baby to think about. I need to worry about us." I placed my hand on my abdomen. "And how I am going to raise him or her by myself." *And here come the tears.* "I'm going to go get my things from Brody's bedroom. I won't be long."

Racing up the stairs, I grabbed everything of mine I could see. I left the gifts, jewelry and toys. I didn't need any more reminders of Brody than I already had. Throwing the duffle over my shoulder, I went back down to get Ruger.

"Jane, I think I have everything. If you see anything else, would you please just set it to the side and call me. I could meet you somewhere." I hit the bottom step. "You know, so I don't have to come back out here."

A look of panic flashed on her face and I knew.

He was home.

FML. Part of me wanted to run out the front door, but I could hear him talking to Ruger in the family room.

Fuck, fuckidy, fuck, fuck, fuck!

I knew he saw my car out front. It was pretty hard to miss. I felt a stray tear slip past and quickly wiped it away.

Jane walked to the foot of the stairs where I was standing and whispered, "Please Leila, just go talk to him. I promise he is calm. You know he won't yell in front of me. Or Ruger for that matter," she said with a little giggle, trying to lighten my mood.

"Jane, I don't think it's a good idea, I need to just go. He made it perfectly clear last night what his decision was. Please, don't make this any harder on me." I bit the inside of my cheek to distract myself from the emptiness and ache in my chest. We were whispering back and forth when I heard him clear his throat. I closed my eyes, looked down and took a deep breath.

You can do this. Just walk out the front door, whistle for Ruger and walk away. Come on, one foot in front of the other.

"I didn't expect to see you here," Brody whispered.

"Yeah, well, I guess I could say the same about you. I just came to get my dog and my clothes. Don't worry, I am leaving now and you won't have to see me again." I barely slowed for a breath. "I'm sorry, if I would have known you were going to be home so quickly, I would've called Jane and met her somewhere else." I whistled and Ruger came trotting over. Grabbing the large duffle bag and a small box off the stairs, I bolted for the front door.

He stood there quietly, not moving and watched me hauling all of my shit out of his house. Jane ran ahead of me to get the door, all the while glaring back at Brody. And let me tell you, if looks could kill Brody would have been bloody and dismembered on the hardwood foyer.

"Leila, wait," he finally spoke and my heart seized. He walked over and reached into the back pocket of his Levi's. He pulled out the sonogram, looked at it once and then extended it out to me. "I thought you might want this back. I'm sure it's the only one and you should have it."

He might as well have pulled a knife out and stabbed me in the chest.

"Thanks." I fought with every last fiber of my being not to cry. I balanced the box on my knee and took the picture from him, our hands brushed. I put the picture on top of the box, turned on my heel and fled. Jane helped me out to my car. She got Ruger loaded up and gave me a long hug.

"Jane, please call me anytime. We could have lunch." I felt like I was losing a friend. *I was.*

"I'd like that my sweet girl. I'll call you later this week and make arrangements." She released me with tears in her eyes. I was grateful I wasn't the only one crying this time.

"Bye Jane. Take care of him please. Even though I hate him right now, I do still love him.…I probably always will."

She smiled at me as I got in my car, started the engine and let the music distract me. Ruger sat in the front seat with his head out the window as I put it in gear and drove away.

I made it all the way home, into the house and upstairs before the dam burst. I sat in the middle of my bedroom floor, holding the sonogram and just wept. I cried for my broken heart, hurt pride, abandoned baby and the end of our relationship.

After who knew how long, I got up, washed my face and went downstairs. I needed to call Drew. He was always my rock, the one person I could always count on, no matter what. Just as I picked up my phone to call him there was a knock at the door. My stomach jumped sideways. Brody?

I ran to the door and flung it open without even looking.

"Jaxon, hey, what are you doing here?" Disappointed didn't even begin to cover how I felt. Which was horrible, Jaxon was a good guy, despite his gruff appearance.

"Hey princess, I just wanted to stop by and check on you. Make sure you got back okay from gettin' your shit." He stopped and looked into my eyes as he stepped just inside the front door. "He was there, wasn't he? Did he give you a hard time?"

"Yes, he showed up while I was there packing my stuff. He didn't stay much of anything. He only gave me the sonogram of the baby back." God, saying it out loud shattered my heart yet again. I sighed and exhaled loudly. "Do you wanna come in?"

"That's up to you. If you wanna talk or just want someone here, I can chill for a while. Or I can go and leave you to your own devices. Up to you," he proposed.

"Honestly, I'm not really in the mood to hang out or talk. I just wanna curl up, go to sleep and wake up from the nightmare that has become my life."

"I'll go. How 'bout I stop over tomorrow and take you to get some breakfast?" he asked, but it didn't really sound like a question. Nothing he ever said sounded like a question or an option. Nope, it just sounded like that's what you were doing, like it or not.

"Sure, sounds good."

"Maybe I can get you on the back of my bike. Before you say no, it's only a few blocks and you'll love it," he said with a grin.

"Yes to breakfast and we'll see to the ride." I wasn't making any promises. Jaxon pulled me into a comforting embrace, leaned down and kissed me on the top of my head.

"See ya bright and early baby girl. I'll text before I show up. Get some rest." He opened the door and stepped across the threshold.

"Thanks for checking on me, and for being so understanding." I gave him a weak smile before he pulled the door shut.

Chapter Two

~Jaxon~

I hated to leave her all alone at her place, but she didn't want to be around anyone. Hell, who could blame her? She just had her heart ripped out and served up on a silver fuckin' platter. I'd give her today to sulk, mope, eat ice cream and cry, but tomorrow, I was taking her out for a ride. She said she'd never ridden before, but said she was scared to even try. I think once she felt her hair dancing in the wind and felt the rumble of power between her legs, she'd be beggin' me to take her for a ride.

I pulled up to the clubhouse of the Marines MC. It was a drab, beige two-story building next to a dirt parking lot. We had occupied this hole in the wall for years. It looked like an old abandoned building, but you know what they say about looks. Once you walk in through the first set of doors, you are stopped another five feet in by a set of secured, thick metal doors. We had the place wired with cameras and an intercom system. No one was coming in unless we let them.

From the looks of it, most of the brothers were here. It was Sunday afternoon and I was late for church. Church was our weekly meeting that just coincidentally was on Sunday this week. I walked in, punched in a code and the metal door buzzed, signaling I could enter. The inner sanctum looked like a nightclub with its long bar to the right, painted black concrete floors, round tables and couches. There were a few other rooms on the first floor. The office, kitchen, liquor cage, bathrooms and laundry room were all situated to the left in the building. On the second floor there were ten bedrooms. Some of us had a permanent room here, while others took turns sharing. Of course, we all had homes, but often crashed here.

Mark, the president, Viper, the sergeant-at-arms, Dig, the secretary, and Drill, the treasurer were all seated around the table in the office when I entered.

"Nice of ya to fuckin' show up, Remi," Dig started giving me shit before I shut the door.

"Fuck off, pussy. I just got home from New York." I took my seat and filled them in on the event. There was much discussion of new prospects, budgets and requests for assistance. We voted on a few items before the official meeting was over.

"You made it home just in time for one hell of a party. One of the prospects is in a band, and they're playin' tonight. Bonfire out back, burgers, beer, the whole nine yards." Viper slapped me on the back.

"I might chill for a while, but I got somewhere to be in the morning." I followed Viper, Dig and Mark out to the bar. Drill was already there talking with one of the new girls whose name I couldn't remember.

"Hey Remi," Kat purred in my ear. "I missed you the last couple of nights. Wanna take a walk with me?"

I knew what she was getting at but I wasn't in the mood to deal with her shit right now. "Nah, I'm gonna have a beer and relax with the boys. Maybe next time."

"Fine, whatever. Dig, you up for some fun?" She was trying to make me jealous, but the joke's on her, I don't get jealous. Especially not over some club pussy.

"Have fun Dig." I slapped his shoulder with a boisterous chuckle.

"Don't mind if I do, since you're not gonna." Dig grabbed Kat around her waist and pulled her to him. "See y'all in a couple hours."

The rest of us sat around drinking and bullshitting until the band showed up and the sun went down. Finally I managed to pry Wendy off me about 11:30 and made a run for the door. No matter how many times I told her I wasn't interested, she still tried. I wasn't in the mood to deal with her. I was eager to get home, so I could check on Leila tomorrow.

*****

~Leila~

I didn't sleep for shit last night. Every time I would fall off, I thought I heard my phone go off or would wake up just to check it. After about 3:30 a.m., I finally turned it off so I wouldn't be tempted.

"He's not going to call or text or email or Facebook message me," I told the ceiling. Then, I put my phone on the dresser and went to sleep.

About 7:45 a.m., I got up and turned on the TV. I watched the news for a little and then remembered my breakfast with Jaxon. Oh shit, he was gonna text me. I jumped out of bed and grabbed my phone. When it finally powered on I saw I had three text messages. One from my BFF, Barb, asking how the weekend went. Ughhhhh, I wasn't looking forward to that conversation. One from Drew, checking in, and one from Jaxon, telling me to be ready at 8:30.

"Shit." I threw the phone on the bed and ran to the shower having fifteen minutes to get ready. Thankfully, it was only breakfast with Jaxon. Okay, that sounded bad, I didn't mean it like that. I just meant I didn't have to dress up for breakfast and Jaxon was laid back. I didn't feel like I needed to go overboard and do my hair and make up for breakfast. He didn't strike me as the high maintenance kind of guy Brody was. Great, there went the leaky faucet that was my face. I had to stop. I was stronger than this.

Shower done, I patted my hair dry, then threw on some clothes. Nothing special just a pair of jeans, a fitted white shirt and my brown oiled Danskos. I let Ruger out the back door just as Jaxon knocked on the front door.

Swinging open the door, I said, "You're early. I still have five minutes left to finish—" Oh fuck, that was not who I expected.

There on my front porch stood Brody, with a brown, double handle shopping bag. A bag, I was sure was full of my shit. Oh dear God, please let me be dreaming. This couldn't be happening.

"Sorry, were you expecting someone?" He looked agitated.

"What're you doing here?" I prayed to God Jaxon was running late.

"You left your dresses and some other things."

"I told Jane I'd meet her, you didn't need to come over here. Besides, the dresses aren't mine. You bought them, so you keep them. Maybe you can give them to the next bed warmer…You need to leave."

"Leila, you aren't a bed warmer—"

"Weren't Brody. As in the past." I seriously wanted to slam the door in his face. "It doesn't matter, I don't want whatever is in that bag. I just want you to go…please." I looked down at my feet, closed my eyes and mumbled, "Don't make this any harder on me."

I started to shut the door because I could feel the tears welling up and my nose starting to burn. Brody caught the door. "I'm sorry Lei."

"No. You don't get to call me that anymore. My name is Leila. And if you were truly sorry, you wouldn't be here. If you were really sorry, you would man the fuck up." He dropped his hand from the door. "Just as I thought. Goodbye, Brody. Please don't come over here again. It's too hard to see you anymore."

I shut the door in his face and slid down the back of the door. I could still hear him through the door. "I am sorry.…Take care of yourself."

Cue the tissues. The dam burst and I was sobbing. I sat there for a few minutes before I heard the familiar rumble of a Harley and picked myself up off the floor. Literally and figuratively. Jaxon had become a friend and I could really use a friend right now. Barb was working and I'm sure Drake was on call. I wasn't ready to tell Drew yet. He would be the first one to punch Brody in the face and the same person to say I told you so. So no, I didn't call Drew. I was sure Brody would be telling him soon enough.

Jaxon knocked on the door as I opened it. "You ready?" he asked with a cocky smile and a gleam in his bright green eyes. He was wearing well-worn Levi's that were ripped and frayed at the hem, a gray USMC T-shirt, leather vest and shit-kicker black boots.

"Yeah." I gave him a forced smile.

"Wait, what's up? Why do you look worse this morning than you did last night?"

"Gee, thanks. Come in, I need to let Ruger in the house and grab my purse." I turned and walked back toward the rear of the condo.

"What happened between the time I left here last night and now?" he barked. His gruff voice startled me, causing me to jump slightly. He must've seen; he modulated his tone. "Sorry, I just wanna know whose ass to beat for upsetting you. I didn't mean to scare you."

"It's okay, you didn't scare me. I was just thinking."

I opened the back door to an awaiting Shepherd that went bounding through the house to Jaxon. I was really surprised he didn't go into "protect mom mode." When I made it back to the living room, Jaxon was leaning on the back of the beige leather sectional petting Ruger.

"So you wanna tell me what the hell's goin' on?"

I really wanted to say no, but instead I went with, "Later. Right now I just want food. Lately, mornings have sucked, but it's getting better, knock on wood." I knocked on the dining room table.

"Well then, let's go, princess."

"My car is out back. We can go this way." I tilted my head toward the back door.

"Oh no, I told you. We're goin' for a ride on the bike, so get your ass out front." He left no room for negotiations.

"But Jax, I'm pregnant. I don't think it's safe." I was no longer just scared to death of road rash. I had this tiny human to take into consideration.

"You'll be fine. We're only goin' a few miles and you'll be in good hands. Enough bullshittin', let's go." He opened the front door and walked out. I grumbled and huffed as I shut and locked the door.

Once out front, I walked over to the black Shadow Rocket, where Jaxon held out a helmet to me. It was an all-black half helmet with a faint grey skull airbrushed on the top.

"Here, I brought this for ya. I had a feelin' you'd use it as an excuse to not ride with me."

I put it on and tried to adjust the chin strap. "Where's yours?"

He looked at me like I had just insulted him. "That's mine," he said nodding up to the helmet covering my head. "I only wear that shit on rides when we go through states that have helmet laws."

"Oh." I wanted to tell him he was stupid and as a trauma nurse just how many guys I had seen in the ER that would have lived if they had been wearing a helmet. But I wasn't in the mood to argue and I really wanted some French toast. Oh, and some turkey bacon. I loved turkey bacon.

He threw his long, thick leg over the bike, sat down and then looked back at me. "What are you waitin' for? Hop on."

Fuck, how did I get on without looking like a complete moron? I put my right hand on Jaxon's right shoulder, lifted my left leg awkwardly and almost lost my balance. This felt all wrong. I rode horses for years and always mounted from the left.

"Fuck that." I walked around to the other side, put my foot on the peg, grabbed Jaxon's shoulders and popped up there like it was a quarter horse. I smiled, proud of myself. "Much better."

Jaxon just shook his head and started the bike. I was ready for the loud roar of the engine, but I wasn't ready for the vibration between my legs. Whoa!

"Wrap your arms around me and hold on princess."

I had to scoot forward and press my chest to his back in order to get my arms around his wide torso. My thighs hugged his ass and my hands felt his taut abs. I was so tempted to rub my hands up and down them to count just how many he had in his pack. I'm guessing six, but as ripped and cut as he felt, he might even have had the elusive eight, but there was no way I was going to find out.

"Feel somethin' ya like?" He turned his head back toward me with a smirk.

"Just drive Jax." I shook my head and rolled my eyes.

He leaned the bike slightly, kicked the stand back and off we flew. I held on for dear life, closing my eyes, too scared to look until we slowed down at the first light. I looked around to get my bearings and he took off again. As we rode, I started to relax and actually opened my eyes. I hate to admit it, but he was right. The way the wind felt against my skin was almost freeing. The cool air on the warm day was refreshing and most welcomed after the shit-show of a day I had Saturday. I laid my head on his back remembering the look in Brody's eyes. I wanted to forget. I wanted to erase the last three months and pretend like I wasn't totally and utterly in love with that raging asshole pile of shit, but God had other plans for me. He left me with a piece of Brody. A piece I would carry for nine months and love for the rest of my life. Brody couldn't take that away, not like he took himself and his love away from me.

We pulled into the parking lot of Toast, which I'd never been to before, but Jaxon said it had the best breakfast around. We got inside and were seated, and as we looked over the menu, the waitress came over.

"Good morning folks, what can I get y'all to drink? Bottomless mimosas are only fourteen dollars and a great way to start out the day." She was an older lady with a thick Charlestonian accent.

"God, a mimosa sounds really good." I wasn't actually planning on ordering one, just stating a fact but I guess Jaxon didn't realize that.

"Oh fuck no, you're pregnant babe. You can't drink anymore," he said and glared at me.

"Would you chill the hell out, I didn't order one. I just said it sounded good. I'm well aware of the fact that I'm pregnant, you Neanderthal. Geesh."

"Congratulations. Is this y'all's first baby?"

We both answered at the same time.

He said yes while I said no.

I turned to the waitress who looked really confused. "Sorry, I'll just have a large OJ and a water."

"Same, thanks," Jax said. I could feel him staring at me, but I kept looking at the menu.

"So what are you getting?" I asked without looking up.

"You wanna talk about what just happened?"

"I don't know what you're talkin' about." Yep, just plays dumb Leila, smart.

"'Kay. Fine. You wanna tell me what happened since I left ya last night?" His hooded eyes bored unrelentingly into me as I looked up at him.

I exhaled a loud, long drawn-out breath. "Fine. What do you want first? My horrible morning or the waitress's loaded question?"

"Waitress, first. I shouldn't have answered the way I did. I wasn't thinking about it being our first child, just that it's your first child. It is, isn't it?" he asked curiously.

I didn't read anything into his question. "Yes, first pregnancy, and first baby."

"So now that that's settled, wanna explain your horrible morning?" He was not going to let it go. He was like a rabid dog with a bone.

"Do I have to?" I picked my menu back up.

Silence.

I guess that was a resounding yes. Great. "Before I say anything, remember we are in a restaurant. Okay?"

"No promises baby girl," he said with his teeth clenched.

"Just before you got to my place there was a knock at the door. I thought it was you, so I opened it and said you were early, but it wasn't you." I pulled the menu back up, pretending to look it over. "It was him...Brody."

"He has some fuckin' balls just fuckin' showin' up. What'd he want?" His words came out like daggers.

"He brought over the dresses he bought me and some other things." Jax groaned. "I told him to keep them for his next bed warmer, that I didn't want anything he gave me. I asked him not to come by anymore, that it was too hard to see him. He, of course, said he was sorry. Which is when I told him if he was really sorry he wouldn't be doing this to me."

A low growl came from Jaxon just before he slammed his menu down on the table. "I'm sorry, he's such a fuckin' piece 'a shit. You deserve so much better. He should be thanking God right now, I didn't see his pathetic ass this morning." The fury rolled off of him in waves.

Our waitress came back to take our order. "What can I get y'all for breakfast?"

"I'll have the French toast with bacon, please."

Jaxon picked up his menu and handed it to the waitress. "I'll have the corned beef hash and eggs, over medium, with toast."

She scribbled down our orders, took our menus with a smile and went to the back.

"Jax, please don't. I know what you're thinking, but it won't change anything. Maybe he just needs time to come around. Maybe after a couple of weeks he will." I stopped myself. I was hoping he would come crawling back and beg me to take him back. Would I? If he came back, would I be able to forgive him? "I don't know, but I don't want you doing anything to him. Please. For me?"

He sat quietly, emerald eyes tense, brow wrinkled. Then he finally agreed. "Fine. For now, I won't do anything."

"And you won't have anyone else do anything," I added wanting to be sure.

"Yeah. Man, that prick's lucky. Here he up and dumped you, while you're pregnant with his baby, and you're still defendin' him."

"Whoa, I'm not defending him. I just don't want anything to happen to him. There's a huge difference."

"All right, let's change subjects. What're you gonna do today?"

"Well, other than breakfast with you, not a whole lot. I have an ultrasound appointment at eleven thirty but that's about it." I took out my phone to check the time. It was only 9:15.

"You gonna go alone?" he asked in a sympathetic voice.

"Yep, that's the plan. I already saw the OB last week and she did a quick scan in the office, but this is to get a measurement to see exactly how far along I am. No big deal." I tried to play it off.

Our breakfast arrived before he could say anything. I was starving and dug right in. Yum, the French toast was out of this world good.

"Mmm, this is delicious. How is yours?" I looked over to his plate that was damn near empty. "Wow, hungry were ya?"

"Yeah, I didn't eat much yesterday." He shoveled more corned beef and eggs in.

We finished our meal and Jaxon insisted on paying. I let him, with minimal fussing. I just didn't have the energy to argue with him. We left the restaurant and climbed back on his bike, keeping my eyes open all the way home. And damn if he wasn't right, I was starting to enjoy this.

We got back to my place about 10:00 and I invited him in. I really didn't want to be alone right now. I knew once 11:30 rolled around I would feel lonelier than I had felt since my mom died. The thought opened a floodgate of emotions that I didn't want to deal with right now. So I did what I do best and I buried it.

"So I have to leave in about an hour, wanna just watch some TV and talk?" I walked over and let Ruger out back.

"Sounds good to me. Whatcha wanna talk about?" he asked as he sat down on the large sectional.

"We talked about what I do and what you do now, but we've never really talked about what you did as a Marine." I wasn't sure if he would even want to talk about that time in his life.

"Don't take this the wrong way, but I don't talk about it." He shut down real fast. His eyes got dark and his shoulders tensed. Okay, touchy subject.

"Sorry, I just wondered where all you were stationed. I've always wanted to travel." I place my hand on my abdomen. "Guess I won't really get that chance now, huh."

"Leila, people travel with kids all the time. You'll still be able to travel." He paused, thinking. "If you could go anywhere, where would you go?"

"Anywhere?" I thought for a second. "I would love to go to Hawaii, or Egypt. I want to see the pyramids and the Sphinx. I'm so fascinated by ancient Egypt."

He laughed. "So mummies and hieroglyphics?"

I just smiled and shook my head. "Oh, and Bora Bora. I love the pictures of the blue water. I've always wanted to stay in one of those little tiki huts, out over the water." My eyes widen at the thought.

"You'll go one day. Just 'cause you're havin' a baby doesn't mean you can't still go places." He made it sound so easy.

"It's not that easy Jaxon." I pulled my knees up to my chest. "Money's gonna be tight. I mean, I make decent money, but as a single mom, it's not going to be easy, ya know? It's not like I have parents I can ask to keep the baby for me."

"Leila, I'll be here. I'll help you as much as you want me to." He turned to look at me. "And you will get help from that asshole. He's more than financially capable—"

"No Jaxon. I don't want a goddamned thing from him. If I take his money, then he will be entitled to see the baby. So no, I won't be asking Brody for anything." I turned back to face the TV. "I'll have a plan in place with Barb and Drew, once I tell him. I do appreciate your offer to help out though. It's very sweet of you and I may even take you up on it." I was touched by his offer. "But if our friendship is going to remain intact, you can't bring him up anymore. I don't want anything from him and you mentioning him doesn't help me to move past this."

"Got it," he said and nodded.

We watched HGTV quietly and before I knew it, the reminder on my phone was going off. It was time to chug twenty-four ounces of water. First, I needed to pee. I swear, I spent more time in my bathroom over the last week than I probably had in the last four years I had lived here. I felt like I had the bladder of a four year old. I ran off to the bathroom, then the kitchen for a bottle of water. When I came back to the living room, Jaxon stood up and turned off the TV.

"I need to head out. Gotta get over to the hospital for my appointment. Thanks for everything Jax." I smiled and put my arms around his waist.

He bent down and kissed the top of my head. "Call me later, 'kay?"

"Will do. Thanks for being here and listenin'."

"Anytime princess." He winked.

I locked the door after he closed it. Set the alarm and went out the back to the Challenger.

Chapter Three

~Leila~

Pulling into the parking garage off Bee Street I found a spot on the third level. Finishing my water on the way, I got to the Prenatal Wellness Center with ten minutes to spare. I hated being late. I pulled the door open and walked into the waiting area, signed in and took a seat. Grabbing my phone, I sent a text to Drew telling him I needed to talk to him and asked him when he could come over. I also sent Barb a text and told her that the weekend was almost the worst of my life and that Brody and I were over. Immediately I got a text back from Barb but replied that I was busy and would call her later.

Ugh, I needed to pee...again. *Damn you tiny baby for hijacking my bladder.* I hoped they weren't running late, I didn't know how long I can hold it. I uncrossed and recrossed my legs.

"I don't think that's gonna help," a deep voice said to me. I looked up and saw Jaxon's smiling face.

"What are you doing here?" I was surprised to see him.

He sat down next to me. "I didn't want you to go through this alone. I knew you didn't want to ask, so I followed you."

I started to silently cry, words stuck in my throat.

"If I was wrong, I can leave. Shit, Lei, don't cry. I'll go." He stood to leave, but I grabbed his hand.

"No, don't go. I'm not crying because of that, I'm happy that you're here. Thank you." I pulled him back into the seat. Well, he let me. I knew better than to think I could make him do anything. He kept my hand in his and gave it a small squeeze of encouragement. "Even if you're kind of a stalker," I said with a giggle.

"I was serious when I said I'd be here for ya. Not all men…never mind." He stopped himself before berating Brody again. "All you have to do is ask, I'll always make time for ya."

"So if I have a two a.m. craving for peanut butter and pickles I can call you?" I grinned, testing our friendship.

"Woman, if you call my ass at two in the morning it better not be for a food craving." His eyes said more than his words. I felt a burst of arousal come out of nowhere. "Peanut butter and pickles?" He made a sour face.

"Leila Matthews," a nurse called. I stood and she held the door.

I looked back at Jax, still sitting in the chair, cocked my head and said, "Are you comin'? Or are you gonna hold my hand from out here?"

"Uh, I can go back with ya?" he asked with uncertainty painted across his face.

"Yes, of course, Daddy," the nurse said before I could answer him.

"Uh, he's—" Jaxon stopped me.

"I'm just a little nervous, that's all," he said and gave me this weird look.

"Y'all can follow me, we are gonna go right in here. Ms. Matthews, please undress from the waist down, use the sheet to cover up and I'll be back in just a minute." She shut the door as she walked out. The room was dim and small. There was a blue exam table, pink chair, ultrasound machine and a large flat screen mounted near the foot of the exam table.

"Uh, I'll just turn around." Jaxon suddenly really did look nervous. "About what the nurse said, I didn't want her thinking you were here alone. Ya know without the dad, like some teenager or some shit."

"Jax, while I appreciate the sentiment, the truth is I am here without the dad. He's not gonna be here for any of these. I don't care what anyone thinks of me." I undressed and hopped up on the table. "Now, can you open the door so she'll come in here and do this scan before I pee myself?"

He opened the door and the ultrasound tech came in immediately.

"We'll do the abdominal first, then you can use the bathroom and then we'll do the transvaginal. Any questions?" she asked as she was setting up the machine.

"Nope, I'm good. Jaxon?" I looked over at him.

"Uh, nah."

"This shouldn't be cold, just a little slimy." She squirted the Aquasonic blue goo on my belly and started rubbing the transducer around. I lay there staring up at the TV and all I could think about was that if she pushed much harder I would be really embarrassed. All of the sudden, like a snowy TV picture getting clear, the baby appeared.

"Oh, there's y'all's little peanut. I'll just take a few quick pictures, then you can empty your bladder," she said as she clicked away on the keyboard.

"Holy shit Lei, I can actually see it." Jaxon was amazed by the technology. "How big is it?"

"I'll be able to get a measurement with the transvaginal wand." She wiped the gel off my belly. "You can use the bathroom now."

"Oh, thank you sweet baby Jesus." I gripped the sheet and jumped down and almost careened right into Jaxon. Luckily, there was a bathroom between each of the rooms. *Ahhh, sweet relief.* I washed my hands and went back out to the exam table.

"If you could place your feet in the stirrups." She got the wand ready. I lay down, put my feet in the stirrups and slid down so my butt was hanging off. I looked over to where Jax was still sitting in the chair, but was now wide-eyed.

"Wait, whatcha doing with—" He stopped as the tech gently slid the wand into my vagina and the screen came to life again. "Oh holy shit, you just put that whole thing up there?"

I burst out laughing. "No Jax, just a little and then she moves it around to see my uterus and the baby. It's okay, it doesn't hurt."

She adjusted the screen and wiggled the wand a little and there it was. My baby. She took a few measurements, then looked at me. "So you seem to be measuring about eight and a half weeks with a due date of April twenty-third." She smiled. "Let's get you some good pictures to share." She stopped and pointed to a tiny fluttering. "There's the heart. Do you want to listen?"

Before I could answer, Jaxon did. "Hell yeah."

With a click of a button the room echoed with the whoosh, whoosh, whoosh, whoosh and big, fat happy tears streamed down my cheeks. Jaxon came over and looked down at me with the biggest smile I'd ever seen him wear.

"That's his tiny little heart beating? Wow, it's so amazing." He swiped his large thumb across my cheek catching the tears.

The tech finished and removed the wand. "I'll give y'all a minute and let you get dressed, I'll meet y'all up front with the pictures. Did you want a video too?"

"Yes," I said with a smile. She closed the door quietly as I continued to weep like an idiot.

"Don't cry baby girl." He cradled me against his chest. "I'm with you through this, here on out. I'm not lettin' ya go through this alone, no matter what." He kissed the top of my head. "Now get dressed so we can go get those pictures of your boy."

I let out a little laugh. "What makes you think it's a boy? The gender hasn't even been determined. It's still little more than an embryo."

"Just a hunch. Get dressed, I'll turn around."

"I have to pee again, so I'll get dressed in the bathroom." I gathered my clothes, happy for the excuse to be alone for a few minutes. I closed the bathroom door, then sank to my knees. The last ultrasound was quick; just to confirm I was pregnant. But today— once I heard the baby's heartbeat, I lost it. Nothing could have prepared me for that. Then, seeing the tiny little fluttering heart was a miracle, and a balm. I forgot all of my heartache and pain. In a rush, my heart filled with joy and with an overwhelming need to protect this child with everything I had. Mixed in the emotional swill was fear; fear of the unknown and fear of failure, for starters. But above all else was an absolute feeling of love. I loved this child, even if Brody didn't.

After a taking a few minutes to compose myself, I used the bathroom, got dressed and walked with Jax back to the front. The tech was waiting with a CD and six 5x7 pictures. We thanked her, left the building and made plans to have dinner at my place later. Right now, I needed some more me time.

I made it back to my place and called Barb. I blubbered and sobbed, telling her the nightmare that had been my weekend with Brody.

"That fucking twatwaffle. Who does shit like that? I mean I know it was unexpected but Jesus fucking Christ, Lei. I can't believe he threw a bottle past your head. I swear to God, if I ever see that ass clown out in public I'm totally junk-punching him." She always knew what to do or say to make me laugh.

"Okay," she continued. "We need to do dinner tonight, you have to make sure you are eating. I know how you are when you're upset, but honey, you have a baby to think about now."

"Actually, I have been eating *Mom*. Jaxon took me to breakfast and—"

"Jaxon? As in the hot biker guys?" she shrieked.

"Yes, the one and only. Anyway, he stopped over to check on me after I went to Brody's—"

"No, no, no we are now calling him the asshat chicken fucker." Barb's interruption caused me to burst out laughing.

"Okay, after I went to asshat's yesterday, Jaxon asked me to breakfast today. When we came back, we talked, then I went to my OB appointment. As I'm sitting there feeling sorry for myself and tryin' to figure out exactly how long I could wait without peeing again, Jaxon appeared." Barb gasped. "Yep. Catch this, he said he didn't want me to be alone. Can you believe?" Barb grunted. "Right. So after that we agreed we'd have dinner here. You okay if I ask him to join us?"

"Hells yeah, that's fine. The least we could do seeing as he took such good care of you."

"Oh my God Barb, when we were at the doctor he said that he wants to be here to support and help me since Br—asshat won't be. How freakin' sweet is that?"

"It is sweet, but how well do you know this guy? I mean, who just steps up to take care of someone else's pregnant girlfriend?"

"I mean, I don't know him like I know your crazy ass, but he's walked me home from work for a few weeks now and we were getting to know each other. Then, the New York thing…he seems like a good guy. Barb, give him a chance, 'kay?"

After a deep sigh she said, "Yeah, okay. I mean he is gorgeous. At least you will have some red hot eye candy while you're preggo. Okay, go call him and text me in a few and let me know what the deal is. Love ya chick."

"Okay, love ya too."

Just before I hung up she added, "Ya know, Lei, it's all gonna be okay. I'd never let you go through this alone."

"Thanks Barb," I said and sniffled.

Just as I hung up with Barb there was a knock at the door.

"Fuck, please don't be Brody." I looked through the peephole and sighed in relief. Opening the door, I said, "Hey there big brother, how's it goin'? Jesus Drew, what happened to your hand?"

"I can't believe you didn't call me." He was pissed. Okay, maybe pissed was an understatement. "I had to hear it from fucking Brody this morning, which is why my hand is killin' me and why he's got a black eye and busted lip. What the hell, Lei?" He pulled me into a bear hug.

"Air...can't breathe..." He released me. "What did you do Drew?"

"I had fuckin' warned him not to screw you over." He fisted his hand in his hair while waving the other hand up and down my body. "And he did this to you and, and...let's just say, he got off easy."

"Aw, Drew. I was gonna tell you. That's why I wanted you to come over, it's not something I wanted to talk about over the phone." Shaking my head, I spun around and walked to the hall closet, grabbing the first aid kit. "What do you want me to say Drew? You were right and I was wrong. You warned me he wasn't relationship material. I have only myself to blame." He growled. "Shut it and sit down. Let me clean this up."

"Shit Leila, is that why you didn't call me? 'Cause you thought I'd gloat or say I told ya so?" He sat down with me as I opened an antiseptic wipe. "I'm sorry you're going through this. Honestly, I thought Brody was different with you. From what I saw and what he said, he was...but this whole baby thing has him so fucked up in the head. Shit, that burns."

"Stop, I don't want to hear about him or how he feels. Don't talk about him to me anymore." After a final wipe, I got up and walked to the kitchen. "You want a drink?"

He came to the bar. "Yeah, Coke is fine. And we don't have to talk about him if that's what you want, Lei. And for what it's worth, I am really sorry he hurt you and I'm sorry you thought you couldn't lean on me. I'm here whenever you're ready to talk or you just need to vent." He picked up the sonogram pictures. "Is this my niece or nephew?" he asked as his eyes widened.

"Yep, that's my little peanut. Jax thinks it looks more like a lima bean though."

Drew looked at me with concern in his eyes. "Wait, Jax? As in the guy Brody swears is stalking you? These are dated today. How does he know what it looks like?"

I turned and handed him the glass of soda, almost sloshing it on him. "Jax is a friend, he's not some crazy stalker like Brody thinks. And he went with me to the appointment this morning. He didn't want me to be by myself. Do you have a problem with that?" Ruger stood up in his bed, eyeing the situation, but quickly plopped back down.

"Whoa, easier there killer. It was just a question." He took the glass and went back to the couch, making the wise decision to leave the Jaxon subject alone for now. "So what are you gonna do? About Brody I mean."

"Nothing Drew." I sighed and sat down on the chaise, pulling a blanket over me. "There is nothing to do. He's made his decision and I made mine. We aren't together anymore and I rather not think about him ever again. Next question detective."

"Well, it's his kid. He's gonna be a part of its life, right?" He obviously didn't ask Brody all of these questions.

"No, he wants no part of my baby or me, and, frankly, I don't want anything from him. Can you please drop it Drew?" I was getting annoyed. "Otherwise, maybe we should get a spotlight and handcuffs to finish this interrogation."

He scrubbed his hand over his face, then dragged it through his hair. A curious smile crept across his face. "So Jaxon, huh?"

"Oh no you don't. There is nothing to tell, we're just friends. He's been really good to me this weekend, when I needed someone. He should be coming over in a little while." I looked at the clock on the wall. "I promised to make him dinner as a thank you for going to the ultrasound appointment with me but then I talked to Barb and she wants to go to dinner, so we might do that instead. Ooh, you wanna go with us?"

"I don't know. Brody's said this Jaxon guy is like fuckin' obsessed with you." My brother was pushing my buttons.

"This coming from the asshole who got me pregnant, then walked the fuck away. Real reliable source, don't ya think?"

"Sorry, but he is usually a good judge of character."

"Then why don't you decide for yourself? Come to dinner with all of us." I wasn't above begging. "Please. It would make me feel a little bit better to be around friends and family. Ya know, since I just found out I was pregnant and got dumped all within a week of each other." And I wasn't above guilting him either.

"Fine, what time and where?" he asked with a sigh.

"I will text you in a little while, once I hear from Barb. I'm gonna take a nap, I'm sleepy."

Drew left and used his key to lock the door behind him, so I didn't have to move. It wasn't long before sleep took me over.

Chapter Four

~Leila~

Maroon 5's Adam Levine woke me up a few hours later. My ringtone for Barb was "Moves Like Jagger." I rolled off the chaise and grabbed my phone and answered, "Yeah?"

"Uh, I've been waiting for you to call about dinner plans. Come on, aren't all pregnant women driven by food?" She had jokes.

"Ha-ha. No, sorry. I fell asleep. Drew will definitely be there. Is Santi's good with you?"

"Mmm, yeah, that sounds delicious."

"Let me call Jax and I'll call you right back." I yawned. "Bye."

I pulled up his contact listing and pressed the little phone icon next to his number.

"Hello," he answered on the third ring.

"Hey Jax, its Leila."

He chuckled. "Lei, I have you programmed in, I knew it was you."

"Oh, right. Well, I know I said I'd cook dinner tonight, but Barb called and wants to go out for dinner. You wanna come with us? We're gonna go to Santi's. Oh, and my brother Drew is coming too."

He was panting heavily into the phone. "Yeah, what time do you want me to pick ya up?"

"Are you okay? Did I"—gulp—"interrupt something?" I wasn't sure I wanted to hear the answer.

"Nah, just at the gym. Let me grab a shower and I'll head over in a little bit."

"'Kay. I'll have Barb and Drew meet us at the restaurant. See ya soon then."

"See ya baby girl," he said and hung up.

I called Barb back and told her we'd all meet her at the restaurant. Then I shot a text off to Drew telling him where and when. A split second later my phone buzzed with his response.

I'll meet y'all there

I got up and took Ruger out to the Battery for some exercise. He loved to play fetch and it was a great day for it. The sun was peeking in and out of the clouds, so it wasn't too hot. There was always a great breeze off of the bay. After about thirty minutes he was tired. His tongue just about dragged on the ground on the way home.

When I got within sight of the house I could see a tall, handsome man leaning on my door. Ruger must have seen him too, because his tail started wagging. Jax was wearing a black button down shirt with light blue jeans and his trademark black Doc Martens. He really did look good. He gave me a nod in recognition.

"Hey, sorry. I needed to let him run for a little. You haven't been here long, have you?" I asked, unlocking the door and going inside.

"Nope, just got here a minute ago." He followed me inside.

"I'm drivin' tonight. Barb and Drew will both have a shit fit if I pull up on the bike with you."

"That's fine. You ready?" he asked, like I was actually dressed for dinner.

"Gimme a minute, and let me change, then I will be." I ran up the stairs and changed into a faded blue, distressed jean miniskirt and a white embroidered, sleeveless top that had tie straps holding it up and a smocked waist. I dressed it down a little by throwing on my favorite brown cowboy boots.

When I came back downstairs Jax stood up from the couch and turned to see me. "Whoa, you look amazing."

"Thanks. Thought maybe if I put on something sexy it would make me feel a little less like I just got dumped."

"Great, I'm gonna have to punch some unsuspecting guy in the face tonight, aren't I?" he joked, laughing.

"No, I'm sure that was a fluke," I said, referring to the night at Jake's. "Besides, with you and Drew around I doubt any man would approach me to ask me out."

"Good." He handed me my bag. "Which way?"

"My car's out back," I lead him to the back door.

We went out to the small one-car garage and the look on Jax's face was priceless. "Fuckin' a Leila."

"Why are men always so damn shocked I drive a Challenger?" I rolled my eyes and muttered under my breath.

"This isn't just any car or any Challenger, for that matter. It's a fuckin' Hellcat—" he started.

"Yes, I know what kind of car I drive, Remi." I knew he didn't like me calling him that, so I did. Just to bust his balls.

"Jaxon or Jax or babe, not Remi."

"What's the big deal? You told Barb to call you that and I've heard your biker friends call you that. Why can't I call you that?"

"My road name was given to me because I was a sniper and I used a Remington M40A5. Don't want you thinkin' about me with killing people. It's meant to be intimidating and I never want you to be scared of me," he said in an unfamiliar soft tone that made me melt.

Oh God, I can't deal with this right now. I'm sure if Brody hadn't just happened to me, then I would be ready, willing and able to eat this man alive, but Brody had just destroyed me and I needed to protect myself so I just responded, "Oh, okay."

We got in the car and I drove to Meeting Street, to Santi's, one of my favorite Mexican restaurants, Drew and Barb were already waiting at a table when we arrived. We ate too much, they drank while I watched and we laughed, a lot. Drew and Jax seem to get along effortlessly, much to my relief. Barb suggested we go over to the Wet Willie's to get a drink and dance.

We finished dinner and all went to the wall of adult slushies. I really wanted a strawberry daiquiri mixed with a pina colada, that's my favorite here. Barb and I left Drew and Jaxon sitting at a high top and went to the dance floor. The music was loud EDM and compelled you to bounce with it. We danced together like we always did; she would dance behind me, really close with her hands on my hips. Then we would switch. I'm sure people who didn't know us probably thought we were together, and that was fine with us.

A few guys came over and danced near us. A few even trying to get between us. We just laughed and ignored them, but there were two guys that were just obnoxious and couldn't figure out we just weren't interested. I looked around to see if I could get the boys' attention for a rescue, but I didn't see them.

Great, they were probably at the bar. Then I felt a strong set of arms snake around my waist and pull me back into a solid chest. The familiar and distinct smell of Jaxon permeated my nostrils. He was staking his claim, or so it appeared to the other men on the floor.

"You lookin' for me princess?" Jax whispered in my ear and held me as I danced against him.

"I was," I said low and seductively as I leaned my head back. He rolled his hips, grinding his impressively large bulge into my ass, as I swayed my hips back and forth temptingly. My arms were up and found their way to the back of his neck. I knew I shouldn't be dancing with him like this, but it felt so good to be a normal person for a moment, enjoying a hot guy.

His giant hands started to gradually climb my body, from my hips to my flank to my rib. My body was hypersensitive to his touch. It seemed to wake up a sleeping monster inside of me. I looked down at his wandering hands to see if I could actually look at the electricity that danced across my skin because it felt that real. Not tingles or chills, but white hot lightning gripping every fiber and cell in my body.

After a few minutes he leaned down, stopping when his cheek was touching my temple. I could feel his warm breath on my skin. I waited for him to do something, anything; finally he spoke. "Let's go get you a drink."

I felt so confused. I knew I wasn't alone in feeliing what had just happened. It wasn't physically fucking possible to feel that kind of chemistry and magnetism from another person without them feeling it too. Then again, I thought Brody loved me. I guessed I wasn't the greatest judge of character right now. Plus with my hormones raging, I could just be horny and Jaxon was a boatload of eye candy, no doubt about it.

UGH men were so difficult.

He took my hand and braided our fingers together, pulling me to the table where Drew was sitting.

Drew stood up and nodded to the dance floor. "I'm gonna go dance with Barb. She's too wild to be left alone," he yelled over the music thumping out of the speakers. "Someone has to look out for those poor unsuspecting men out there."

It didn't go unnoticed that our hands were still woven together. I picked up my drink and gulped it all down. I hadn't realized how hot and thirsty I was until that moment. *It could have something to do with the smoldering, sexy ass man standing in front of me. God the things I wanted to…*

Whoa hormone rush much?

"What?" he asked with this sexy confused look on his face when he realized I was staring at him.

"Not now, later. I don't wanna yell over the music and all these people." I pulled my phone out of my purse, 10:30 p.m. Damn, it was early and I was ready for bed.

"Stay here, I'll be right back," he hollered, but I barely heard him, it took a minute to register. He made his way back out to the dance floor. I sat down and waited, wondering what he was doing. Less than a minute later he returned with Drew and Barb in tow.

"You ready?" he asked as he held out his hand to me.

Part of me wanted to ask for what, but the other part won. I took his hand and followed him, looking back at Barb who was right on my heels. When we made it out the doors onto East Bay Street, Barb announced she was going home. Drew immediately went into cop mode and took her keys, forcing her to ride home with him, even though she lived a few blocks away. Jaxon's bike was at my place, so he rode home with me.

"Why don't you stay at my place? I don't think you're in any shape to ride home." *Who am I kidding? He lives within walking distance.*

Honestly, I wanted him to stay. I felt safe when he was near me and I didn't want to be alone tonight. Over the last few months, I had become accustom to falling asleep next to Brody. *Jesus Leila, you can't just substitute Jaxon in.* Was that what I was doing? I knew Jaxon wasn't Brody. Boy did I know. Being with Jaxon felt natural, easy, like I had known him for years.

"That's fine, I'll crash on the couch."

"I have a guest room, you can sleep in there. My couch isn't the best to sleep on. It's too soft. You'll wake up tomorrow morning and never want to speak to me again," I said and laughed.

I parked the car, unlocked the back door and disarmed the alarm. Jaxon held the door so Ruger could go outside.

Dropping my bag, I kicked off my boots in the dining room. I turned to tell Jax I was going to bed and to make himself comfy, but I walked straight into his chest and he caught me in his arms.

"Whoa there, you okay?"

"Damn, you're too fuckin' quiet. I didn't realize you were right behind me." I righted myself.

"Sorry, I didn't mean to freak ya out," he said, laughing at my jumpiness.

"It's okay. So the bedroom is over there. You know where the kitchen is, please make yourself at home. Get whatever you'd like. I'm gonna crash, I'm exhausted." I tried to sneak away before he could remember to ask me why I was staring at him in the club.

Grabbing my arm before I could make my getaway, he leaned down to me and gave me a hug and kissed the top of my head. "Night baby girl. Sweet dreams."

He let me go and I slowly made my way upstairs to my room. I was asleep before my head hit the pillows.

Chapter Five

~Leila~

October and November passed by with no word from Brody. I still held out hope. *Yes, I know. I'm a dumbass.* I couldn't help but wish he would change his mind and want this baby.

I spent most of my free time with Jaxon. We seemed to fall into a comfortable routine. Tuesday through Friday, I would see him when he walked me home from work, just like always. Friday night through Monday night, he would come over or we would go out.

Mostly, we hung out at my house watching football on the weekends. He learned really fast not to talk during football unless it was about football.

We got to know each other, talking about our families. His parents lived in Greenville a few hours away and he was an only child. One topic seemed off limits. He never elaborated on his tours with the Marines. We talked a little about the motorcycle club; he was pretty vague about them too, but said they were as much his family as his mom and dad.

Mid-December, we still were walking Ruger around the Battery and sometimes Folly Beach. Jaxon always held my hand and he kissed the top of my head. So many times over the last few months I had thought about what it would be like to be more with him. When those thoughts crept into my head I saw Brody and quickly shut them down. I couldn't let myself be vulnerable like that again. My inner lioness had other thoughts though; she wanted a playmate. She wanted out of her cage to prowl and devour and only one thing would sate her sexual desires.

On a chilly December Friday night, exhausted from a long shift, I sat on my bed with Jaxon, popcorn between us, watching *Knocked*

Up. We just finished the scene where the sister finds her husband sneaking around to play fantasy baseball, and she starts crying asking why he can't have fun with her anymore and that he does things that hurt her. I don't know why, but it made me sob.

I felt the bed shaking and looked over to see Jax trying to hide his laughter.

"What's so funny? It's sad. She loves him so much and he is a selfish asshole. What's funny about that?" I sniffled. "Do you wanna go hang out with your friends and play fantasy baseball? You don't have to stay here with me"—sniffle—"it's not like I'm your problem."

Now he wasn't trying to hide it, he just about fell off the bed laughing. So, I decided to help him along. I grabbed my down pillow and slammed it into the side of his head. All I saw were his feet go flying straight up as he flipped backward off the bed.

Jaxon popped back up with a devious look on his face and then launched himself at me across the bed. "You think you're funny, huh?"

I laughed as he held me down and tickled me.

"Stop. You're gonna make me pee." I was now crying for different reasons. I tried to escape, which ended with him on top of me.

Nose to nose.

Suddenly, I wasn't laughing anymore and he wasn't tickling me. I waited there for what seemed like an eternity, not moving, in the hope he would make the first move. I couldn't trust myself or my judgment because baby hormones seemed to control my brain. He brushed a few curls out of my face and just as he started to go for it, Ruger started barking like a banshee.

Really Ruger? You're killing me Smalls.

Someone was knocking on the door. I looked at the clock and saw it was almost 11:00.

"Who the hell is knockin' on my door at this hour?" The only person I would expect this late would be Jaxon and he's already here. Dressed in a little gray ribbed tank top and a pair of cotton pajama pants, I went to answer the door. Before I could even get out of the bed Jax was halfway down the stairs.

"Jax, wait, don't answer it. Let me look and see who it is." I bounced down the steps after him.

"Fine, but don't open the door. You hear me?" he said, his voice gruff. "You expectin' anyone?"

I shook my head and looked through the peephole.

"Holy motherfuckin' shitballs," I mumbled, turning back around.

"What the fuck Lei? Who is it? You're white as a ghost babe." He started over to open the door.

"No. Don't."

"Why Leila? Who's at the fuckin' door?" he asked quietly but clearly annoyed.

"Oh God, this is not happening. It's Brody. Brody is here. Why the fuck is he here?" I started rambling like I did when I was nervous.

"Well, let's just see, shall we?" Jax sounded chipper, but was starting to scare me.

"No, don't. I don't want to see him and I have nothing to say," I whispered but it was too late. Jaxon ripped the door open enough that Brody would be able to see him…and me tucked behind him.

"What the fuck do you want?" Jaxon gripped the doorknob.

"It's none of your fucking business. I came here to see Leila." He pulled his eyes from Jaxon down to me. "Can we talk?"

"No, she has nothing to say to you."

"I think she's more than capable of answering for herself," Brody snarled at Jaxon, then turned to me, "or does your boyfriend here talk for you now?"

"Stop it, both of—Oh!" I gripped my little belly and looked down.

Jaxon was immediately at my side. "What's wrong? Are you in pain?" He picked me up and carried me to the couch, leaving Brody standing in the doorway.

"Jax, put me down, I'm fine. Jesus man, chill." I looked down at my belly. "He kicked. Give me your hand, I know you'll be able to feel it this time." I moved his massive hand to where the baby had just moved. "Give it a minute."

Brody shut the door and was standing behind the couch watching us. "Are you okay?"

"Yeah, it's just the baby kicked really hard," I explained.

His eyes widened. "Is that the first time you've felt it move?"

Jaxon looked up at him. "No, he's been moving for a few weeks now, but then again, you'd know that if you hadn't abandoned her, right"—KICK—"oh shit I felt him, Lei, I actually felt it."

"Right, it's hard to miss that, huh?" I beamed.

"Wait, did you say him?" Brody chimed in.

"Not that it's any of your business since you made it that way, but Jax thinks it's a boy. We won't find out until next week." I looked back at Jax and starting biting the inside of my cheek. "What did you want Brody?"

"I wanted to check on you. See if you needed anything and well…can we talk?" He looked at Jax. "Alone?"

"No fuckin' way," Jax growled.

"Jax, please it's okay. Just let me hear what he has to say so he can go and we can finish the movie. It will be fine, I promise."

"Yeah, it will be fine. It's not like I'm going to do something to the mother of my child," Brody said flippantly.

"Watch it Brody. And you don't get to call me that. I'm the mother of *my* baby, you made that perfectly clear months ago, but I am willing to hear you out. Five minutes, that's it." I turned back to Jax. "Please. I know you're not comfortable with this, but I can handle it. Will you run over and get that ice cream I've been craving all week?" I pouted out my bottom lip. "Pleeeeease?"

He blew out a frustrated breath. "Fine, five minutes and I will be back, with your Ben and Jerry's." He stood up, kissed the top of my head and went upstairs.

"So, he's living here now?"

"Not that it's any of your business, but no. He stays over some." I heard Jax coming back down.

"Be back babe. You want anything else? You got enough cream cheese and salami?" He knew me so well.

"Ooh no. I ate the rest yesterday." I scrunched my nose. "But don't worry about it tonight, we can get it tomorrow at Bi-Lo. Good lookin' out though." I didn't want him to leave me alone with Brody for that long.

Jaxon shut the door. My place had never been so quiet. I wasn't sure where to start.

"All right, you've got your five minutes of undivided attention. So get on with it."

"Lei, I'm sorry. I know I've said that before—"

"Eight weeks ago, get to the point Brody."

"I just wanted to see if you needed anything. See how you were feeling?" He paused. Then the real reason came out. "I miss you. I talked to Drew the other day and he said you were starting to show and…I don't know. I guess I wanted to see you."

"Wait, what?" I shook my head. "You've been getting updates from my brother?" I was pissed. "The last I heard he kicked your ass."

"Uh, not really updates, I just ask every once in a while. He didn't kick my ass, he got in a few lucky shots, but I deserved them. For the record, he doesn't offer it up or anything if that's what you're thinking," he said to cover Drew's ass.

"No, I told him not to tell you a damn thing. What the hell?" I got up and walked to the kitchen for a bottle of water. "To answer your questions, no I don't need or want anything. Especially from you. I think you've done quite enough. Jesus Brody. I just started pickin' up the pieces of me that you shattered almost three months ago."

"So what does that mean for us?" he asked. "Have you given up on me?"

"Given up on you?" I asked incredulously, almost laughing. "You walked out on me the same minute you found out I was pregnant. I didn't get a choice. You made that one for me, and now, what? You expect to come by and we would just pick up where we left off?"

"No, not exactly. I just thought maybe we could try. I certainly didn't expect to see him here, in your bed," he said, his voice getting more and more strained.

"Oh hell no! You don't get to be pissed about Jaxon. He has stepped up and been here when I needed someone. When I needed a shoulder to cry on after you crushed me. Someone to hold my hand during ultrasounds and doctor's appointments. Someone to hold my hair while I got sick." I sat back down on the chaise. "So, no. You don't get to be pissed he was doing *your* job. He's my friend, and not that I owe you *any* fuckin' explanation, but that's all it is, right now."

"You know I still love you." He scooted over toward me on the couch, reaching for my hand before I pulled it away. "I fucked up. I get that Lei, but please let me try and fix this."

"Brody, if you would have said all of this to me six or seven weeks ago things might be different." I put my hand on my belly where the baby was doing flips or some shit. "Oh geez, settle down in there."

"Can I feel?" Brody asked sheepishly.

I looked down, contemplating with an exaggerated sigh.

"Yeah." I wasn't totally comfortable with it, but I wasn't a bitch. Although, I really wanted to say fuck no, you didn't want this baby so why should I let you feel him moving around. "Here, put your hand right here."

He stared at my stomach and then waited.

"Give it a minute, sometimes he gets shy." I moved his hand around to the left side just as he kicked again. "There, did you feel that?"

Brody shook his head, but then the peanut did another flip. "Whoa, that feels fucking weird." Brody's eyes grew.

Needing to break the moment, I got up. "Okay. You said what you needed to say, but it doesn't change anything Brody. I can't trust you anymore. How do I know you're not here just because you're lonely and horny?"

"I'm not here because I want sex. If that's all I wanted I could get that whenever." I could see he immediately regretted saying that. "I love you Lei. Please just think about it, about us."

"You're not gettin' this. It's not just us anymore Brody. There's a child I have to think about now. You've already dumped us once. I won't let you do that again."

He looked devastated, but I stayed strong in my convictions.

"I think you should go home. Jaxon will be back in a minute and I'm tired," I said, shaking my head. "Nothing has changed. Maybe it could have, if you didn't wait so long to figure out what you want, if you even have. Next time, just call. Please. I'm trying to move forward."

"Forward. With Jaxon?" he asked frankly.

Is that what I wanted? Did I want to move forward with Jax? Did he want to move forward with me?

"Yes," I admitted quietly, sort of surprising myself.

"Don't make any decisions right now. Please just think about what I said." He turned to leave. "We could be a family. A real family. I'm not saying I'm not terrified, because I am, but I want try, for you."

Ohmygod. Just shut up man. Was he trying to guilt me into taking him back? "Good night Brody."

He stopped and reached for my belly. He rubbed it softly for a split second and opened the door. "Night Lei. Call me if you need anything."

Jaxon was standing in the doorway as he opened the door. "All done then?" Not waiting for an answer, he said quickly, "Great. Bye."

"Jax, Brody was just leaving." I shot him a pleading glance to be nice.

"Bye Lei. Please think about what we talked about."

The two pushed past each other with a solid shoulder bump. Once inside the house, Jax stared out into the darkness before slamming the door. He didn't say a word, just put the ice cream in the freezer and picked up his pack.

"Where are you going?" I said in a panic and a few octaves higher than normal.

"You obviously need some space to think about whatever it was he said, so I'm gonna go."

I reached out and grabbed his arm.

"No, please don't leave. There is nothing to think about or to figure out. I figured it out while he was here."

He hung his head.

"All the more reason I need to leave," he said, and hurt rang in his voice.

"How long were you standin' at the door? How much did you hear?" I started to doubt myself, and how I thought he felt about me.

"Long enough to hear him ask you to be a family. With him."

"So then you didn't hear me tell him I was trying to move forward?" I had hope again.

He turned and looked into my eyes, hesitating. "No."

I grabbed his wrist and pulled him over to the couch, sitting down close enough our legs touched.

"I told Brody I was trying to move forward. That I couldn't trust him anymore, not after he left me the second he found out about the baby. I told him that maybe if he would have come to me the day after with his remorse, I might, big might, have been able to forgive him, but that's not what happened. I told him I was moving on"—I exhaled loudly, trying to build up the courage to tell Jaxon—"with you."

"With me?" He looked at me with shock and awe. "You told him you couldn't be with him, because you wanted to be with me?"

"You're freakin' me out here." I jumped off the couch, before he could grab me, and walked to the kitchen. I took out a spoon and the Ben & Jerry's Americone Dream ice cream.

"Wait, Lei. Don't shut down on me. Talk to me." He got up and came into the kitchen blocking the opening. "I'm sorry, I'm just a little caught off guard. I thought you only wanted to be friends."

Oh great. What the fuck did I just do? Ugh.

I shoved the spoon in my mouth. "I did, but over the last couple of months something changed. I don't know. Maybe I am imagining it or it is the hormones influencing my brain."

"No, don't do that. Don't write off how you're feelin'." He reached me in one stride and took the ice cream away. "Talk to me. Tell me."

"No, just leave it alone. I was wrong to say anything. You're right, we're just friends." I couldn't look him in the eye any longer so I looked down at the spoon in my hand. I walked over and dropped it in the sink with a loud clank. "I shouldn't've said anything."

He stopped my exit.

"Tell me what you want. If I wouldn't have said anything, tell me what you were going to say." His green eyes pleaded silently with me.

Well, hell. Here goes nothing.

"I would've said that I wanted more with you. There, are you happy? Now that you know, you can ride off and leave me here too." I walked out of the kitchen trying to hide my tears. I got about two feet away when I heard him turn around. I couldn't bear to watch him walk out the door, so I retreated up to my bedroom.

The movie was still on pause, pillows still strewn about the room and bed and the popcorn bowl was on the bedside table. It had been such a good night, then Brody had to come over and ruin it. He ruined our relationship months ago, and tonight, he sabotaged my relationship with Jax. I picked up the burgundy covered down pillow and fell awkwardly face first down onto my bed. A few seconds later I heard the familiar creak of the stairs.

Dear God, can I not have a little dignity? Just a little, is that too much to ask?

"Babe," he called to me from the foot of the bed, but I didn't look at him. "You've had your turn, I was wonderin' if I could talk now? Without you running from the room?"

"I didn't run," I spoke into the pillow. "I walked."

He playfully smacked me in the ass. "Okay smart-ass, sit up so I can see your smilin' face."

I rolled over and crawled up so I was surrounded by pillows. He came around the side of the bed and sat down next to me.

"Leila, I know we agreed to just be friends, but from the first moment I saw you, I wanted you. That never changed. I stopped askin' you out, yes, but I never stopped wantin' you. That won't change."

"Even when I'm huge and fat?"

"Even when you're huge and fat," he said with a laugh. I slapped him in the shoulder. "Ow, what the fuck? You said it first, I just agreed."

"God, you suck at this. You're not supposed to agree with me. You're supposed to say no Lei, you're not fat, you're pregnant." I lay down on my side, facing him.

He roared with laughter. "Okay, okay, you're missin' the point babe." He looked at me with this soul-consuming passion. "I do want you. Now, four months from now and four years from now. I want more. I've always wanted more. I was just waiting for you to realize it and for you to be ready."

"What about the baby? That changes things. We're kind of a package deal Jaxon. Could you really see yourself raising this baby?" I didn't really want to ask, but I had to know before I got in over my head with him. "I mean it's not your child. Could you raise Brody's child and not look at him or her with animosity?"

He put his head down on the pillow and lay down next to me. "I haven't seen this little guy yet, and I'm already in love with him. No, he won't be mine, biologically, but he will in every other way that matters." He slid his hands around my jaw, behind my ear. "I want both of you."

He propped himself up on his elbow, looked down into my eyes and leaned in. Holy shit, he's finally going to kiss me. His lips were soft as he touched them to mine. He sucked in my top lip gently while his tongue danced around it, teasing and tantalizing. I angled my head slightly to the right and captured his bottom lip mimicking his actions.

Jax slipped his right arm around my waist, hauling me hard and fast to his body. My leg wrapped around his butt and pulled him as close as I could get him without becoming a part of one another. His head dropped to the pillow as he reached for my cheek. He rolled me over so I was on top of him, but never broke the kiss. His dick was hard and I was grinding against him. His hands were palming and squeezing my ass. I stilled.

"You okay?" he asked.

Quietly I looked at him, taking in all of his gorgeous features. Bright jade eyes, strong jaw, perfect lips. Even his nose with its little bump at the top from where it was broken years ago. I held myself up with my locked arm and ran my hand from his temple down his cheek, then behind his neck.

"Yeah, never better."

"Good," he leaned up and whispered against my mouth. "'Cause we aren't even close to being done."

We kissed until we were gasping for air. I sat up, crossed my arms over my body, grabbing the hem of my tank and pulled it over my head. I fell back down against his chest and grazed my lips over his once, then he sat me up. Ripping off his own shirt, he flipped me on my back and watched me looking him over, taking in the beauty of his muscles. They were thick and defined but not grotesquely like a bodybuilder. His tattoos stopped on his arms, not reaching his taut, flawless chest. I smiled when I saw he had the elusive eight abs, like I imagined. When I looked up, he searched my face for any doubts.

"Are you sure you want to do this? This changes everything. If we do this, you're mine. I won't let you go Leila and I don't share." His eyes confirmed his possessiveness.

"I'm sure. I've thought about this moment for weeks, but Jax, be gentle with me," I got out before he attacked my mouth. His tongue swept back and forth, swirling and dancing with mine. Pulling back, he took hold of the sides of my pajama pants and tugged them down my legs. He progressively kissed me from the knee up the outside of my thigh, skimmed his tongue along my hip bone to my navel. He placed his enormous hands on my protruding belly almost covering it completely. He placed tiny little pecks all over it, trailing up to my chest.

"God, I love your tits." He pinched my nipples between his calloused fingertips. "Are they still sore?" He remembered I had said they were bothering me.

"No, that feels so fucking good. Just not hard, 'kay?" I moaned as he bent his head to my breast and licked a small circle around my nipple. I closed my eyes in bliss. "Oh fuck Jax, mmmm."

He took his time licking, nibbling and rolling my nipples until they were achingly hard. Suddenly it stopped and I felt his weight disappear from the bed. My eyes flew open searching for the reason he left. He was standing next to the bed, slipping out of his jeans. Oh God, his thighs were huge. They looked like tree trunks, so thick and sturdy. As he reached for his grey boxer briefs, all of the air left my lungs in a sudden rush.

My eyes and face must have shown my astonishment. Without thinking, the words left my mouth. "Holy fucking shit Jax. You're gonna kill me."

Brody was large, but Jaxon was scary big. At least nine or ten inches and his girth was thicker than my wrist. I doubted seriously if I'd even be able to make my fingers meet when I gripped him.

"Baby, I promise we'll take it slow. I'd never hurt you." He pulled his wallet from his pants, which caught me by surprise.

"What're you doin'? Get up here," I rushed him.

"Condom babe. Unless you have some?" he asked.

"We should probably talk before…ya know," I said warily. "I have only had unprotected sex once and we know where that got me," I said looking down. "But I've been tested since then, standard when you find out you're pregnant. You?"

"Well, I haven't been tested in about three months, but I also haven't been with anyone since then either." His words threw me for a loop.

"Huh? You haven't had sex since the middle of September?" My head cocked to the side.

"Nope, not since I knew I had a chance with you. I couldn't even get hard for one of the girls at the last club party I went to. Well, until I thought about you, then—"

I cut him off. "Whoa, stop right there. I sooo don't wanna hear about you fuckin' some girl while you were thinkin' about me. Too much."

"So, we are both clean and we don't have to worry about…" his words fell off.

"An unplanned pregnancy? No, I think I got that box checked."

"So no condom?" He grinned like the Cheshire cat.

"Jaxon Henderson get up here and fuck me," I spit out.

"Baby girl, I'm plannin' on fuckin' you senseless, but right now, I wanna take my time with you." He climbed up, kissing me while his fingers found their way down my body, between my legs. "Oh fuck Leila. You're fuckin' drenched."

He slipped his middle finger between my folds, grazing my clit and subsequently slid it inside of my pussy. "So tight. No wonder you're worried I'll hurt ya." He pumped his large finger in and out of me a few more times.

"Ohhhh, Jaxon. Mmm, don't stop. Oh God." I was so turned on and it had been so long. I knew it wouldn't take much.

"I wanna see if you taste as sweet as I've dreamt you do." He knelt on the foot of the bed and lay down between my knees. "Bend your knees and let me see you."

I pulled my heels up and let my legs fall apart, exposing myself to him.

"Mmm, so fuckin' perfect," he murmured as his tongue took its first swipe through my lips, grazing my clit, sending a shockwave through my entire body.

"Ahhhhhh!" I rocked my hips in need of more pressure. "Oh fuck. Oh Jax, yeah ohhhhh." My body shuttered against his mouth as he again started plunging his middle finger in and out of me. That sent me sailing over the edge, careening headlong into a heart-stoppingly powerful orgasm like I had never experienced. It lasted so much longer than any other time before. Jaxon had a way of elongating my pleasure with just the right amount of pressure here and there. I swear I might have actually blacked out for a few seconds.

"Mmmm, oh God, I can't move. Jax…that was…incredible."

He kissed his way back up my body to my neck, then my jaw. He positioned himself between my legs, reached down and rubbed his hard, wide cock across my clit, coating himself in my wetness. "Lei, last chance."

"I'm not changing my mind Jaxon. You're who I want, just don't hurt me." I wasn't talking about physically, but I think he knew that. He rested on his elbows and gave me the most sensual, intimate kiss. All lips, no tongue. It was soft and slow. It helped to relax me as he pushed his massive cock slowly into me.

"Aghhhhhh," I whimpered in pain, so he stopped moving. "Don't stop. I'll be okay, just keep going."

"I don't want to hurt you or the baby, Lei." He looked at me with so much compassion and love.

"Jaxon, it's okay," I reassured him and rolled my hips slightly. It moved him further within me.

"Damn baby. You're so fuckin' tight I can barely move."

He filled and stretched me, pushing my body past its limits, finally stopping when he was all the way in. He pulled out and then slid back in again. Faster this time, but with little force. Soon he was gliding in and out in a fluid motion. My body welcomed the invasion and wanted more. God, he felt so good.

Jaxon was so different from Brody. Brody was hard, intense and unrelenting. He fucked me. Jaxon was intense, but was tender and careful. He made love to me. He took care of me. There was a level of intimacy between us that I never found with Brody. Unspoken communication that our bodies sensed from one another, and responded to with urgent passion.

"Oh God, Jaxon, yeah, oh yeah, don't stop." He started to thrust deeper and faster. Each time the wide head of his dick plunged into my pussy he caught my G-spot.

"I want you on top." He pulled out of me and flipped me. Oh hell yeah, I couldn't wait to ride him. I had dreamed of this moment so many times over the last few weeks.

I eased myself down, inch by glorious inch, until I could go no further and gyrated my hips in a circular motion as I slowly rose.

"Oh god baby, you're killin' me. You're gonna make me lose it." He closed his eyes and gripped handfuls of sheet.

"Not yet, I'm so close." My lungs heaved. "I don't wanna stop yet." I started bouncing and rocking my pussy up and down on his rigid dick. "Oh God Jax, yeah, right there."

He pulled me down so our chests met, wrapped his arms around my waist to hold me still and began thrusting unrelentingly.

"Ohhhhh fuuuuuck. Harder Jax, oh God. I'm—" I screamed as he continued his assault on my pussy. I could feel my whole body tense, muscles contract and nerves all fire at once as I reached my climax. I rode out my orgasm as he still drove into me.

"Lei, I'm close baby. I want you under me." With that he turned me on my back, without withdrawing. I swear he was going to tear me. He rested his forearms beside my face, allowing him to rest his forehead to mine. He slowed his pace, opened his eyes and trapped me with his gaze. I looked so deep into his eyes, I could see all of the emotions and feelings he had admitted, and the ones he still kept bottled up inside. I could see the passion and lust, but beneath the surface, I could see something else, the tenderness in him, the affection and devotion he felt for me. His green eyes were forever burned into my memory, with their vibrancy and tiny yellow flecks. While his lips and tongue explored every cell of my mouth, my eyes memorized his face. Every line, smooth plane, scar and dimple were seared into my brain.

He yelled out my name as he reached his climax. I could feel his dick get harder inside of me as he exploded. His face tensed and then relaxed as he slowed his attack.

"Oh God Lei." He kissed me softly. "Why did we wait so long?"

I chuckled quietly. "Hmm, let's see…for starters I had a boyfriend. Then there is the whole fact I had my heart broken. And then…I got to really know you." He kissed the tip of my nose.

I realized I had to go clean myself up. "Hey, uh, I kinda need to go to the bathroom."

"Oh fuck babe, I'm sorry." He pulled out and helped me out of the bed.

As I walked to the bathroom, remnants of our passion ran down the inside of my thigh. I jumped in the shower and washed off. About a minute in, Jax strutted his fine ass into the bathroom and leaned on the granite vanity.

"See somethin' ya like big boy?" I looked at him from the corner of my eye as he ogled me while he stroked his semierect shaft.

"Oh babe, you have no idea." He pulled open the large glass shower door and joined me. "We might as well stay in here because I'm getting ready to make you dirty all over again."

"Promises, promises," I taunted. "Me first."

I dropped to my knees in front of him, taking him in my mouth. I could only manage half of his long dick. It had to be nine or ten inches. I could wrap both hands around him and still get a mouthful.

"Oh shit babe, that's so good. Oh yeah, suck my cock." He threw his head back and leaned against the wall to steady himself.

I jerked my hand back and forth as my tongue sucked and swirled around his broad tip. I moaned and vibrated my throat as he thrusted down almost gagging me. I sucked as hard as I could and slowly pulled my head back until I released him with a *pop*.

"Here or the bed?"

"Here, bend over. I want you from behind." He spun me around and gripped my hips. "Mmm, damn your ass is fuckin' perfect. Put your hands on the wall to balance yourself."

He held his now fully erect cock in his hand, rubbed it up and down my slit, coating himself to ease in.

"Oh God Jaxon, easy."

"Baby, if it hurts, tell me, we can wait." He rocked out a little, then back in a little more this time.

"No, I want this, but you've gotta go slow." This position allowed him deeper access and it was almost uncomfortable. He pushed into me slowly, allowing my walls time to expand around him. He withdrew and pushed back in with more force this time.

"You okay?" he grunted out as his pace increased.

"Mmm, God, yes. Oh Jax, don't stop." And he didn't. He drove and thrust into me. He'd go fast and hard, then slow down and take his time as my muscles tightened around him. He slipped his hand around my waist, and he found my clit and I exploded. My walls contracted and squeezed his thick girth.

"Shit babe, I can't hold it." He groaned as I felt his body straighten and pump his release into me. "Fuck."

He pulled out and turned me around, his lips found mine and roughly nipped and sucked at them. "We definitely will be fucking in here often, the mirror is in the perfect position. I can't wait until I can make you watch as I fuck you from behind against the glass wall," he whispered against my lips.

Well, thank God I was in the shower and not wearing panties, because that just caused a flood.

We showered. For real. Jaxon washed my hair for me and even combed it through while the conditioner sat. Exhaustion took over now that the adrenaline and oxytocin had dissipated from my body.

"Babe, can we just climb in bed and finish the movie tomorrow?"

"Yeah, you sleepy?" He stepped out, grabbing two towels and wrapping one around me.

"Yeah," was all I could manage and followed it up a long yawn. I tucked the large, soft towel around my body after I dried off. In a surprising move, Jaxon scooped me up and carried me to the bedroom, laying me gently on the bed. He threw on a fresh pair of boxer briefs from his pack.

"You wanna drink baby? I'm gonna grab a water."

"Yeah, if you're going down." I smiled, thinking about the evening's turn of events. He returned a few minutes later with one bottle of water.

"I thought you went down for a drink?" I asked, wondering where his bottle was.

"Okay, I lied. You always take a bottle of water to bed with ya and I knew you were too tired to go yourself. If I would've asked, you would've said no. This was easier than arguing with your stubborn ass." He climbed into my bed, lay on his side and looked at me. He reached over and placed his hand on my belly. "You sir, need to stop drainin' all your momma's energy."

Jaxon was always so serious and tough. I wanted to take a picture of him just like this, so vulnerable, lying here talking to my belly. It would serve as a useful reminder for times when *he* was being a stubborn ass.

"You are so certain it's a boy, huh?"

"Yep."

I closed my eyes and listen to him whispering away about motorcycles and football. As I drifted off, I felt him pull the comforter up around us and kiss my forehead.

Chapter Six

~Leila~

The week passed by quickly since we both had to work. Before I knew it, my next ultrasound appointment was here. I was twenty weeks into my pregnancy, halfway. Woohoo! I couldn't wait to see this little munchkin. I was really showing now. Well, I was before, but now you could tell in anything I wore, not just snug clothes. I needed to go buy more maternity clothes. I had a pair of jeans I could wear and a pair of normal yoga pants. Of course, my scrubs still fit since they were drawstring, but even they were getting too tight.

I called Drew the day after Jaxon and I finally had sex. Of course I didn't announce that fact, I just told him that we had decided to try being more than friends. Drew was honest in his response. He didn't like it, but then again he didn't not like it. He was worried about me getting hurt again; I was too. Reluctantly, Drew agreed, I needed to move on and he appreciated that Jaxon had been by my side since New York.

Barb and Drew met Jaxon and I at the Prenatal Wellness Center. Jaxon insisted on getting the 3D/4D and I wanted them to be there with us. I was really torn about finding out the sex. I wanted to be surprised at delivery, but Jax wanted to know so we could plan better. It would be easier to buy clothes and decorate a nursery. I was starting to freak out about the nursery and having the baby on a different floor. Jaxon suggested I start looking for a new place, but I didn't want a new place. I loved my place and the location. He was right in the fact that it was too small. In a few short months, I will have outgrown the small two bedroom condo.

"So are we ready to see the baby?" the tech asked.

"We are." Energy radiated off me in waves.

"Have y'all decided if you want to know the sex? We should be able to determine that today, if ya want."

I looked at Jax and he looked back down at me. "This is your call babe. You know how I feel. I just want you to be happy."

Drew somehow thought it was a good idea to chime in right now. "Did you ask Brody if he wants to know?"

I could see and feel Jax rile up. He was holding my hand and I had to let go because he had it in a death grip. "Brody has been by to see Leila two times in three months. So no, that fucker doesn't get a say in this. This isn't his baby anymore."

"Sorry man, I just thought if y'all were tied he could be the swing vote. I didn't mean anything by it. You know where I stand about you two." Drew and Jax had gone out for beers one night this past week, a few days after our phone call. They talked. I asked, but neither would say what was discussed.

"Well, I think you should find out what my little godbaby is gonna be. That way I can start spoiling it now." Barb reached over and rubbed my belly. She did that a lot these days.

I smacked her hand away for the umpteenth time. "I told you, I'm not a Buddha statue, stop rubbing my belly for good luck bitch."

"Haha, I told you, I would rub my baby whenever I wanted hooker." We always had such loving names for each other.

"Since this is your baby, you mind carryin' it for a while. My bladder could use a break from the somersaults and springboard action. Okay, okay, we're so far off topic." I turned to the tech, who had finished setting up the machine. "Yes, we want to know."

"You sure Lei?" Jax squeezed my hand.

"Yeppers, let's do this thing."

She squirted goo all over my round little belly and rubbed the transducer back and forth, spreading it around.

"Aww, there's a face." She pointed to the area with the mouse. "Looks like they're sucking on their thumb." She continued to point out little things here and there. "Anyone wanna place bets before we get down to the other end?"

Drew and Jaxon both agreed on a boy, Barb said girl and I didn't care either way. I just wanted a healthy baby.

"Man, this is one feisty little baby ya got here. Every time I get close, they move or cross their legs." She kept moving around until she finally paused the screen. "Oh, there we go. It's a girl."

A tear fell down my cheek. A daughter, I was going to have a baby girl. I looked up at Jax to see a look of terror on his face. "Oh fuck."

"Jaxon Austin Henderson! What is wrong with you?" I scolded.

Barb was cracking up, but Drew wasn't laughing either.

"Oh God, this is payback. I can't have a daughter. I'll go to jail." This crazed look came over him. "She's never allowed to date. Ever."

Now everyone but Jax was laughing, even the ultrasound technician.

"Baby look at me." I tugged on his hand, pulling him from this demented rant. "It'll be okay. We have years before we have to think about that." That seemed to calm him down a bit.

We finished the scan, then got our video and pictures. Drew insisted on taking all of us out for lunch at Hyman's.

After lunch, Barb and I went shopping for some maternity clothes at the mall where I found tons of cute tops that accentuated my swollen stomach. I also did a little Christmas shopping since it was only three days away. I never thought to ask Jax what his plans were for the holiday. Since I didn't have a family to travel to, I sort of forgot other people did.

When I got home it was after 4:00 p.m. I put everything away, then called Jaxon. It went straight to voicemail, so I left a short message asking him to call when he got a few minutes. He was probably riding or in the middle of club business.

I decided to wrap his presents and put them under the tiny Charlie Brown Christmas tree we bought and decorated. Jax wanted to get a huge tree and I didn't want one at all, so we compromised. Luckily, Ruger hadn't tried to water it, yet.

I cooked a light dinner and left it on the stove, waiting for Jax to come over. I sat down on the couch and turned on the TV to kill the time.

Next thing I knew, I woke up and it was 10:24 p.m. I grabbed my cell to see if I had missed a call from Jax, but I hadn't. I knew I was just being neurotic, but my skin tingled with angst. It wasn't like him to not call or not come over. I mean, I knew we didn't live together and we weren't married, but he had been staying here every night, when I wasn't working.

Suddenly my heart began to race, my hands shook and I felt sick. Oh God, he doesn't want this. He doesn't want me or my baby girl. He was totally freaked out when we found out it was a girl. I started to cry. He's left me just like Brody did.

No! Stop this. Your hormones are getting the best of you again. Call him. Don't freak the fuck out until you have a reason. It could be something completely unrelated. I picked up the phone and called him, which still went straight to voicemail. I called Barb next to ask for Viper's number. She was reassuring and calmed me down, then offered to come over, saying she would call him on the way. Ten minutes later, Barb used the key to let herself in.

"So, I talked with Cole, they're at the clubhouse. He's fine, uh, well maybe fine isn't the word." She sat down on the end of the chaise. "He's trashed. He went to the clubhouse to share the news, and well, he may or may not have celebrated a little too much."

"Oh, thank God." I was so worried, now I was just pissed. "I'm gonna kill him. Wait, who's Cole?"

"Viper. His real name is Cole. I told Cole to have Remi, err, Jaxon call you."

"Thank you. Jesus, I'm sure I sound like some clingy, nagging wife."

"Ha, if it was me, I'd be halfway to the clubhouse. I don't trust those whores down there." She rose and went to the refrigerator.

"Excuse me, what did you just say? Whores?" I was confused.

"What? He didn't tell you?" She looked at me with this look of sympathy. "Shit, I should've kept my big mouth shut."

"Spill it bitch."

"All right." She grabbed a diet coke and sat back down. "The clubhouse is full of, okay, maybe not full of, but there are women there for the brothers', um…disposal. And let me tell you, these hooches go far beyond throwing themselves at the boys. They'll fuck anyone, anywhere and at any time."

"Oh God." A new worry crept into my hormone riddled brain.

"Stop, I don't think you have anything to worry about. Re— ugh—Jaxon clearly cares for you. I don't see him as a cheater." She set her drink on the coffee table. "And if it makes you feel better,

Cole said Jaxon hasn't been with anyone in months." Confirming what he told me.

Suddenly, I became aware of the fact that I felt wet. "I need to pee." I swear my bladder had shrunk. Normally, she would be using it as a trampoline, but she had been still tonight. She must be sleeping.

I closed the downstairs bathroom door, pulled my black yoga pants down and screamed for Barb.

The door flew open and bounced off the door stop, almost hitting her in the face. "What the hell Leila? What's wrong?"

"Barb, I'm bleeding. Like, a lot. Get me some new panties and pants please. I've got pads down here. Then we need to leave."

She was up the stairs before I realized she left. Seconds later she came running down the steps. "Here babe, gimme those."

"Barb, please call Jaxon. Tell him what's going on and that I'm going to the hospital." I put on the clean clothes.

"I'll drive. The Jeep is out front." Barb threw my blood-soaked clothes in the sink. "I'll clean those later. Are you cramping?"

"Not really, my back hurts a little, but no abdominal pain. Just call Jax. Oh, and Drew too, but tell him not to come up there, that I will call him later."

She already had her cell pressed against her ear. "Cole, babe, listen. You need to tell Remi I'm taking Leila to the hospital." She was quiet a minute. "Yeah, she's bleeding...no you fool, she didn't cut herself. Just get to MUSC. Okay, hang on." She handed me the phone. "Jaxon wants to talk to you."

I took the phone in my trembling hand. "Hello?"

"Babe, whas goin' on?" He was clearly drunk.

"Jax, I'm bleeding. Barb is taking me to the hospital to get checked out. I can't talk, we've gotta go."

"We'll meet you there Leila," his voice sobered with a gravelly tone.

"Be careful." I handed the phone back to Barb. She told Viper which building and then rushed me out the front door.

We made it to the ER in minutes. Oh shit, I hadn't thought about this part, I really didn't want the people I worked with seeing my vagina. I'd never be able to look at them the same way again.

Barb grabbed a wheelchair and went into nurse mode. "Twenty weeks, bleeding, back pain, denies abdominal cramping."

"Hey Leila." Derrick trotted over and took me from Barb. "Talk to me girl, when did it start?" He wheeled me into a room.

"Fifteen minutes ago, give or take. No real significant cramping, mild discomfort in my lower back, no fever or chills," I rattled off answers to questions I would've asked.

"Okay then, you know the drill. Everything from the waist down off. I'll be right outside the door, holler when you're done. I wanna get you on the fetal monitors."

Barb helped me get undressed and started pulling out the receivers. "Come in Derrick."

He returned with Mary and Dr. Miller. I was relieved to see Dr. Miller. "Talk to me, start to finish."

I ran through the series of events leading me to where I currently was. With lots of corrections and input from Barb.

"Looking at the EFM, the baby's heart rate is good. You are having small contractions that aren't regular, which is good. I'm gonna run a UA, CBC and chem stat." Dr. Miller took my hand in his. "Try not to stress, okay. While we are running those, I'm gonna find an ultrasound machine. I'll be right back."

"Barb can you please call Jaxon and find out where he is?" I asked as Mary drew blood.

"Of course, I'll be right back."

She stepped out into the hallway, but I could hear her telling someone my room number. She poked her head back in. "Do you want me to call anyone else?"

I knew where she was going with this.

"No. I don't want him here. Especially if Jax is drunk, God only knows what he'd do." That's when I heard him in the hallway, raising all kinds of hell, cussing at the nurses, demanding to be allowed in to see me.

"I'll get him." Barb shook her head with a smile and opened the door. "She's in here you caveman. Settle down or they'll throw you out and she doesn't need that," she chastised him as he entered the room.

As soon as I saw him, all of my fortitude and resilience died and I was a blubbering hot mess. "Shh baby, I got you. Don't cry. It's gonna be okay." He sat down on the bedside and wrapped me up in his strong arms. "Talk to me, what're they sayin'?"

I tried to slow my breathing and contain my sobs. "I'm bleeding and having contractions."

"Fuck. This is my fault. I shouldn't've left you."

"Jax, no, you couldn't have known. No one is at fault. Dr. Miller went to get the ultrasound, I'm sure he's checking for a placenta previa." I pointed at the machine. "Barb will you turn it up for a sec."

Barb reached over and adjusted the volume on the monitor and her heartbeat filled the room.

"See, she's okay."

"Oh, thank God." Relief washed over his face. "I want to—"

He was interrupted by Dr. Miller and a tech coming in with the ultrasound machine. "Leila, let's see what's going on, shall we? Oh, hi. Sean Miller."

Jaxon shook Dr. Miller's hand. "Jaxon. I'm Leila's, uh, boyfriend." He looked at me for direction.

"Nice to finally meet you." He wheeled the machine to the bedside.

Barb and Viper stood in the corner out of the way. Jax took position at the head of the bed, holding my hand. The screen was much smaller and hard to make out anything.

"It looks like you have a partial previa. Only a very small part of the placenta is covering the cervix, so it may still migrate up and away, allowing you a normal delivery."

Taking a deep breath I relaxed slightly. Jax kissed my temple and whispered to me, "See everything's gonna be just fine."

Easy for him to say. He didn't know the protocol for previa patients. "Can I do the bed rest at home or are you admitting me?"

"As long as someone can be with you, at all times, then home is fine."

"I live alone," I started to say, but Barb and Jax cut me off, both agreeing to be there. "Okay, since that's settled, when can I go home?"

"I'm still waiting on the blood work. You're UA is clear. I'll check and have Derrick come back in a few minutes." They all cleared out, taking the ultrasound machine with them.

"So what does bed rest mean exactly?" Jax sat back down next to me.

"Relatively flat on my back or side until the placenta moves up a little more. Probably an ultrasound in a week or two to check progress." The next one was sure to get his attention. "And pelvic rest… no sex for a while."

"What? What's a while?" He sat straight up.

"At least a few weeks. Worst case scenario until after delivery," Barb explained.

"Dude, that fuckin' sucks for you." Viper chuckled a little, earning himself a quick jab to the ribs from Barb. "Ow babe, I was just teasin'."

"Knock it off asshat." She came around to the opposite side of the bed. "Jax and I can take turns staying with you."

"Shit, I gotta ride up to my parents' in two days. I'll call and cancel."

"No, absolutely not. It's Christmas. You will go and see your parents, you hear me. Barb will be here and Drew too. I'll be fine." He started to argue. "Besides, it's only a partial. Hopefully, it'll move and everything will be fine. End of discussion."

An hour or so later we got the all clear to go home. By this time, Jax had sobered up and explained he left his charger at my house, so his phone was dead. Barb drove us both back to my place and dropped us off. She agreed to come over Wednesday, so Jax could drive to Greenville. It was only a three hour drive and Jax insisted on coming home the same day. I argued with him, telling him he needed to spend some time with his mom and dad. I begged him not to take that time for granted; they wouldn't always be there. He finally conceded.

Chapter Seven

~Leila~

The next day was spent in bed watching movies with Jax. He made chili and even brought me some salami with cream cheese. It sounds really nasty, but it's a-mazing! It was my one weird pregnancy craving.

Wednesday was Christmas and I couldn't think of a better way to wake up, than tangled around Jaxon's body like wrapping paper. I wanted to give him his present, but I wanted him to get on the road before traffic got crazy.

"Merry Christmas." I kissed him good morning. "Hey, would you be upset if we did presents tomorrow when you get home?" I asked running my hand across his chest.

"Why? It won't be Christmas tomorrow. The drive can wait a few hours."

"No, honey. You told your Mom you'd be there by noon."

"That was before you were on bed rest. I think she'll understand if I'm late." An odd look crossed his face. "Unless you're trying to get rid of me?"

My shoulders slumped and my face drooped. "No, of course not. Why would you say that? I just don't want you to ever regret not spending as much time with them as possible Jaxon." He knew how I felt about my mom and how I wished I had more time with her.

"You're right."

"Wait, what was that? I'm right?" I sat tall and cocky.

"Don't let it go to your head, smartass." He rolled his eyes, climbed out of bed and went to the shower.

Ten minutes later, Jaxon strutted out of the bathroom, wrapped in just a towel. Oh my…Merry Christmas to me. "Is that my present wrapped up in that towel?"

He threw his head back and laughed. "Babe, if we are gonna make it through the next couple of weeks not having sex, you can't say shit like that."

I crossed my arms and pouted. "This sucks. The second trimester is when you're all horny and want it all the time."

"Not helpin' babe. You're makin' my dick harder with each word." He pulled on tattered Levi's and a tight black T-shirt. He smiled. "It's only a few weeks and the end result will be more than worth the wait." He rubbed my belly. "Have you started thinking about names?"

"Not really. You?"

His eyes closed briefly and his face softened. "You want my input?"

I scooted over to him and wrapped my arms around his broad neck. "Of course I want your input honey." I pulled back. "I mean, you still want to raise her with me, right?"

"You know I do. Never doubt that." He leaned in and kissed my forehead, then held me against his chest. "No matter what happens, I'm here with you. Things won't always be perfect. We'll have fights, that's a given, but I'm not going anywhere." He pulled back and looked at me. "I love you Leila. Nothin' will ever change that."

Hormones took me hostage, tears streamed down my face. "Oh Jaxon." I was terrified to say it because of what happened with Brody, but Jaxon was nothing like him. He was honest, loyal and devoted to me and the baby. He has been since the first minute I told him I was pregnant. It dawned on me that whether I wanted to be or not, I was in love with him. And I told him a half second before I launched myself into his arms. His hand tangled in my curls as he gripped the side of my head, kissing me.

We were torn apart by the sound of the front door shutting.

"I guess I need to get on the road. Are you sure you don't want me to just stay here with you?"

"Jaxon, we've talked about this. It's only twenty-four hours and you need to see your parents. It's Christmas." Was he trying to make this harder for me?

"Exactly, it's Christmas. I wanna spend it with my woman and our baby girl. In bed."

My heart soared. "Go see your mom. I'll be right here waiting when you get home tomorrow."

Barb strolled into the bedroom. "Hey y'all. Merry Christmas."

We all exchanged greetings before Jax kissed me, then grabbed his pack and left. I did good and held it together until I heard the door shut. "Damn these stupid hormones, I don't even know why I'm cryin'."

Barb jumped in bed with me. "Cheer up, I brought you a present!"

I sniffled once. "Can you go downstairs to the tree and get me yours?"

"Yeah, or we could get ya outta bed, get a shower and move ya downstairs for the day."

"You always know just what I need. Thanks honey."

Barb started the shower and gathered clothes for me to put on once I got out. She ran downstairs and made us breakfast while I rejoiced in the hot water. I got dressed and made my way carefully down the steps.

"You should've waited until I was there to help you."

"Okay, that's enough." I was annoyed at everyone's hovering. "I'm not ninety years old, I didn't break my leg and I'm certainly not an invalid. It was just one episode of bleeding. Y'all need to stop all this." Changing my tone I added, "I appreciate y'all taking turns to sit with me, but I am fine to walk down the steps alone Barb."

"I'm sorry, I know it's gotta be hard to have everyone fussin' over ya. I'll try to relax a little. Now eat your breakfast young lady." She smiled like the smartass she was.

We exchanged Christmas presents, ate, watched TV, took naps and sat around most of the day. Jaxon called to let me know he made it to his mom and dad's safely. About 5:00 p.m. Barb got a call on her cell from someone at work who was trying to make her come in. A bunch of people were out, myself included, and they desperately needed nurses. She tried to explain she was with me and I couldn't be left alone, but after a minute of arguing, she relented.

"Damn, I have to go to work. Put your shoes on, you're coming with me. Miller said you could stay in one of the ER beds, so you're not alone. I need to steal a pair of scrubs." She went upstairs and came back down a few minutes later.

"I'm not going, I'll call Drew." I grabbed my cell and called him.

"Merry Christmas little sister. How are ya feelin?"

"Merry Christmas bro. I'm feelin' okay. Hey, listen, Barb is with me today and tomorrow because Jax went to see his parents. She just got called into work and I need someone here with me in case I start bleeding again."

Before I could even ask, he cut me off. "I can stay with you. I'm out with a friend getting dinner, so it'll be about thirty to forty-five minutes."

"Shit Drew, I'm sorry. Just stay there. I'll be fine here by myself, I have my cell phone. Just come over after you're finished."

"I'll bring dinner with me. Are you hungry? I could get you something too."

"Do you really need to ask?" I was always hungry.

"Okay, I'll bring extra. See ya in thirty."

"Drew's comin' over to stay with you?" Barb only heard half of the conversation.

"Yep, he'll be here in just a little while so you can go to work and not worry about little ol' me. He'll crash here tonight and Jax will be home tomorrow about noonish."

"Okay, but you call me if you need anything or if you get bored." She hugged me. "I'm going to bring your iPad over and get you a drink before I head out. Anything else?"

"Nope, I'm good sweetie, thanks." She took Ruger out, then left for work.

Ruger came over and put his head in my lap. "My sweet boy, you wanna come up?" I patted the couch and he climbed up. It was few and far between that he was allowed on the couch. He curled up right next to me and quickly drifted off. "Lazy dog."

There was a light knock, then I heard keys in the deadbolt. Figuring Drew had his hands full with dinner, I went to the door and opened it. Boy I was so not prepared for what greeted me.

"Lei, why are you up? Aren't you supposed to be on bed rest?"

"Well, hello to you too Brody. Why are you here?" I turned to my brother who I was ready to kill. "What. The. Fuck. Drew?"

Brody pushed past Drew, slipped his arms under my knees and cradled me to his chest as I struggled against him. "Damn it Brody, put me down. Now!"

"Not until you lie down. Stop fighting me." He held me tighter.

"Would you stop being ridiculous? I am allowed to walk from the door to the couch. Put me down, I need to pee." That got his attention. Pointing at my traitorous brother, I said, "Drew, I'll deal with you in a minute." I was gonna light his ass up for bringing Brody with him.

I got to the bathroom and my night went even more to shit.

"Drew," I hollered.

"Yeah," he answered from the other side of the door.

"I need you to get me a pair of panties and pajama pants." I was starting to shake as I took a pad out of the cabinet.

"What's wrong with the stuff you got on?" he asked.

"Asshat, just get the stuff. Panties are in the top drawer of the tall dresser and pants in the bottom left drawer of the long dresser." I took off my wet clothes and wrapped a towel around my belly.

"Seriously, Leila open the door," Brody demanded.

"No, go away. I don't need…" Oh fuck. I quickly sat down on the floor when I started to feel faint.

"Lei, open the fucking door." He sounded so far away. I tried to crawl over to the door, but my body was so heavy. I looked down and saw blood.

"I can't," was all I could manage.

"Leila, are you near the door?" he hollered. I tried to respond, but I just couldn't make my voice loud enough. "Leila, if you can hear me get away from the door."

I heard wood splintering and caught a glimpse of Brody as he broke down the door; Drew was behind him. I must have fallen unconscious, because I woke up in Brody's arms in the back of Drew's Tahoe.

"Hey, stay with me. Keep your eyes open baby, look at me," he pleaded and I tried, I really did.

"Drew," I managed to mumble.

"I'm right up here sis. We're takin' ya to the hospital." He rolled with lights and sirens.

"Save your energy, don't try to talk. Drew called Barb," Brody explained, "they're on standby." He brushed the hair out of my face.

"Why didn't you call and tell me what was going on Lei? I would've been here before now."

"You...left...us," I got out slowly. "Jax, call Jax. Please. Drew, Jax." The look on Brody's face said it all. I might as well have just gutted him. He'd made his choice, and I had made mine.

"I will later, right now we need to take care of you and the baby." Drew put the SUV in park and jumped out in front of the ambulance bay.

Brody handed me off to Barb, Drake and another nurse I couldn't make out right away.

"Barb," I called out for her. "Jax, I need Jax."

"I called him ten minutes ago sweetie. He's on his way." She held my hand as they wheeled me into a trauma room.

A flurry of activity surrounded my bed. I tried to keep my eyes open, but they started to get really heavy. Barb fitted an oxygen mask on my face while Mary started an IV and drew blood.

I heard Brody yelling as he pushed past and was at the bedrail. "Leila keep your eyes open damn it. Stay with me. Don't go to sleep. Fight Leila. You have to keep your eyes open."

Struggling against the burn, I kept blinking at him. I turned and looked around the room, then focused back on him. I reached up and pulled the mask down. "No matter what, save her. Promise me, Barb." I looked over to Barb. "Jaxon..."

*****

~Jaxon~

I rushed out of the house in the middle of Christmas dinner, promising to call my mom once I was at the hospital with my woman and child, then hopped on my bike and took off.

Damn it, if I just would have stayed home.

I had driven from Greenville back to Charleston in a record two hours and twenty minutes. When I arrived at the hospital, I was told she was in trauma room two. One of the nurses took me back and said that everyone was saying a prayer for Leila and the baby. That's when I realized it must have been worse than last time.

I pushed the curtain back and saw her tiny body curled up on the stretcher, wrapped in white and blue blankets. Even sick in a hospital bed, she made my dick twitch.

Then I saw him.

"What in the hell are you doin' here? Haven't you done enough? Get the fuck outta here. Now." I roared from her bedside.

"Fuck you, that's my kid. I'm not going anywhere."

"Oh fuck no, that's my baby. You walked away you motherfuckin' piece of shit. You left her and this child months ago. You don't get to come back in here, like you give two shits. She's told you she doesn't want to see you." I realized I was really loud. I looked down at her sleeping peacefully. "Leave now, or I swear to God, I'll break my promise to her, beat your fuckin' ass and throw you out."

Drew stepped in. "Brody, I think he's right. You should probably go." He tipped his head toward the door. "I'll call you if there's any change. Thanks for your help."

His jaw tightened and he looked at Leila, then back to me.

"Fucker." Brody punched the wall as he left.

I turned to Barb. "Tell me what's—" Leila squeezed my hand. I looked down at her, squeezing back. "Hey babe, can you hear me? Come on princess, wake up."

"Jax," she said and blinked sluggishly.

"Yeah, I'm here. Wake up sleepy head."

"I'm..." she trailed off and closed her eyes again. "I'm awake. Is she okay? I didn't lose her, right?"

I looked at Barb for some guidance, as she smiled and nodded her head. "Yeah, princess, she's doin' great. Just like her beautiful momma." I rubbed her hand and kissed her lips. "How are you feelin'?"

"Tired. Can we go home now? I just wanna sleep."

Barb shook her head no and said, "You need to stay here for a little longer. The bleeding has stopped, but they need to do some more testing. Just go to sleep and we'll wake ya when it's time to go."

"You won't leave me, right?" she asked me, her voice small and fragile.

"I'm staying right here, I'll be next to ya when ya wake up. Wild horses and a team of mercenaries couldn't drag me away from you." I kissed her pale lips. "I love you."

She sighed and closed her eyes. "I love you Jax."

I turned to Barb. "Why is she so tired? How much blood did she lose?"

"She didn't lose much. Thankfully, Drew and Brody were there and broke down the bathroom door. They got her here in plenty of time. This bleed was worse than the last one, but still not too bad."

"So why is she so out of it? She wasn't like this last time."

"I think it might be because she didn't eat enough today. Add on top of that the bleeding, it's enough to make anyone faint," Barb reassured me.

"Oh, thank God. Hang on, you were with her. Why didn't you make her eat?"

She stifled a chuckle. "We're talking about the same person, right? Have you ever been able to make her do anything she didn't wanna do?"

"Point taken." I paced around the room. "Will she have to stay here?"

The doctor and nurse walked in. "Drew, do you wanna step out into the hallway so we can talk?"

"You can talk in here." He walked to the end of her bed.

"Jaxon, it's nice to see you again, hate it's like this though." He extended his hand to me.

I took the proffered hand. "Dr.Miller. So what's going on? Is she gonna be okay?"

"Yeah, all the tests indicate so. It looks like another small bleed, sometimes this happens as the placenta moves up the uterine wall." He turned to Barb. "She didn't eat again today, did she?"

"She ate a little breakfast, but then she took a nap and I got called in here."

"Okay, so what's the plan? Can I take her home now?" I asked.

"Yeah, but she has to stay in bed. Up only to use the bathroom and I don't want her up and down the stairs."

The doctor left and the nurse went over discharge instruction. They wanted to wheel her out, but I scooped her up in my arms and carried her to Drew's SUV, then followed him back to her place on my bike. After we got her situated, Drew agreed to stay with her so I could run over to my place. She was still sleeping when I left.

Chapter Eight

~Jaxon~

I was only gone for a few minutes, but when I got back a gray Venom was parked in front of the house.

I'm gonna fuckin' kill him.

Opening the door with my key, I scanned the room. No one. Then I heard voices coming from upstairs.

"Brody, please," she spoke in a meek tone. *What the fuck*? I ran up the stairs two at a time.

"I'm just asking for you to think, for one minute," the asshat was pleading with her. "We made her together. She's a piece of me and of you. He's not her father and never will be." My bullshit meter was just about to overflow. I stood at the top of the stairs listening. "I want you back. Watching you today, I've never been more terrified in my life. I know I fucked up royally and it'll take time to earn back your trust, but I want that chance Leila. I want to raise our daughter, together, as a family." I could hear Leila sniffling. Fucker was making her cry. "I can give you anything and everything you could ever want or need. You just have to give me another chance. I know you still love me. Tell me you still want me."

"I've told you this already," she said. "I don't think I'll ever be able to get that image of you that night out of my head." Sniffle. "I don't trust you. You shattered my whole world when you shattered that bottle. I loved you. I told you we were having a baby and you threw a bottle past my face." Sniffle. "And maybe I could've gotten past all of that, but you walked away and didn't come back for months. Months, Brody. I have moved on with Jaxon. He's a good and loyal and devoted man." He huffed. "Stop it. You don't get to come in here and huff at me or my choices. Jaxon may not be the biological father, but he's been here a hell of a lot more than you have." No more sniffles now. "He wants her and has since the beginning, which is a hell of a lot more than you can say. He doesn't have any doubts and isn't scared to grow up. He will be her daddy. If you actually stick around, then we can discuss your role in a few months."

"I will be here and she's my daughter. I will be a part of her life. I don't want to fight with you Leila. Please, just take some time to consider what I've said." I thought he was done, so I started to walk the rest of the way to the bedroom, but he started talking again.

"Let me ask you something, if he wasn't here, would you give me another chance?"

"I want you to leave Brody." She was quiet and sounded exhausted.

"Just answer me Lei, if Jaxon wasn't in the picture, could we be a family?"

"It doesn't matter Brody, I am with him. I love him. He's good to me. I can trust him not to run out on me, like you did and just like my father did to my mom."

And there it was.

"He's why you won't try again, because you think I'm gonna be just like your father?"

She was quietly sniffling. "Brody, please just go." Part of me wanted to drag him out by his balls, but she needed to handle this her way.

"Baby, look at me. Please." Silence. "We have a few months to figure this out. I want to be a part of everything else going forward, doctors appointments, ultrasounds, emergencies, all of it. I'm gonna be by your side from now on, I swear."

I turned the corner and saw him sitting on the bed next to Leila, his back to me. She was lying down on her side facing the bathroom, with a tissue in hand wiping her tears. Neither of them saw me. He leaned down and kissed the side of her head. It took all my self-control not to rip him off the bed and beat the shit out of him.

"Brody, don't. You have to stop. I love Jaxon. You and I are over. You made that decision, not me. And yeah, some part of me will always love you. You are a part of me now, but it's not the same way I feel for Jax." I stepped through the doorframe causing the floor to squeak.

"I should've known you'd be a fuckin' pussy and wait to corner her when I wasn't here to throw your fuckin' ass out." I crossed the room. "You're leaving. Now."

"Fuck you, I'm here to see the mother of *my* child." The asshole was pushing all the right buttons if he was looking for me to beat the shit out of him.

"Both of you stop," Leila scolded.

"What? You want him here?" I set my sights on her.

"Lei, we need to finish this conversation," Brody chimed in before she could answer.

"Jaxon, I do need to finish—" she started.

"I guess I'm the one who needs to be leavin'." Anger reverberated through every cell in my body. I couldn't believe she was going to let that fucker stay and continue to manipulate her. Why couldn't she see him for who he was—a selfish prick.

"No, Jax, please. Don't leave. It's not like that. I just need to finish telling him I'm with you. There is nothing left for him and me. I'm with you, don't go." Tears streamed down her beautiful face. Watching her cry, knowing it was my doing, almost broke me, and although I hated staying in the same room as that fucker, I wasn't gonna do one more thing to hurt my Leila.

"Drew can stay with you tonight and I'll come over tomorrow. You can finish whatever this is and then we will talk." I needed to get away from her. She was slowly destroying all my defenses. I was trying to make the right decision for her, for us and for this innocent child.

"No. I want you here, not Drew, not Brody. You! Stay and talk to me now. You promised you'd be here with me no matter what."

Fuck, she was right. "Fine, I won't leave. I'll sleep in the spare room and we can talk later." I turned and looked at Brody. "You might not think you need time to figure things out, but from what I heard, you do. I'll be downstairs if you need me."

"Please Jax, stay up here. Brody is leaving. I don't know what you heard or think you heard, but I want you. I love you," she started to get out of the bed to come to me.

"Leila you can't—" Brody started to tell her what to do.

"Fuck you Brody. Haven't you done enough," she hissed.

I rushed to her side as she stood up. "Okay, you made your point. Now lie back down. Please."

"No. Not until you promise to stay with me, up here." Damn, if she didn't know exactly what to say to make me cave.

"Fine, we will talk—"

"Tonight," she butted in.

"Yes, tonight." Yep, totally just caved.

"And stay up here?" Her bloodshot eyes looked up at me.

"Yes, now lie down."

"Leila, please think about what we talked about and call me tomorrow." Brody stood in the doorway staring at her.

"Get out." I tightened my hands at my sides.

"Fuck you," he shouted.

Leila grabbed my forearm before I could go after him. "Babe, just ignore him." She turned to Brody. "You heard him. You need to go Brody."

After helping her to the bathroom, I got her back in bed. Okay, I carried her. I loved her fiercely and would do anything to protect her and this child. "I'm gonna go talk to Drew. You wanna drink or somethin' to eat?"

"Yeah, will you bring me up some tea and salami with cream cheese?" She batted her long, black eyelashes at me. As if she really needed to. We both knew she had me wrapped around her tiny little pinky.

"Yeah." I gave her a quick peck, then went to find Drew.

We needed to get some shit straight and fast.

*****

~Leila~

Jax didn't come back for half an hour. I could hear him arguing with Drew downstairs, but they were too quiet to make out what they were saying until Jax raised his voice and said, "That fucker isn't welcome here. We clear?"

When he came up with my sweet tea, he sat beside me on the edge of the bed.

"Listen," he started. "I know we've said we would raise this baby together"—he rubbed my little bump—"but, I don't want you to feel obligated to stay with me. He is the father and I would understand if you wanted to try again, for the baby's sake."

Oh hell no. He did not just say that. "Are you done?" I waited, but he gave me this bizarre look. "Finished? As in, I can talk now?"

"Uh, yeah."

"Good, sit back and listen real good and carefully." I pushed up to sitting in the bed. "Number one, I would never stay with you out of obligation. Two, I've said it before, but I will say it again and again if I need to. Brody may have donated sperm, but you're who's been here for me. Three, I know you heard me say that a part of me would always love him, but you took it completely out of context. A small piece of me will always love him, because he gave me this little miracle." I rubbed my stomach. "Who, by the way, is hungry. Four, I want you Jax. All six feet four inches of frustrating, loving, compassionate and sexy you. Yes, the situation is less than ideal, but it's the hand we were dealt." I took a deep breath. "Now, you're gonna scoot your fine, tight ass over here and hold me for the rest of our first Christmas together."

"You wanna know what I want?" He turned back to me.

I shook my head.

"What's for dinner?" He smirked. "Really, what do you want? I can make a quick sandwich or—"

"Frozen pizza, pepperoni." He scrunched up his nose. "What? Don't make that face at me. It's what the baby wants. Ooh, and she wants buffalo wings and cheese fries." I didn't realize how hungry I was.

"What? We don't have wings and fries, and it's Christmas night. I doubt any place that is open serves either of those. How about a grilled cheese?"

For a half a second I contemplated messing with him, but I was too tired and hungry to work up the energy. So Jax went downstairs, made grilled cheeses and brought them to bed. We watched movies until I remembered his Christmas present.

"Can we do presents now?"

"Yeah. Wanna tell me where you hide mine and I'll grab it while I get yours?" He walked over and opened my closet.

"Nah, I can reach them." I hid them under the bed.

He came back with two wrapped presents, one about the size of a large shoebox and the other a small jewelry box. Seeing the tiny box made my heart race, surely it wasn't a ring. We hadn't been together long enough for him to propose, and I certainly wasn't ready for him to ask me to marry him.

I pulled out his presents and sat them on the bed in front of my crossed legs. "Let's take turns opening so I can watch, 'kay?"

"Whatever you want baby."

I handed him the first present. He tore into the silver wrapping paper, opened the box to reveal the silver frame engraved Daddy's Little Girl with the 4D ultrasound picture of her sucking her thumb. "Lei," he said then paused. "It's perfect, I love it."

"Okay, my turn." I held out my hands, letting him decide which one to give me first. He handed me the large box first. Ripping back the green and red paper, I stopped to run my fingers across the words Jimmy Choo embossed on the box. "Jax what did you do?"

"Open it and see," he said, giving nothing away with his deadpan face.

Carefully, I lifted the box lid and pulled back the tissue paper. "Oh my God, Jaxon." I was stunned at the luxurious black Jimmy Choo diaper bag with double handle top and quilted leather bottle pockets on the sides.

He just grinned. "You like it?"

"Oh Jaxon." My eyes leaked. "It's gorgeous and way too much. You shouldn't have done this." I took the bag out of the box and hugged it in my arms. "I love it, really I do, but we can't spend this kind of money with a baby coming in a few months."

"Says who? You let me worry about that 'kay?"

I leaned over and kissed him. "Here, open," I instructed, handing him the larger box of the two.

"This one's a little heavier." He shook the box.

"Just open it." I was excited for him to see what was inside.

He tore into the paper. "Holy shit babe. You got me a camera?" He pulled the black Nikon box out of the wrapping.

"Well, we were lookin' at them a few weeks ago and you said you wanted to get one before the baby came," I explained. "Now you can take all the pictures you want."

"Awesome." He started pulling things out of the box. "Did you charge it?"

"No pictures tonight." I put my hands up in front of my face.

"All right." He lifted the last present to me. Inside was a silver key.

I held it up. "Is this the key to your heart?"

"Nope, front door."

Now I really was confused. "The front door? To what?"

"The front door to my house around the corner. I want you to move in with me." Thank God I wasn't drinking or else it would've come out my nose.

"Huh? As in, live with you? Sell my place?"

"Yes, as in, live with me."

"You want me and the baby to live in your house?" I still needed him to spell it out. "I thought you were renovating? We can't move in with a newborn if there is hammering and sawdust." I realized it sounded like I was rejecting him. "I'm not saying I don't want to, but how could we live there while you are workin' on it."

"First of all, you're right, I have been remodeling, but I am about a week or two away from being done. Just have to finish the master bathroom and decorate the nursery. I would never move y'all in if it wasn't perfect, but I do want you to help me pick out the finishings."

"How long have you been planning this?" I wondered.

"The remodel or moving y'all in?"

"Moving us in. I mean, I knew you bought the place and gutted it, but when did you make changes to your plans to include a nursery?" I wanted to know how long he had been so committed to me without me realizing it.

"First time I considered moving you and the baby in with me? Probably the middle of October. I changed the plans to include a nursery six weeks ago, and I canceled all of the tile, flooring, mirrors and vanities for our bathroom about the same time."

I sat watching him. His excitement blazed across his handsomely rugged face. "This is real? You want us to move in with you and you want me to sell my place?"

"I do. I'm committed to both of you. Talk to me." He took my hand and rubbed circles on the back with his thumb. "What part freaks you out?"

"I'm not freaked out. Why do you think that?" I was a little bit freaked, but excited too.

"Come on Lei, I know you. I know your faces and your noises. This face"—he lifted his chin—"says you're having a tiny panic attack, but refuse to admit it to anyone."

Holy fuck, he does know me.

"Okay, cards on the table?" He nodded. "I'm scared that if I move in with you and you have to deal with Brody about the baby all of the time, you'll get sick of it and want us to leave. If I've sold this place, then I won't have any place to go. I'm just as committed to us as you are—I'm just scared Jax."

"Slow down and take a breath, babe. I won't let him come between us. I will never get sick of either of you. And I will always want you. I don't doubt your sincerity, love or commitment." He leaned forward and pulled me to his chest. "You need to protect yourself and always be prepared. It's one of the things I love about you. If it will make you feel better, don't sell this place, just rent it."

"What did I do to deserve you?" I kissed his chest. "I love you Jax. More than I ever thought possible."

"I love you too princess." He held me for a minute. "So is that a yes or a no?"

"Yes, I want nothing more than to fall asleep with you every night and wake up with you for three a.m. feedings."

He let out a deep breath. "Good. Now let's go to sleep. I'm exhausted."

"Sounds like a great idea. Night Jax."

"Sweet dreams baby girl."

Chapter Nine

~Leila~

Over the next week, Jax brought home design books, tile samples, paint colors and pictures of the bathroom in its current state. We reviewed the blueprints, made a few changes and settled on a color scheme. Since I couldn't get out of bed to see the real thing, this remote planning would have to do.

During the day, when Jax worked on the house or was at the clubhouse, I lay in bed with my tablet looking at nursery themes and paint schemes. I picked out a pale pink and gray bedding set with a paisley pattern that was handmade. Jaxon found the most adorable white furniture in a Pottery Barn Kids catalogue and were having her name made in wooden painted letters to match.

Barb and I were lying in the bed Sunday morning, flipping through baby books shouting out names. We had decided to see who could find the worst name, then we asked Jaxon to pick between them. Obviously, we weren't actually going to name her one of these awful names, and, knowing him, he'd cotton on to the game soon enough.

"Jaxon," I called from the master bedroom.

"Yeah babe, what's up?" He trotted up the stairs.

"So Barb and I have narrowed the name list down and we want you to pick. Whichever one you chose is what we will name our little peanut."

"Okay, so let's hear it." He sat down on the foot of the bed since Barb was propped up on his side of the bed.

"I thought maybe Bernice Geraldine," I said it straight-faced. The inside of my cheek was probably bleeding from biting it so hard. Jax had this look of sheer horror on his face.

Barb played along so well. She jumped in before he could say anything. "I pick Edna Mae. So what do you think?"

Jax looked back and forth between us. "You seriously want to know what I think?"

"Yeah baby, which one do you like better?" I smiled sweetly at him.

"I think you both need to go back to your crack dealer and ask for a refund, 'cause he sold y'all some really bad shit." He looked at me like I had three heads.

"What? What's that supposed to mean?" I feigned hostility.

"Yeah, what's wrong with our names?" Barb shot out.

"You can't be serious." He looked back at me. "You're not actually suggesting we name our daughter Bernice Geraldine or Edna Mae," he said, his brow furrowed.

Game over. He said, "our daughter."

Awwww. How can I mess with him after that? I crawled down to him at the end of the bed and wrapped my hands around the back of his neck.

"No," I said and gave him a quick peck, "we were just fuckin' with ya." I smiled and quickly scooted away.

"Damn you woman. You're so lucky you're pregnant and on bed rest." He shook his head as he walked back out of the room. Barb and I laughed as we heard him grumbling all the way down the steps.

"I'm gonna go and let you rest." She bent down and spoke to my belly. "Bye my sweet girl. Be good to your momma."

Grabbing the remote, I turned on FX and started watching the *Twilight* marathon but I don't think I made it through the first movie. I woke up during *Eclipse* and went to the bathroom, then climbed back into bed and checked my phone. There was one text message waiting from Brody, wanting me to call or text him and let him know how I was feeling and when my next OB appointment was.

Hey, I feel fine. No cramping, bleeding or fainting. Thx for—
"Who you textin'?" Jax appeared in the doorway.

I jumped. "Geez Pete. You scared me."

"I'm sorry babe, didn't mean to."

"I was just texting Brody back. He sent me a text while I was sleepin' wanting to know when the next doctor's appointment is."

Jaxon walked over and plopped down, grumbling, "I liked it better when he wasn't in the picture."

I grabbed his elbow and pulled him back to me. then wrapped my arms around his strong, bulky bicep. "I know it's not easy to have him in the middle of this, but he is the father." I sensed him pulling away.

"Jax, look at me." He turned his icy stare to me. "Brody might be her father, but you will be her daddy. You'll be the one singing her to sleep, rocking her when she cries, getting up at three a.m. and it will be your voice she recognizes. Don't let him come between us."

"Babe, I'm tryin' but he has made it perfectly fuckin' clear he wants you. He wants to be a family with you. And he keeps throwing that shit in my face."

"Well, I guess it's a good thing I want you, and it's a good thing that we are gonna be a family. The only one who has the power to change that is you." I lifted his arm and curled into his side.

"Promise me he's not gonna steal you away from me." Wow. For first time since the day I met him, I realized there was something that could make Jaxon feel insecure. And I didn't like that I was the cause of him feeling that way. It killed me to know that he thought Brody could ever take his place.

"Jaxon, I love you. I'm not going anywhere honey. I'll be here as long as you want me to be." I pressed my hand to his chest and lifted my lips to his, flirting my tongue along his bottom lip, earning myself a little growl. Reaching up and tugging him over to me, I fisted my hands into his hair, pulling him into my mouth. I needed more of him. Breaking our connection long enough to pull his shirt over his head, I traced the lines of his pecs with my tongue and squeezed his nipple.

"Fuck. Babe you gotta stop, we can't," he groaned as I reached between us, unzipped his jeans, reached in and stroked his shaft. He grabbed my hand, stilling my motion. "Babe, the doc said no sex."

"Right, but he didn't say anything about me goin' down on you." I shoved him onto his back. I tugged his jeans down just enough his cock could spring free. "This is the game we're gonna play. Your hands are going to stay behind your head. If you touch me, I will stop. If you want to come, you will follow the directions. This can go as fast as you want or I can drag it out for an excruciatingly long time."

"Mmm, I love it when you're pushy. Jeez, babe, I'm not gonna last long." He threw his head back as my mouth enveloped his engorged dick. I moaned and sucked as I slid him in and out of my throat and lightly scratched his balls, causing him to grab a handful of my curls. Immediately I stopped and pulled all the way back. "Babe what th—Oh shit." I gave him a knowing look.

He released his hold and I began to work his cock with my tongue. He groaned and thrust his hips, gaining deep access to my throat. I tried my best to fit all of him, but I just couldn't. Using my hand, I stroked it in unison with my mouth. Slipping him out of my mouth to trace his tip with my tongue, I teased and licked him up and down, then took him fully in my mouth and bobbed up and down until I felt his balls tighten and dick swell with his impending orgasm.

"Babe, I'm so fuckin' close," he spoke at the ceiling.

"Come in my mouth Jax."

"Mmm, you sure?" he gritted out.

"Mmhmm," I hummed as I slid his shaft in and out of my mouth. With a curse, his release hit the back of my throat. I swallowed as much and as fast as I could. I milked him, sucking every last drop until he began to relax. I climbed down from the tall bed, leaving a euphoric Jax flat on his back, arms still behind his head. I went to the bathroom, peed and swished some Listerine. Walking back out, I found Jax in the same position.

"Babe, fuck that was awesome."

I smiled lasciviously. "Yep. Bask in my awesomeness."

Chapter Ten

~Leila~

Having to spend yet another week in bed, I was bored out of my mind. I listened to music, watched a few movies and found a bunch of kickass books. My favorite was a tie between the Consumed series by Skyla Madi and the Driven series by K. Bromberg.

New Year's Eve was quiet.

"Here babe." Jax handed me sparkling apple cider.

Setting the bowl of popcorn down in the middle of the bed, I reached out and took the crystal flute. "Thanks. What do you wanna watch?"

"Don't care, whatever you want." He dropped to the bed as Ruger's sniffing nose appeared. "Come on buddy." Jax patted the bed and up came one furry, begging Shepherd.

"No begging," he warned Ruger, then slung his arm around my shoulder. "I'm sorry this is how we are spending our first New Year's Eve together."

"Don't be sorry, it's perfect. There isn't anywhere else in the world I'd rather be than curled up here with you." I scooted closer to him. "Seriously honey, I'd rather be here with you just like this than be at a bar with hundreds of drunken idiots."

He leaned down and kissed me, slow and seductively. "I love you Leila."

"I love you too Jax. Happy New Year." I hooked my arm around the back of his neck and pulled him back down to me. We spent the next thirty minutes kissing in the new year. I couldn't think of a better way to celebrate.

Okay, I lied. I wish we had been making love at midnight.

The next Monday Jax and I went to the Prenatal Wellness Center to see the OB and have another ultrasound. Dr. Rogers wanted to check and see where the placenta was in relation to my cervix. I'd been praying that it had moved for any number of reason; including sex. Just satisfying Jax's needs was getting old; I needed sex.

Unfortunately, Brody had called me on Friday to say he would meet us for the appointment. He actually had the balls to ask if I would meet him there alone. I laughed and told him, "No way." I mean *really.*

We arrived a little early, and beat Brody there. After a twenty minute wait the nurse called my name. Still no Brody. Jax couldn't have been happier. I told the receptionist that Brody might show up late and to send him back whenever he got there.

"Hi, Leila." Dr. Rogers popped her head in the room. "Jaxon. How are y'all doin'?"

"Hi, Dr. Rogers, we're good. No more bleeds. It's been three weeks, I'm so ready to be off bed rest," I said.

"Yeah, we need to get her out of the house. I'm being compared to fictional characters," Jax muttered, sitting in the chair to the right of the exam table.

Dr. Rogers laughed. "Well, I just wanted to say a quick hello before you had your ultrasound. I'll see y'all in a few minutes, 'kay?"

"Yep." I wiggled, crinkling the exam table paper. Dr. Rogers shut the door and I turned to Jax. "Can you please hand me my phone babe?"

"Yeah," he said, sounding annoyed. He must've known I was checking if Brody texted me.

The notification light blinked.

Sorry Lei, I had an emergency in NYC on my way to airport now. I can't make appt. Text me so I know what Dr. said.

I wasn't sure why I was slightly disappointed. I was glad Brody wasn't there, but I didn't want my baby to grow up feeling her father didn't love her enough to hang around.

"Is it my lucky day?" Jax looked happier than he had since we left the house.

"Yep, it's your lucky day. He's not coming. He's on his way to New York for work." I sighed.

"What the hell Lei? Why do you sound upset? Did you want him here?" Jax asked gruffly.

"Jaxon, please don't take this the wrong way, but yeah. I'm pissed. He made this big fuckin' deal about being here for his daughter and the first opportunity, he's absent."

"So you're pissed? Not disappointed?"

I sighed. "Mostly pissed, but, yeah, I'm a little disappointed." I could see he was not happy with my answer. I felt the need to explain.

"Jax, you don't get it. My dad walked out on me. You will never understand how that feels. It makes you feel like it's your fault. That you were the reason he didn't want to stay. That he didn't love you enough to stay. I never want that feeling for her." I touched my protruding stomach. "She'll have you, but when she gets older we'll have to sit her down and explain all of this."

He stood and walked over to me. "You're right, I don't understand what that feels like, but I'll make sure she never feels like she's not loved." His face softened. "We'll make sure she understands his choices are not her fault and that it has nothing to do with her."

"How is it that you always know the perfect thing to say?" A lone tear skated down my cheek. I tugged on the front of his shirt, pulling him closer and wrapped my arms around his waist. A knock on the door gained our attention.

"Hi, I'm Polly. I'm gonna do your ultrasound. All ready?" the petite brunette in pink scrubs asked.

"We are," Jax answered with a nod.

"Great, let's get started. Can you lay back for me please?" She coated my belly in the warm goo and slid the transducer around. "Ahh, there she is. I will take measurements, then we will get y'all some pictures, 'kay?"

"Sounds good." I smiled as I watched the screen.

She went about her business and then printed out four pictures. She handed me a small towel and told us Dr. Rogers would be in shortly.

I handed Jax the pictures to put in my purse while I cleaned myself up a little. Dr. Rogers was in about five minutes later.

"Do you want the good news or the bad news first?" She set her tablet down on the counter with a straight face.

Bad news? I can't take any bad news. I've had enough bad news to last three lifetimes.

Jax grabbed my hand.

"Good news, I guess," I answered timidly, taking a deep breath.

"The good news is the baby looks great, measures right at twenty five weeks. She's about a pound and a half. And, the placenta has migrated away from the cervix." Dr. Rogers smiled.

"Oh thank you baby Jesus." My shoulders finally relaxed and Jax kissed the top of my head.

"But that's where the bad news comes in," she said, cutting short our celebration. Really? Couldn't she just leave it at that? "Since the placenta has moved, you are cleared to go back to work."

"Wait, that's it?" I looked from her to Jax and back to her.

"Yeah, moms that are almost in their third trimester beg to be written off of work. I guess from your reaction, you're not one of those moms." She chuckled.

"No, Leila definitely isn't one of those women," Jax answered.

The doctor went over the measurements and reassured us everything looked fine. Just as she seemed ready to leave Jax nudged me. "What?"

Quietly, he muttered under his breath for me to ask about sex. A huge grin spread across my face. I shook my head and nodded from him to her, suggesting he ask.

"Uh, hey, doc. I had one more question." Jax was red as a Jersey tomato. "Um, is it, uh, safe for us to…ya know?"

I sat back biting my cheek trying not to giggle. Dr. Rogers must have picked up on it and played along. "I'm sorry, safe to do what exactly?"

Jax groaned. "Sex. Can we fuck or what doc?"

"Jaxon Austin Henderson," I scolded him like a small child.

Dr. Rogers burst out laughing. "Yes, you can have sex, but take it easy the first couple of times. By next week, you should be able to resume a normal sex life."

"Thank fuck." He dropped into the chair like a rock.

"I'm sorry Dr. Rogers, please excuse him. I think all of the pent up…testosterone is starting to back up into his brain." I cut my eyes in his direction.

She left the room still smirking. I dropped the sheet and reached for my panties and jeans. Even though my back was to him, I could feel his eyes on my naked flesh.

"Don't even think about it," I said.

"What?" he asked, playing coy.

"Don't what me Jaxon. I can feel your eyes practically fuckin' me over the exam table, even though I can't see them." I pulled up my maternity jeans. "You can wait 'til we are home babe."

He snatched up my purse, hoodie and our pictures, grabbed my hand and practically dragged me out of the doctor's office. As he stalked through the lobby the receptionist tried to get our attention.

"Excuse me. Ms. Matthews would you like to schedule your next appointment?" she hollered across the room.

Jax didn't even stop walking. He looked over his shoulder. "She'll call you tomorrow. Or the next day."

"Sorry," I squeaked out before he pulled me out the door. "Jaxon, slow down. I can't walk as fast as you."

"Sorry babe. I just can't wait to get you home." He pushed the lobby doors open and the wintery air swirled around us. Jax must have seen me shiver. "Shit Lei, I'm sorry. Here, let me help you with your jacket."

"Thanks." I shrugged on the thick gray hoodie.

He drove us home like the car was set with explosives. When he spun tires at a red light I finally spoke up, "Hey Kevin Harvick, this ain't Daytona. Slow down!"

He backed off as we pulled onto East Bay. We turned into the garage a few minutes later. He was out the car and opening my door before I could unbuckle my seat belt.

"Whoa killer, calm down. There is no rush. I'm as eager to have sex as you are, but damn." I closed the door to the Challenger as he unlocked the door and turned off the alarm. *Play time!*

"Hey, you hungry? Wanna sandwich or something?"

"Nope and neither do you. Upstairs now."

"But the baby's hungry Daddy," I said, trying to stall.

"Babe, no fuckin' around. Upstairs. Naked. Two minutes. I'm takin' Ruger out, then I'm comin' for ya." He turned around in the hallway once he called Ruger. "It's either upstairs naked or bent over the first available flat surface I find you near."

If I was further along, I would be concerned my water just broke. He turned me on that much. *Don't judge.* It had been almost four weeks since we'd had sex. I was a puddle of horniness.

After dropping my stuff on the dining room table, I climbed the stairs, used the bathroom, then changed into a sexy black and pink lace bra and panty set I had bought a week before I went on bed rest.

I was in the bathroom with the door shut when I heard him running up the stairs. He sounded like a herd of elephants. The bathroom door burst open.

"Holy shit babe. You look so fuckin' hot."

I could see the bulge in his jeans. "Really? I don't look fat?" I was starting to be self-conscious about my pregnant body.

"Oh baby, no. You're sexy as fuckin' hell." He grabbed my hips and our chests collided. Our lips and tongues ravaged each other's mouth as he slipped his hands around my backside and lifted me off the floor. "Bed or wall?"

"Bed."

His tongue probed as I locked my ankles behind his back. He carried me from the bathroom to the bed and laid me down gently.

"Wait, Jaxon, wait."

He halted. "What? What's wrong?"

"Nothing. I just wanted to remind you to be gentle with me."

His mouth was back on me as he pulled the lacy cups down, giving him access to my breast. He took his time licking and tonguing my nipples until they were so sensitive it hurt. Slowly, he kissed his way down to my pussy.

"Hope these aren't special," he growled. Before I could say a word he ripped them off me. Oh fuck, those were brand new—and I couldn't have cared less. He pushed my thighs apart and dipped his tongue into my wet slit.

"Oh fuck." I rolled my hips and moaned. I wasn't going to last more than thirty seconds. He flicked his tongue up and down my clit as he eased his finger into my greedy pussy. "Oh God Jaxon, yeah. Right there, oohh."

He pulled back and my eyes shot down to his. "Eyes on me."

I propped myself up on my elbows and our eyes locked. His talented tongue went back to work, slipping and swirling around my throbbing clit. The first wave hit me as he curled his finger around and massaged the front wall of my pussy. Our eyes never left each other as I screamed his name and my whole body quivered and shook. He slowly ascended my body, eyes still locked on mine.

"Mine," he whispered against my belly as he laid soft, lazy kisses up my navel to my breast. He palmed them, squeezing my nipples between his thumb and middle finger. He rubbed his index finger over the peak of my nipple causing me to moan loudly. That sent me over the edge. I grabbed his arms and pulled him up to me.

"Stop playin' around Jax. I need you in me now," I begged like a wanton slut. He gripped his thick shaft and rubbed it up and down my soaked slit.

"Is this what you want baby?" he teased.

"Ugh, stop teasin' me. You know that's what I want."

"Then say, 'Jax I want you to fuck my pussy.'" His eyes were dark with need.

"Please," I continued to beg.

"Say it baby. I can tease you like this for hours." He rubbed the head of his dick across my clit.

"Fuck, Jax please."

"Say it Lei."

Fine. "Jax, fuck me."

"Nope. Say it."

I knew what he wanted me to say, but God, it sounded so whorish. He pushed just the tip of his dick into me and then pulled back out. It's like he knew what incentive I needed to push me over the edge.

"Oh God, Jax." I caved. "Jaxon I want you to fuck my wet pussy. Now!"

He growled and shoved his deliciously fat cock into my tight slit. He pushed all the way in, balls deep and paused. "You okay?"

"I will be as soon as you kiss me." I pulled his face down, my lips seeking his out. He pumped into me, slow and deep. I threw my head back. "Oh Jax, don't stop, right there, oh God."

He picked up his tempo all the while his face searched mine. "Oh fuck Lei. You still okay baby?"

"Yeahhhhhhh," I moaned out. "Harder Jax. I need more."

"Baby, I don't wanna hurt ya. I gotta hold back for now." His thrusts were deliberate and planned. He went fast and shallow, then slowed and went deep, rolling his hips.

"Oh God Jax, I'm gonna come, don't stop."

"Wait baby, I'm almost there, wait...." His eyes stayed fixed on mine as he slid in and out of my wanton sex. "Now," he roared. I felt him stiffen inside me, then empty himself deep within my walls. The sight of ecstasy on his face sent me over the cliff. I came all over his cock as he finished pumping his own release into me.

"Oh God Jax, is it possible that's better than I remembered?" I lay there unable to get myself up.

"Fuck babe. That was un-fuckin-believable. You sure you're okay? You want me to help ya to the bathroom?" He rolled off me. He took care the entire time not to put much weight on me.

"Yeah, I'm okay, honey. I probably should get up before I make a mess on the sheets." I hated the cleanup.

"Babe," I hollered out of the bathroom. Jax was in the doorway like a madman in a split second.

"What? What's wrong?" he said quickly with panic written all over his face.

"Geez, relax, nothing is wrong. Actually the exact opposite. No bleeding, at all." I stood up from the toilet and flushed.

"Jesus Leila, you damn near gave me a fuckin' heart attack." He scrubbed his hands over his face with a huff.

"Did you just huff at me?" I approached him, intending on playing with him a little.

He scrunched his forehead in disbelief. "What if I did? Whatcha gonna do 'bout it?"

"I may have to spank that incredibly sexy ass of yours." I bounced my eyebrows with a smirk.

"Is that so? What makes you think I'd letcha?" He wrapped his arms around my chest, under my arms and picked me up. He walked backward and over to the bed. He sat down and I wrapped my legs around him. He grabbed a handful of curls and pulled my head back exposing my neck. "I think you may have overestimated yourself sweetheart."

With that, he attacked my neck with rough kisses and playful nips. I could feel him hardening beneath me. I was frozen in my position because of his hold on my hair. With his free hand, he reached between us and stroked his shaft, rubbing it against my core to ensure easy access.

"Oh fuck yeah," he gritted out as he slipped into my greedy, needful body.

He felt like home.

Chapter Eleven

~Leila~

The next day, about an hour after Jaxon came home from working on the house, my cell phone chimed. Brody. Crap. I had forgot to let him know about the doctor's appointment.

"Who you texting princess?" Jax came in from the kitchen where he was cooking dinner.

"Brody. He's texted me twice and I forgot to reply earlier. He wanted to know about my check-up," I answered without looking up. "He also wanted me to meet him this weekend."

"What the fuck for?" Jax growled.

"I don't know, I told him I'd see if we had plans and that if not *we* could meet him." I looked over my shoulder at my sexy brooding alpha who had two fistfuls of couch. "What are you feeding me for dinner?"

With a snort, he seemed to drop it. "Chili and cornbread."

"You didn't—" I started to ask.

"No, I didn't make it too spicy babe," he answered my question before I could finish it.

"Okay goodie." I got up from the couch. "I'm gonna pee, then we can eat."

"Good, we can talk about your work schedule," he said, walking back into the kitchen.

Groaning and rolling my eyes, I waddled to the bathroom. When I came back, I saw the dining room table set for two, with bowls of chili, and a plate full of cornbread muffins. I loved that my man cooked for me. It might not be a gourmet five course, but it was delicious and it was made with love.

I pulled the chair out and spied Ruger sitting just outside the kitchen entryway. Begging, of course.

"You want cheese for your chili?" Jaxon asked as he threw a piece of cornbread in the air to Ruger.

"No, and stop feeding him people food. He's gonna weigh a hundred and fifty pounds if you don't." I sat and put my spoon in my chili for a little taste. "Jesus Jaxon. I thought you said it wasn't spicy."

"Lightweight," he muttered as he sat down at the table with my water and the cheese. "What if I said I wanted you to put off going back to work for just a little while?"

"I would say you're nuts. I love working. You know that. Besides, why would I?" I added some cheese to my chili.

"You've had a rough pregnancy. I just think you should give yourself a little more time to relax. I don't want to see you in the hospital bleeding again because you pushed it too much too soon. And we both know you would." He picked up his longneck and took a swig. "I'm not saying you shouldn't go back to work. I just think maybe take another week. Maybe during that time we can move some of your stuff to my house."

I took a bite just as the baby kicked the crap out of me, which caused me to cough and sputter all over myself.

"You okay?" he asked and sat his spoon down.

"Yeah, I'm good." I cleared my throat.

"I'm not tryin' to be an asshole babe, I just want you to take care of yourself. That's all."

"If you think an extra week off will make a difference, then I'll take one more week before I go back," I compromised. The beginning of this conversation actually started last week. He'd said he wanted me to wait to go back to work until after the baby was born. Moving off that notion was his compromise.

Over the next week he slowly started moving my stuff to his—our—house. Drew's lease was going to be up in a few weeks, so he agreed to move into my place and pay rent. I told him to just pay the utilities. That was another argument. After an hour of back and forth, we finally agreed to five hundred dollars a month. Which I thought was too much, but he told me his last place was paying twelve hundred a month, so it would save him a ton of money.

Monday morning, in our new home—which was weird, I had to admit—I woke up early and told Jaxon that I was going to go over to the hospital and see about picking up my shifts again.

When I returned home I found an empty house. He left a note on the gray quartz countertop in the kitchen.

Had to go to the Clubhouse. Will probably be late. Don't wait up.

Opening the crate door, I let Ruger out the back door to the small side yard to use the bathroom. As I stood in the covered breezeway between the back door and the garage I looked around my new home. Jaxon had done a beautiful job remodeling this place. It would take some getting used to, but I loved the extra space and the large gourmet kitchen.

Ruger trotted back over after chasing a few squirrels and one very irate mockingbird. "You ready to go in boy?" Opening the back door, Ruger went to the kitchen and sat by the corner where his treats were. "Just one mister. You're starting to get a little too fluffy."

Grabbing my phone, Ruger and I went to the living room and watched a little television. An hour or so later I tried to call Jaxon, but after two rings it went to voicemail. Correction, he sent me to voicemail. I left a message asking him to call me and that I was starting back to work Tuesday night. That was at 2:00 p.m. and it was now 10:30 p.m. No call back, no text. I was starting to get pissed. Then I got worried. Then I would get pissed he was making me worry. I was my own worst enemy.

Stop this, you're makin' yourself crazy.

I locked up the house, set the alarm and went upstairs to the third floor master bedroom. It was really more a master retreat since our room took up the whole third floor. Half of the floor plan was our bathroom and walk-in closet, the rest was our bedroom. Jax also set up a bassinet and portable changing table in our room for the baby. That way, for the first few weeks, she was right there next to us. Of course, Ruger has an oversized orthopedic dog bed near the foot of the bed.

Our bed was set off to the right of the stairs. A solid-wood, black, four-poster king-size bed with a crème-colored upholstered headboard adorned with crème gossamer curtains that encompassed the edge and draped to the floor. A large plasma screen hung over a traditional floor to ceiling, brick exposed fireplace. Jaxon had done an amazing job and now, it was starting to feel like home. Our home.

*****

~Leila~

I woke to Ruger's growl. Jaxon was finally home. I heard his heavy Docs trudging up the stairs. I was still angry with him for not bothering to call or text me so I closed my eyes and pretended to be asleep. I wasn't ready to have this fight, and a fight it would definitely be. He sat on the edge of the bed and cussed his boots, which hit the floor with a loud thud. He stripped and climbed into bed.

Ugh, he reeked.

A large palm curled around my chest and pulled me backward as he tucked in behind me and whispered in my ear, "Lei, babe, you awake?"

"No Jaxon. Go to sleep." I tried to pull away, back to my side of the large bed.

"I don't think so babe. Not goin' anywhere."

"Jax, unless you want to have a conversation right fuckin' now about why you smell like a skanky stripper, you'll let me go and do not push the issue." I tried to pull his arm off of me.

"Well, I guess we are havin' this shit out now then. 'Cause I ain't lettin' ya go babe," he said, holding his ground..

"Fine." I rolled toward him and planted both palms on his muscular chest and pushed him back. "You can start by explaining why you didn't call me back or text me for that matter. Then you can explain where you've been for fifteen hours and finish it all up with why you smell like a dirty whore."

"Babe," was all he said.

"Don't babe me. If you aren't gonna explain then fuckin' say so."

"One, I was handlin' club business, that's all you need to know about that." I had come to accept there were certain things he didn't share about the club.

"Second question, same answer as the first. Club business. And three, I don't smell like a whore," he said, agitation grated in his voice.

"Fuck you Jaxon. I can deal with you being vague about the club bullshit, but what I can't ignore is why you smell like those whores down at the club. I can't believe you." I ripped myself away from his hold. "For weeks I was on bed rest. Is that when you started fuckin' around?"

"You gotta be shittin' me. Do you fuckin' hear yourself? Leila, I haven't fucked anyone else since we have been together. Hell, even for months before we were together." He slung the covers back and leapt from the bed.

"Then why do you smell like pussy? Just be fuckin' honest."

"I swear to fuckin' Christ Lei, you're losin' your shit. The hormones have gotten to you. I have *not* fucked anyone other than you." He got about three feet away and was yelling back at me before Ruger's training kicked in. I heard him before I saw him. He was growling and even though he hadn't barked, I was scared for Jaxon. Ruger put himself between us, but Jax didn't take the threat seriously and kept coming toward me. I knew he was only trying to hold me and make me listen, but Ruger didn't and that's when he lunged and snapped at Jax. "Ruger *pfui*."

Ruger did not stand down. Jax put his hands up in surrender and looked at me for help.

"Ruger *pfui*! *Nein*." I grabbed his thick brown leather collar and regained his attention. He lay down. Quietly, I said to Jaxon, "I would suggest not yelling at me."

"Fine." He sat on the foot of the bed on my side. "I'm sorry Lei." Tears welled in my eyes. Bastard. He did fuck around. "I should've called. I got back from the run about one a.m. and me and the boys decided to grab a few beers at the clubhouse."

I grabbed a pillow and curled myself around it. "Oh God, this is not happening right now," I muttered under my breath.

"We drank, a lot. And yeah a couple of the girls tried, and they rubbed up on me, but I swear nothing happened. Okay, well, nothing happened between me and anyone. Not sayin' the guys didn't bend a few over the pool table, but I swear on my life, I didn't touch any of them." He reached for my hand and moved up to the pillows. "Babe come on. Look at me." I lifted my eyes to his. "Babe don't cry. You know that fuckin' guts me."

I grabbed a tissue with my free hand and blew my nose. "Why didn't you call me? You had to know I'd be freakin' the fuck out."

"I'm an asshole. I shoulda. I promise I'll do better baby. Come here." He pulled me to his hard, bare chest. "I love you Lei. You're mine and I'm yours. You mean the world to me darlin'. Just 'cause we have a fight, doesn't mean I'm gonna fuck that up."

"I love you too," I whispered against his naked skin.

"Thank God. Can we please go to sleep now? I'm fuckin' exhausted."

"Oh no, if you're sleepin' in this bed, you have to shower. I'm not havin' our bed reek like cigarettes, stale beer and skank. I'd have to burn the sheets, I don't think you want that." I pushed him toward the edge of the bed. Muttering a few choice words, he stalked toward the bathroom.

Chapter Twelve

~Leila~

The next few weeks came and went. I was back at work in the ER, which I loved. I didn't realize how much I enjoyed my job until I couldn't do it. I missed the adrenaline rush I got when EMTs sprinted in the ambulance bay with someone coding. I missed being perched over someone and doing chest compressions and watching them come back to life. I missed the calm all of that insanity brought me. It sounds ass-backward, but it was true. When shit went south in the ER, I found my zone and became methodical. My actions were precise and even in split second decisions, my actions were well thought out. It made me feel alive.

Jaxon didn't understand it until I asked him why he did so many tours in the Marines.

"What do you mean why did I do it?"

"I mean exactly that. Why go back into war zones so many times?"

"Lei, I've already told you I'm not talkin' about my deployments." He threw up the familiar brick wall when I asked about his time in the service.

"Babe, I'm not asking what you did. I'm asking why you kept going back when I'm sure you saw and had to do some awful shit."

"It was my job and I was damn good at it. It was exhilarating. Not knowing what would happen from one minute to another."

"And the ER is the exact same for me. That's what you're not gettin' Jaxon. I love the thrill of not knowing what is going to come through the door next. It's an adrenaline rush knowing you have the chance to save someone's life." I walked into the bathroom while he turned the shower on.

"Oh."

"Yeah, it's the exact same thing. Well, except you were killin' people and I'm saving them."

It was like I flipped a switch and the lights were finally on.

We got into a comfortable routine. Jaxon would drop me off at work in the evening then pick me up in the morning if he wasn't on a run for the club. The two times that happened, Barb had been on the same shift so she brought me home.

Jaxon had been going on more club business recently and I wish I could say I was okay with all of it. At first all of the secrecy and disappearing for hours at a time didn't bother me much. But recently it had been happening too often.

This week alone he had been out of the house for almost three days straight. When he came home, I had asked where he was going. He'd looked at me blankly. "Babe, you know the drill."

"Well maybe that's not good enough anymore. There is this whole other part of your life I don't know anything about. I understand that you can't go into details, but—"

"Then just drop it if you're so understanding. I don't want you a part of that world." He grabbed the keys to the bike from the counter.

"Why? What are you doing? Is it illegal? For fuck's sake, my brother is a cop, Jaxon."

"Would you just leave it alone? I can't say and it's in your best interest to stay the hell out of it." With that, he stormed out of the house and I spent another night alone with Ruger.

Even though I was living with someone for the first time in my adult life that wasn't my brother or Barb, I spent as much time alone in this house as I did with Jaxon. I tried to take advantage of the quiet time and read or take Ruger to the Battery, but I felt lonely and confused. He'd wanted me here so badly, pushed so hard for us to live together and now where was he and what was he doing?

Tonight, I wasn't in the mood to cook myself dinner and eat alone, so I called Drew. "Hey bro, what are you doin' tonight?"

"Just chillin' here at the house. Why, what's up?" Drew asked hesitantly. "You okay?"

"Yeah, I just don't wanna eat alone. Jax had MC shit to do and Barb is working."

"Oh so what, I'm your last choice?" he asked, pretending to be hurt.

"Yep, absolutely my last resort. Dork. Do you wanna get a bite to eat with your little sister or not?" I chuckled while I watched the little nub slowly move from one side of my belly to the other. It still fascinated me to just sit and watch her.

"Yeah, come over here and I will order Chinese."

Weird being back at the condo and it looking like a bachelor pad already. We sat around the coffee table with cartons of food and watched a movie, laughing until we cried. It felt great to have some down time with my brother.

My cell phone starting playing Big & Rich's "Run Away With You," Jaxon's ringtone. Looking down at my watch, I realized it was almost 11:00 p.m. "Hello?"

"Where are you? Are you okay?" Jaxon sounded frantic. I hadn't left a note or texted him where I was going or when I would be home.

"I'm fine. I'm at my brother's. We had dinner and watched a movie."

"Oh. Why didn't you tell me you were goin' over there? I got home and freaked the fuck out. I thought something happened to you."

"I'm sorry. I should have left a note. You're right. Give me a few minutes, then Ruger and I will be home."

"All right, be careful," he grumbled.

Jaxon was waiting on the front steps as I got out the car. He was still in his tattered jeans and black cut, but his feet were bare. Ruger took off ahead, excited to see Jaxon. "Hey."

"Hey," he repeated as he held the door open for me. Once we were all inside he caught my arm before I could make it out of the foyer. "Lei, we should probably talk."

My heart started pounding and my palms got sweaty. Nothing good ever came after those four words. "Can we do this in bed? I'm really tired and my feet are killing me."

Jaxon reached his hand out and tucked my curls behind my left ear. "Of course babe."

Leading the way, I followed him up the stairs to the third floor, then climbed into bed after kicking off my flip-flops. I watched as he stripped down to his gray, tight boxer briefs. This man could be covered in engine grease and I would still melt every time I looked at him. His body was mesmerizing. I could stare at him for hours committing every curve, dimple and muscle to memory.

"I'm sorry for the shit I said earlier. I know you're just worried about me and I shouldn't have been such an ass." I took a breath to speak but was stopped before I was able. "No, just listen. You asked questions that I cannot give you answers to right now. I will tell you that it's MC business and there are some aspects of it that aren't exactly on the up and up, but I try to distance myself from those runs and those dealings.

"I love you Leila. I will always want to keep you safe and sometimes that means being left in the dark. Some of the people that we deal with in the club will exploit any weakness they can find to get ahead. You are my weakness. You are the only thing in this world that could break me. So the less you know the better and the further away from that side of my life the better."

"So you expect me to be okay with you living two lives?" I was a little outraged.

"I'm not living two lives babe. I'm just keeping you shielded from the dirty parts." He finally got into bed next to me. "It won't be like this forever. Just for now."

"You promise?"

"I swear. As soon as I can, I will tell you what you want to know."

He was trying. That was clear.

"Babe, remember, for years and years there was no you. I'm aware things have to change. Just for now, Lei, it's gotta be this way, 'kay?"

I nodded. "Okay." I could accept that. For now.

Jaxon leaned over and kissed me what was probably supposed to be a good night kiss, but I caught the side of his face just as he began to pull back and I kissed him. Without a word, he slipped his hand under my back and sat me up. Slowly he pulled my shirt over my head, then undid my bra as I whispered, "Make love to me Jaxon."

For the next hour that is what he did. Slow, deliberate and restrained; then unremitting and reckless. All of our cares and worries fled, as we melted into each other and found our nirvana.

Chapter Thirteen

~Leila~

Today was Valentine's Day and Jaxon was acting weird. He hadn't mentioned anything about the day or if he had made any plans. About 4:00 p.m., I grabbed my keys and kissed him goodbye. He didn't ask where I was going or when I was going to be home, which for him was way weird. He seemed so preoccupied and I couldn't figure out why.

Driving to the grocery store, I decided to pick up rib eye steaks, baking potatoes, pencil asparagus and fresh lettuce. I had already picked up his present earlier in the week. It wasn't anything extravagant or expensive. I bought him a thirty-two gig iPod touch and loaded a playlist for tonight. I also got him a Bluetooth headset he could wear on the bike.

When I returned home about forty-five minutes later, there was an unfamiliar woman walking out the front door. She was dressed in jeans and a chartreuse polo. If I had to guess, I would say she was probably in her mid to late thirties. Not drop dead gorgeous, but pretty. Oh, and get this, she waved to me.

I just looked at her out the corner of my eye and kept unloading the groceries from the car. I muttered all the way to the back door, kicked it open and damn near dropped all of the bags I had strategically arranged in my arms. Jax rushed to my side and tried to help, but I was already pissy about some strange woman coming out the front of our house.

"I got it." He still tried to take the bags. "Jax, I'm fine. I said I have it. Just move so I can put them down."

He moved out of the way with his palms raised as I neared the center island. "Just tryin' to help babe."

"Who was just leavin'?" I tried to play it off as curiosity instead of jealous pregnant woman paranoia.

"Why don't you set the groceries down and walk into the dining room." He was suspiciously calm.

I did as he asked, then locked eyes with him, searching for any clue of what I was walking into. I was met with a vacant stare. I kept my gaze on him as I walked through the kitchen.

As I entered the dining room, it felt like someone sucked all of the oxygen out of the atmosphere. Arranged artfully around the room were dozens and dozens of long stem red roses. They all surrounded our dining room table, which was set impeccably, and tall pillar candles were lit everywhere.

"Oh Jaxon, they're beautiful." I turned back and I launched myself into his strong arms.

"I love you. Never ever doubt that princess," he whispered against my lips as they captured his. "There's more."

"What did you do? You didn't have to do all of this," I said.

"I wanted to surprise you. I had dinner delivered, thought you might like to stay in and have a night alone." He kissed me softly. "Maybe we can have a naked dinner?" He lifted his eyebrows suggestively.

"Right, naked meal? With me? The whale? Only if you want to lose your appetite."

He smacked my ass. "Stop babe. You're fuckin' gorgeous. I love your body, but you're right, naked dinner's probably not a good idea. I don't think I'd make it through a meal without fuckin' you on the table."

"Why didn't you tell me before I left you were plannin' something? I wouldn't have bought stuff for dinner." I remember all of the groceries on the island. Thankfully Ruger was in the small side yard and not enjoying the steak.

"Well, for one I needed you out of the house. Secondly, I didn't want to spoil your surprise."

I looked down and realized I was in a pair of maternity yoga pants and one of Jax's old USMC sweatshirts. "I'm gonna run up and change clothes."

"Don't. I love you just like you are. It doesn't matter what you wear or don't wear. You could put on a burlap sack and I'd still want to fuck you on the first available surface." He spun me around and walked me to the head of the table closest to the kitchen wall and pulled out a chair for me. "Sit."

"Yes, sir." I sat as ordered.

"Mmm, I like that." He lifted off the stainless steel lids and revealed the five-star quality meal. "Beef Wellington, roasted fingerling potatoes and asparagus with Hollandaise sauce."

"Wow. Honey, this looks amazing."

He took his seat opposite of me. "Let's eat. I have other plans for you."

Eeep!

We finished dinner and I tried to clear the table. He all but snatched the plates from my hand.

"Can you grab Ruger?" he asked. "He's in the side yard."

"Sure." I gave him a chaste kiss and exited the back door.

I rounded the side of the house and saw Ruger lying in the grass next to the patio set and square gas fire table. The fire table emitted a soft glow that danced around the yard. I noticed a small gift bag sitting on the black wicker sectional. There was a note on ivory parchment paper leaning against it that read, "Open Me Lei." I opened the bag to find another folded piece of parchment that said, "Turn Around." I pinched my brow together in confusion, cocked my head to the side, then slowly spun around. And almost passed right the fuck out.

There was Jaxon, clothed in his distressed Levi's, a long sleeve gray Henley and black Doc Martens, bent down on one knee. My hand flew to my mouth as I gasped and tears brimmed in my eyes. He reached under the cushion and pulled out a small blue Tiffany box. He slowly opened the box and rested it on his knee.

"I've thought about this moment for months. I never thought I'd find myself wanting to get married, let alone getting down on my knee, but when I walked into that ER a year ago and you flat out rejected me, I knew I had to have you.

"Not only were you the first woman to not be enamored by my charismatic charm, you laughed at me. You're stubborn, strong-willed, vivacious, beautiful and intelligent. You have captured me, heart and soul. I want to spend the rest of our lives showing you, telling you and making you feel how much I love you.

"Leila Carolyn Matthews, will you marry me?" He lifted the box. Inside was a scintillating one and a half carat princess cut diamond set atop a platinum band laid with brilliant round diamonds.

I, for the first time ever, was absolutely speechless. I just stood there, mouth wide-open, gawking at him.

"Lei, babe?" He looked up at me, his brows drawn together.

"Oh my God Jaxon. Oh my God." I finally got part of my brain to cooperate. "Are you sure you wanna marry *me*? I come with so much baggage. The baby. Brody. Are you sure?"

"I love you. Unequivocally and unconditionally. I couldn't love our daughter more if she was my blood. I want you to be my wife. No doubts, no hesitations and no reservations."

The tears broke through the dam. "Yes! I'll marry you Jaxon. Oh baby, I love you so much." I threw my very pregnant self at him as he stood. He caught me and kissed me senseless. Ruger picked up his head briefly, then went back to ignoring us.

"I love you Lei," he murmured against my lips as I kissed him fervently.

"Take me inside and make love to me Jaxon."

"Don't you wanna put on the ring? Or at least look at it?" he asked.

"Oh, right," I said with a giggle. "I mean, I looked at it and it's beyond gorgeous. Of course, I want to wear it. Will you put it on my finger?"

He pulled the ring from the box, held my left hand with his and slid the ring into place. "Do you like it? We can exchange it if you don't."

"Jaxon, I love it. It's perfect." He scrutinized my face. "Really. If I would have picked one out myself, this is exactly what I would've chosen. I love it." I held my hand out in front of me, then kissed him again. He bent down, hooked his thick arm behind my knees and lifted me to his chest like I weighed nothing.

Wrapping my arms around his neck I whispered in his ear as I lightly traced his lobe with my tongue. "I want to go inside and fuck my fiancé."

He carried me inside, up the staircase to our bedroom and laid me down in our bed. Our room looked like a church altar with white candles were strewn about.

Jax took his time and worshipped my body. He made love to me for hours. Sweet and slow, fast and hard. I lost count somewhere after orgasm number four or maybe it was five. Around midnight, we finally fell asleep twisted around one another.

Chapter Fourteen

~Leila~

On Sunday we met Barb, Drew, Drake and a few of Jaxon's brothers from the MC at Toast for brunch. I decided not to say anything until someone noticed the sparkling, brilliant engagement ring on my finger.

We all sat down while Jax made introductions. Viper and Mark already knew Barb, but Dig was new to everyone but me. Viper and Barb were there before anyone else and got a table. They were sitting awfully close and I couldn't help but notice the little glances or subtle way he brushed the outside of his hand against hers.

Note to self, dig into what's going on there.

"Holy shit, Lei! What's on your finger?" Barb snatched my hand from the menu and almost clotheslined Jax in the process.

"Whoa, Barb. Face." Jax leaned back out of the inspection.

"So that's kinda why we asked everyone here this morning. Jax asked me to marry him last night, and I said yeah."

I looked at Drew. "I know it's early, but I was hoping you'd walk me down the aisle."

He stood from his chair and came around the table. "I'd love to." He pulled me up into a warm brotherly hug.

We sat back down, ordered our food and continued to have an uneventful brunch—until Jax was paying the bill.

"Babe." Jax tilted his head. "What's up? You look funny?" He leaned in. "You gotta use the bathroom or somethin'? Your face is all scrunched up."

I placed my hand on my belly as a contraction eased off. "No. I don't need to 'use the bathroom.'"

Barb looked at me, and her eyes widened. "No"

I cut my gaze to her and shook my head slightly, as if to say, "shut up."

"Gentlemen, if you'll excuse us. We're gonna run to the little girls' room real fast." She jumped up from her chair with Viper giving her a nod. She reached for my hand, trying to look nonchalant and gave the boys a big, fake-ass smile as she dragged me away.

Once we entered the restroom, she halted and spun to face me so quickly I ran smack into her. "How long and how intense?"

"Chill Barb, they're just Braxton-Hicks. It's only been a few today. Nothing regular and nothing painful. It was just that the last one was a little uncomfortable. It just caught me off guard, is all."

"You sure, hussy?" she quizzed.

"Positive slut. We're good." I rubbed my belly.

"Fine, but I'm watchin' the clock bitch." She scowled as I rolled my eyes at her before we left the bathroom.

"Y'all ready?" Drew lifted his chin at Barb and me.

"I suppose so." Barb turned to Jax, who was reaching his hand out to me. "Thanks for brunch and congratulations again. Love ya girly."

Pulling away from Jax momentarily, I gave Barb and Drew a hug goodbye.

"You sure about this sis?" Drew asked. "It's not like y'all have been together very long. Don't get me wrong I like Jax, but marriage? That's a huge step. I just want you to be sure you're ready."

"I am Drew. I love him like I never thought possible. And the best part is that we started as friends. Marriages that started as friendships have a good base. Lust and passion can wear out over the years, but friendship like that is timeless."

"I just want you to be sure. I don't want to see you get hurt, that's all."

Again. He wanted to say again.

"I know and I love you for it. I'm good."

Jax said his goodbyes to Viper, Mark and Dig, which were a grunt and a slap on the back. *Cavemen.*

As we were walking out to the parking lot, Mark mentioned a run that was to take place in about a week or so. Jax didn't seem surprised and said he'd be there.

Later that night, I asked what the run was for and was quickly told to not ask questions. I stood in the middle of our newly renovated gourmet kitchen, jaw hanging.

"What?" was the only word I could form in my stupefied mind.

"What, what? You know the deal. I can't talk about the shit that goes down at the club." His eyes darkened. There was something about this run that was different. "It's nothin' new Leila. We've had this talk, nothing has changed."

"Jesus Jax. I didn't ask if you're plannin' on fuckin' killin' someone."

He was quiet. Too quiet. He turned and walked out of the kitchen. On his way he just muttered, "Leave it be Lei."

"Where are you goin'? You're just gonna shut down and walk away when we have a conversation you don't wanna have? What the fuck is going on? Are you're doing something illegal."

No response, but he stopped in his tracks.

"Oh my God, that's it. Isn't it? It's illegal and..." Jax whipped around and was in front of me in one stride.

"I swear to Christ, Leila. Just fuckin' drop it," he roared. "I'm not talkin' about this. Conversation is over." He grabbed his jacket out of the hall closet before coming back toward me.

"Where are you going?" I stood between him and the back door.

"Out. Don't wait up, it'll be late," he growled as he shouldered past me.

As he slammed the door, I whispered under my breath, "Fuck you Jax. You will not make me cry." I took a few deep breaths and looked at the clock. It was 6:41 p.m. when I heard him rev the bike and roar out the driveway.

Great. Less than twenty-four hours after we got engaged and we were fighting.

A few hours later I put the iPad down and called Drew, but it went to voicemail, so I hung up and called Barb.

"Hey babe, what's up?" she said all chipper.

"Jax and I had a fight and he walked out almost four hours ago."

"Aw, I'm sorry hon. What did y'all fight 'bout?" She listened as I explained the situation.

"It's not about what he's gonna do. Okay, maybe it is a little, but more than that it's the way he fuckin' talked to me, Barb." She quietly agreed. "Now he's probably at the club, drunk off his ass."

"You wanna go get him? We'll come pick ya up."

We?

"Shit Barb, why didn't you say you were busy? I don't want to interrupt. Thanks for listenin' to me rant."

"Lei, you're fine. Cole and I'll come pick ya up. That way he can drive his bike back. Be there in five." Before I could argue or ask about Viper, she hung up.

I reached down and rubbed my round little belly. "Guess we're gonna go pick up Daddy, sweet girl."

I changed into a pair of maternity jeans and a fitted purple sweater and grabbed my phone. True to her word, Barb and Viper were there in just a matter of minutes. We headed out to the club with Viper driving the Jeep. We pulled into the parking lot and got out. It was after 11:00 and I was tired.

As I walked up to the club my nerves danced up and down my body. My skin tingled with anxiety and my stomach sank as Viper entered his code into the keypad at the front entrance.

We walked down the hallway with Viper leading the way. It opened to a large room with a long bar and several pool tables and couches. Viper stopped abruptly and turned back to me.

"Why don't y'all wait out front and I'll grab him?" I could hear the edginess in his voice as he blocked my view of most of the room. Off to the side, I could see a tall, broad-shouldered guy with a blonde head bobbing up and down on his crotch.

"Oh my God," I muttered as I looked at Barb. "Viper, get out of my way." I tried to push past him, but he wrapped his massive hands around the tops of my shoulders, stopping my progress.

"Barb, babe, help me out here." He looked to her for some assistance. She put her hands up and shook her head.

"Fuck," he gritted out as I slipped away from his grasp.

Across the room at a table was Jax with Mark and two other guys. In his lap was a topless bleach blonde slut. She was straddling him with her arms around his neck and grinding up and down on him. She grabbed the sides of his face and shoved her tongue down his throat. His fist went to her hair and pulled her head back, which shoved her tits in his face.

I stood there unable to move or speak, watching it all unfold in front of me. The sick, sinking feeling I had in my chest was unbearable. I turned with tears streaming down my face and ran to the front door with Barb hot on my trail.

"Get me outta here Barb. Now."

We climbed into the Jeep and started to back out as Jaxon came barreling out the front of the club with Viper hot on his heels. I could hear him yelling my name and pleading for Barb to stop.

"Drive Barb, don't stop. Just go, please."

"Oh honey, I'm so sorry," she started.

"No, don't. I don't wanna talk about this. Just take me home." We drove the rest of the way home without speaking. My phone rang once before I turned off the power.

As we pulled up in front of Jax's house her cell rang.

"Yeah," she answered. "Cole, she doesn't want to talk to him. No. I said no. Maybe tomorrow, but not right now." She hung up and turned to me. "Cole said Jax was pretty hammered."

"Drunk or not, I don't care. I wonder how long I've been a fuckin' fool. How long has he been doin' this?" I stared straight ahead, eyes wide, unable to blink.

"Leila, he adores you. I think it was just a lap dance that got—" I cut her off.

"Stop Barb, I'm not talkin' about this. I can't. Really." With that I got out and went inside.

I grabbed a bag and shoved a bunch of clothes in it from the closet and dresser, then threw in my toothbrush, deodorant and comb. I turned on my phone, called Drew and left him a voicemail telling him I was coming over. As I hung up, my voicemail alert chimed and six text messages came in, all from Jaxon. I shoved my phone in my pocket and ignored all of them.

I whistled for Ruger and went to the kitchen, snatched my purse and keys off the counter and went to the back door, set the alarm, then locked the door behind me. I opened the driver side door to the Challenger and threw my bags in the back. Ruger hopped right in.

I drove to the condo and pulled around back. Drew's vehicle was missing from the garage, so I parked inside and lowered the garage door with a quick press. I unlocked the back door and was surprised the alarm wasn't set. Ruger went bounding through the house, and I was startled by a familiar voice. *Fuck.*

"Ruger. Hey buddy. What are you doing here?" Brody scratched Ruger's neck, then lifted his head and saw me at the back door. "Leila? What's going on? Why are you here?"

"Uh, this is my house. Why are you here?"

"Well, Drew and I were hanging out until about twenty minutes ago when he got called in. I just stopped in with a pizza and had a few beers. He said he wouldn't be too long, to hang out. Your turn. Why are you here at midnight on Sunday? You okay?"

Walking past him to the kitchen, ignoring his question, I grabbed a water bottle out of the refrigerator and walked over to the sectional.

"Seriously Lei. What the fuck is going on? You're freaking me out here."

"I don't want to talk about it Brody. Just leave it alone, please." I chewed on the inside of my lip to curtail the tears trying to escape as I plopped down on the chaise.

"Not a chance. What'd he do?" he asked, his voice gravelly and raw. He sat down next to me and grabbed my hand. "Talk to me babe."

His pulling out babe was the last stick holding the dam together, I broke down and sobbed. I didn't say anything, just cried. Brody pulled me over to him and held me in a warm, familiar embrace. His strong arms circled my chest, pushing my growing belly against his tight obliques. My arms were folded in between us. He leaned back and lifted my chin up to face him. He swiped his thumb along my tear stained cheeks. "It's gonna be okay. Just talk to me."

"We got in a fight." I sniffled loudly as my diaphragm spasmed and my breath caught. "Then he left. I sat around and waited. Like, four hours later, I called Barb, who came and picked me up. We went to the club. And...and he was there." I wasn't going to tell Brody everything. Not in a million years. The tears had finally stopped and my anger was starting to set in. "He was being an ass so I went home and grabbed some stuff and came here."

Brody didn't speak, but his jaw clenched and flexed as he stared at the coffee table. He finally turned his eyes to me.

"I'm sorry he hurt you." He looked down and saw the newest piece of jewelry adorning my left hand. He didn't seem surprised, but rather, dejected. I tucked my hand under my leg. "It's okay Leila, Drew told me earlier. Well, actually it's not okay, but I don't want you to feel like you need to hide from me. I fucked up. You moved on."

"I'm sorry Brody, I don't want to hurt you. Maybe I should just go upstairs." I started to try to lift myself off the couch.

"No, stay. We don't have to talk about him." He changed topics. "How are you feeling?"

"Fat. And now depressed." Cue the tissues. More waterworks. "Probably why he's getting drunk and staying out, because I—"

"Don't you dare finish that sentence. You're gorgeous. You're not fat, honey, you're eight months pregnant." He pulled me back against his firm chest. "Honestly, I've been a little worried you haven't gained enough weight."

I cried harder as I relaxed into him. "Why did he do this?"

The front door slamming startled us apart. Standing in the foyer was all six feet four inches of pissed off, drunk Jaxon. "What the fuck's goin' on here?"

"Jaxon, what're you doing here?" I used the arm of the couch to pull myself up and wiped the tears from my face.

"I had a feelin' you'd come runnin' straight over here. Sure didn't expect he'd be your first fuckin' call though Lei."

"Jax, I didn't call him. He was just here…No. You don't get to do that. You're not turnin' this shit around on me." Now I was pissed as I walked toward him. "Fuck you, Jaxon. I wasn't the one dry humpin' a fuckin' cunt in front of you. I wasn't the fuckin' one who kissed that whore. No, you motherfuckin' asshole, that was *you*." I shoved him but he didn't budge.

"Lei, it's not what it looked like. I swear, just let me explain." He grabbed at my hands.

Brody heard everything. Of course. He came around the couch to stand in front of Jaxon. "You need to get your fucking hands off her and go. I think you've done enough for one day."

"Brody, I got this." I held my palm up into the chest of a livid Jaxon.

"Fuck you Brody. I'm sure her runnin' over here is your fuckin' dream come true."

"Stop Jax, you're drunk. You need to go home. I have nothing else to say to you right now."

Brody grumbled as he stalked over to the kitchen.

Jax turned his eyes back to mine. "Come home with me Lei. We need to talk. You have to let me explain, baby," he pleaded.

"Jax put yourself in my shoes. If you walked in here and I was straddlin' Brody on the couch, kissin' him and he buried his face in my tits, what would you do?"

The vein in his forehead bulged and throbbed as he gritted his teeth. "I'd fuckin' kill him."

"So, you might have a small idea of how I feel. Of course, your anger is hypothetical and mine's fuckin' real," I hollered, "because I fuckin' watched you do those things." I turned and winced at the stupid Braxton-Hicks contraction. "Go Jax."

"You're gonna stay here? With that asshole?" he barked.

"Right now, I don't owe you any answers, but yeah, I am stayin' here. And Brody is going home. Unlike you, I can't just jump from one bed to another."

"That's not true, Leila. I swear to you, I'm not cheatin' on you and I never have. Please just come home with me."

"Go! Now!" I was fighting back the tears as I screamed at him. Ruger had now placed himself between us in defense mode.

"God damn it," Jax yelled as he turned around and threw open the thick wood door. "You got tonight, but tomorrow we will talk."

"Please, just go, Jaxon," I whispered as I looked at my swollen midsection.

"I love you Lei." Jax pulled the door closed as he stepped into the cold winter night.

As soon as the door shut I was hit with another Braxton-Hicks. I placed my hand on the right lower quadrant of my abdomen as I winced. I prayed it would pass quickly before Brody came back into the room or noticed my discomfort.

"You okay?"

Shit, too late. "Yeah, I'll be fine. I'll deal with him tomorrow." I was hoping he'd be distracted by my answer.

"That's not what I was askin' Lei. You're holding your side."

"I'm fine. She's just strechin' out, it's just a little uncomfortable sometimes." He started walkin' toward me. "Listen, I don't wanna sound like a bitch, but I'm really tired and I just wanna go to sleep."

"Why don't you let me stay with you until Drew gets back? I'll hang out on the couch and you can go sleep."

"Brody, please. Can you please just go? I just wanna be alone." I grabbed my bag.

"But—" he started.

"No. I'm fine, just go home Brody." Exhaustion had settled in and I was ready to crash. "I don't have the energy to fight with you, so please don't make me."

"All right. You need anything before I leave?" he asked as he grabbed his keys and phone.

"No, but thanks for listening to me and not sayin' anything. I'll text you the time for the next OB appointment. I mean, if you still wanna go." I walked toward the door to lock up behind him.

"Of course I do. I'm sorry I missed the last appointment. It was something that couldn't be avoided." He reached out and rubbed his palm gently down the left side of my belly. Bending forward, he quietly whispered to our daughter, "Bye sweet girl. Daddy loves you."

It was the sweetest thing Brody had ever done or said. I took a deep breath as my throat tightened and eyes swelled.

"Night Lei. Call me if you need anything." He turned and walked out the house. I locked the front door, let Ruger out the back for a minute, then locked up the rest of the house and turned on the security system. I grabbed my phone, water and bag, then scaled the stairs to the master bedroom. I brushed my teeth and washed the black streaks of mascara from splotchy face, before climbing in bed.

Chapter Fifteen

~Leila~

I heard the alarm sometime in the early morning and Drew woke me long enough to tell me he talked to Brody. He said he'd take the spare room and see me in the morning.

A wet nose nudging my cheek woke me at 10:30 a.m. "Hey boy," I said as I scratched his head. "You need to go out?"

I got my answer in the form of a wagging tail and prancing feet. His whole body wiggled as he waited for me to get out of the bed and open the bedroom door. As soon as I did, he took off like a bat out of hell. I heard Drew greet him.

"I'll let him out Lei," Drew hollered up the stairs.

"Thanks, I'll be right down."

A few minutes later I was sitting at the granite peninsula in the kitchen watching Drew scramble some eggs.

"You wanna talk 'bout it kiddo?" Drew looked over his shoulder at me.

I drew in a long breath and chewed the inside of my cheek. Did I want to talk about it? I did, but I didn't. I'd cried myself to sleep, cried in my sleep and cried when I woke up. I thought I was done feeling like this. And as much as I wanted to bury my head in the sand and try to ignore the massive chasm in my heart, I needed to deal with Jaxon before I discussed the situation with anyone else.

"Nah. Thanks, though. I need to deal with Jax, and the sooner the better."

About an hour later, I collected my purse, phone and keys, said goodbye to Drew and climbed in the car. Parking in the back in my normal spot, I got out and unlocked the door. Jax was seated in a barstool at the kitchen island. He must have heard me coming, because he had his sights on the back door as I entered.

"Hey babe," he said as he slid off the barstool.

"Hey," I spoke softly as I dropped my stuff on the old wooden chest at the back entry. He walked over and tried to pull me into a hug. "Please don't Jax. We need to talk."

His face sagged at my rejection. "Yeah, I guess we do. Let's go sit in the living room."

The living room was at the front of the house; the furniture deep and fluffy. I loved this room. We decorated it with the beach in mind. It was soothing and calm. It was a good choice for the ensuing conversation.

"Jaxon—" I began, but he stopped me.

"Wait, please let me explain before you say anything. I've been dyin' inside since last night." He sat down facing me with his arm slung over the back of the couch. I tucked my right foot under my butt and draped my arm in the same fashion. "I swear Lei, it looked so much worse than it was."

"I seriously doubt that," I muttered under my breath, barely audible.

"I know I shouldn't have left like I did, and I definitely shouldn't have talked to you like I did. It's just…there's shit goin' on I don't exactly agree with, but I'm not the Prez, so I have to follow orders. I still can't say what's happenin' but I will tell ya, I'm not feelin' it." I sat quietly and listened.

"Anyway, I left here and just rode for a while. Eventually, I ended up at the club and I drank too much. Not an excuse, just explainin'," he said as he saw my head tilt in annoyance. "Mark and Dig came over, we did shots. They didn't ask why I was there. They actually thought I was celebratin' our engagement. Then all of a sudden, Kat was there and she was in my lap. Dig and Mark told her about us and told her to give me a lap dance." I really wanted to throw up listening to this shit. "I know you saw everythin' else, so I won't go any further, but I swear to you, Leila, I have not and won't ever cheat on you." He held my hand between his, making it look miniscule.

"From where I'm sitting, you kissing her and then pulling her hair back so her tits were in your fuckin' face is pretty much cheating."

"Wait, let me explain. I pulled her hair back to get her mouth off me. Kat and I have a history, I'm not gonna lie, but I told her in September that I was done because I was in love with you. She seemed to be happy for me. I swear it was only a lap dance."

"So is that why you came home last week stinking like a slut? 'Cause you were getting fuckin' lap dances?"

"What? No," he answered. "Last night was the only lap dance I've gotten in six months. You're the only one I want givin' me lap dances or shovin' your tits in my face. Yours is certainly the only mouth I want on me. I love you."

I wanted to believe everything he was saying, but I just couldn't. Especially after I had been given good reason to be skeptical. "Jaxon, I'm gonna be completely honest with you. I want to believe you, but you have to put yourself in my shoes. Like I said yesterday, if you saw me like that you'd be pissed."

"You're right, I'd be fuckin' furious. I don't know what I'd do if our roles were reversed and I saw you kissin' on Brody. It was hard enough to see him holding you while you cried." He hung his head. "It fuckin' ripped my heart out. Then to hear you ask him why I did this to you, Jesus Lei, I wish I could go back to yesterday and change everything that happened. I wouldn't have walked out."

"But you did. You didn't trust me enough to talk to me and that's part of our issue. You don't trust me Jaxon." I pulled my hand away from him. "And after last night, I don't know if I can trust you."

"Tell me what I can do to fix this and I will, baby. I'll do anything."

"You can't fix this. Not right now. I need time to think and to figure this out. And I can't be here with you until I do." My heart split as I said it. It was one thing to think it, but as it came out I felt absolutely destroyed.

"Baby, I need you here with me. I can't imagine my life without you. I don't want to wake up again like I did this morning," he pleaded.

"I need some time Jax."

"Is this about Brody?" he hissed.

"Ya know what Jaxon—" I stood up. "Brody happened to be there, I didn't call him and I didn't ask for him to be there, so don't turn this shit around on me. I didn't fuck this up. That's all on you."

"Yeah, well, you didn't seem too upset that he was there," he muttered.

"I'm gonna go, I have to work tomorrow. I need to grab some clothes from the bedroom, but then I'm gonna stay at the condo with Drew for a couple of days." I started up the stairs, but before I made it to the fourth step I was overtaken with a massive contraction. "Ahhhh!" I doubled over, holding my stomach.

"What the hell babe? What's wrong?" Jax flew off the couch and was by my side in the blink of an eye.

I blew out a few hard breaths as the contraction eased off.

"Lei, talk to me. What's goin' on? Is it the baby?" He rubbed his hand up my back.

"I'm fine. It's just Braxton-Hicks contractions." I straightened.

"Are you sure? Maybe we should take you to the ER just to have you both checked out."

"Jax, we're okay. I've been having them since Saturday. It's completely normal." I continued up the stairs to our bedroom leaving him standing there.

As I came back downstairs, I found him sitting on the second step with his head in his hands.

"Please reconsider babe. We need to fix this, not run from it." He stood in front of me halting my forward progress.

"I just need some time. I can't think around you and I need to get my head right. I'll call you tomorrow." I stepped around him as he grabbed my left hand.

"I love you Leila. I'll be here when you wanna come home, but I'll give you your space. For now."

"I love you too Jax," I whispered. "That's what's making this so hard."

He pulled me to him and kissed me softly. Then he bent down and kissed my belly. "Can I call you later to say good night?"

My throat tightened. I knew I should say no, but I couldn't. I missed him already and I hadn't even left. "Yeah."

I walked down the hall to the back of the house. Before I opened the back door, I turned around and looked back at him standing in the foyer. God, I wanted to run to him. It hurt so much to see the pain and anguish on his face, but it had hurt much more to see him with that woman all over him. And I did, every time I closed my eyes. That memory would be imbedded in my mind for a long time.

Opening the door, I left before I talked myself out it. We needed the space. He needed to feel the consequences of his actions. I needed to figure out if I could forgive him and move past this. Cheating was one thing I wasn't sure I could get past. I know he said it wasn't cheating, but damn.

I spent the next day on the couch in the condo. Taking turns between reading and weeping. Drew respected my wishes and let me be. Jax called around 9:30 p.m. to tell me good night and ask if I had any more contractions. I lied and said no. I didn't want him to worry and come barreling over here like a caveman.

The next two days, I worked my ER shifts and came back to the condo. I missed Jaxon. I missed the way he would rub my feet in the morning after my twelve-hour shift, before he went to the clubhouse to do whatever it was he did there. I missed curling up next to him and falling asleep on his chest. I missed how he eased my fears with a simple "Babe." But I wasn't ready to forgive. I wanted to, but I just wasn't there yet.

Thursday, Barb and I met for dinner and went shopping for the baby. She told me I need some retail therapy. It was just an excuse for her to shop.

"So have you decided what you're gonna do?" she asked as we looked around the baby superstore.

"No. I just don't know how to unsee him with her. Every time I think about forgiving him, I see her kissing him and shoving her boobs in his face. Plus, for weeks, he's been secretive and going on runs. Hell for all I know this may have been happenin' all along." I picked up a tin of Bag Balm and put it in the cart. "And Brody keeps calling me. I think he thinks since I've moved out that he has another shot or something. I've told him in no uncertain terms, that's not gonna happen, but he's relentless."

"Gee, Brody? Relentless? I'm shocked." Barb was the queen of sarcasm.

"Ha-ha. You're not helpin' here." I pushed the cart over to the bottles and breastfeeding section. "What should I do?"

"Brody, I'd tell to chill and Remi…Well, I'm not really sure about that one honey. I mean, you love him, right?"

"Yeah, that's not the problem though."

"So tell me, what's hanging you up on forgiving him?" She reached out and stopped the cart.

"I told you. I keep seeing him with that skank." I turned to face her.

"I think it's more than that. I think you're looking for an excuse to bolt. He can't leave you if you're already out the door. Hear me Lei, he's not your dad. You can't put your dad's fuck-ups on Jaxon."

"I know he's not my dad, Barb. I'm not trying to bail. I just agreed to marry him for cryin' out loud."

"So then, what is it? 'Cause I know you girl, and something else is going on." I grabbed a package of bottles off the shelf and pretended to read the label. "Stop ignoring me, bitch. I will kick your ass, pregnant or not."

"I don't know, okay? I don't know. Anytime something in my life is goin' good, I let myself be happy and then it all goes to shit. I swear the universe hates me or something." I took a deep breath and put the bottles back. "And another thing, that Club. For Christ's sake, I don't even know what he does. I know he goes there. He goes on 'runs' whatever the hell that means, and he does some construction work. Oh, and the charity stuff, which is cool, but he's so secretive. When I ask, he says"—I deepened my voice and shook my head—""it's club business.'"

"And there it is. That underlying thing I knew was there. You think he doesn't trust you. Right?" Barb made a crazy face as she lifted a package of breast pads that were shaped like hearts. "What the fuck are these?" She held them up to her voluptuous chest and we both burst out laughing.

"Maybe that's part of it, but it's not just that I don't think he trusts me. I don't understand why he has to have all these secrets, Barb. I almost feel like he's leading another life or something."

She looked at me with a doubtful glance and kept walking. "Now I know the pregnancy hormones have gone to your head. You're making no sense. You know where he is and, for the most part, what he's doing. His life is with you, Lei." We strolled through the highchairs, car seats and strollers. "Have you talked to him about this?"

"Yes. And no. I mean, I've tried, but I always get the crap about it being club business and not being able to discuss it with me. He asked me to accept that for now, but I don't even know what I'm accepting." I stop to look at a soft pink and gray playpen.

"Well, now is a good time to talk to him. He wants to fix things, so maybe he'll talk," she suggested. She turned to look at the price tag. "Holy sheep shit Batman. Two hundred and twenty dollars for a playpen? Shit, for that price it better put them to sleep for you."

Chapter Sixteen

~Leila~

Jax and I talked on the phone once a day over the last week. I kept it brief because I couldn't deal with the pinging emotions when I heard his voice. Then, when I shut my eyes, I remembered what I saw and I was back to square one. He told me he was out on a run to somewhere in Tennessee and was due back on Sunday. We made plans to get together at the house to talk.

It was Friday night and after sleeping all day I woke up in the late evening and was ravenous. For the first time in the two weeks that I had been back in the condo, Drew was there the same time I was. He had asked if it would be okay to have some of the guys over to play poker and throw back a few beers. Of course, I didn't care; it was his place too. I planned on staying upstairs, out of the way. I grabbed some pizza and a bottle of water, then went back upstairs to my cave. I put *The Notebook* in the DVD player and surrounded myself with pillows. An hour into the movie, I was blubbering like a fool. Still sniffling, I paused the movie, grabbed my empty plate and headed downstairs, hearing the guys bullshitting as I got further down.

I hit the bottom step and saw our houseguests. Sitting around the sectional was Drew, Bobby, Jasper, Johnny, Damon and...Brody. *Well hello universe. I see today was a good day to fuck with me a little more...thanks for that.* "Hey guys, just need a drink and I'll get outta here."

I prayed no one, especially Brody, noticed I had been crying. They were playing Texas Hold'em, from the look of it, and there were already several empties on the table. I made my way into the kitchen when Jasper started talking.

"Hey honey. How are ya feelin'?" When I turned he was standing at the bar.

"Hey Jas. I'm good. How about you? Everything good at home? Donna doin' okay?" I set my plate in the sink.

"Everything's good darlin'. How much longer you got left?" He lifted his chin.

"Seven weeks. I can't believe it, I'm so ready. All these damn contractions are getting annoying." I rubbed my side. "Plus, she thinks my ribs are monkey bars."

"What contractions?" Brody sidled up next to Jasper. Obviously, I wasn't quiet enough or Brody was eavesdropping.

"Brody, simmer down. It's nothing." I grabbed my water and exited the kitchen. "Jasper, I'll see ya Sunday at dinner." Kissing his cheek, I started for the stairs.

Brody caught my arm and stopped me in my tracks. "What contractions Lei? You said you'd tell me what's going on."

"Dear God in heaven. What is the matter with you Neanderthals?" I blew out a dramatic breath. "They're just Braxton-Hicks. It's completely normal. I'm an RN for fuck's sake, I think I'd know if it was a problem and at that point I'd tell you. I'm fine. Go finish your game." I turned away and went back upstairs and opened the door to a frisky Ruger.

"You need to go outside?" I asked in a silly high-pitched voice. He heard "out" and took off. Once I waddled down the stairs, he was already pacing at the back door. I grabbed my sweater on the way down and wrapped it around my shoulders and opened the door to the small backyard, which was fenced in with high black wrought iron gate that was tied in to a six-foot high brick wall. The patch of grass was about the size of a two-car garage. Enough for a quick Ruger nighttime visit.

I sat down and hit the switch to ignite the flame for the small propane fire table. As I looked up at the stars, enjoying the heat, I heard the door open. Ruger was lying in the grass chewing on a large bone, only stopping long enough to acknowledge our intruder.

"Ya know, it's a little cold to sit out here."

Brody. "It's not too bad. Between the fire, sweater and all my fat, I'm pretty toasty."

"Damn it Lei. I've told you, you're not fat. You're eight months pregnant. And what, you've gained twenty pounds?"

"Actually, twenty-five, if you must know."

"Right, so you probably still weigh less than most women. You're beautiful and even more so pregnant." He sat down next to me.

"Brody, I need you to understand that just because I'm not living with Jaxon, that doesn't mean we aren't still together." *We were still together, right?* I had started to wonder myself.

"Babe, you have to know I'll never stop trying. You're carrying my daughter and I love you. That has not changed." He reached for my hand. "I understand you need some time to figure things out, but I don't. I know what I want, and I want you. I will wait as long as I need to Lei. I know things got really fucked up between us, but I want to fix it."

I got angry as I thought about that night, six months ago. The night my world started spinning out of control. The night he threw me out of his life and I fell into Jaxon's. My chest still ached and my throat tingled at the memories. I had cried over it for weeks.

"Brody, I can't do this with you." I looked down at my hand. On my ring finger was Jaxon's beautiful engagement ring. Seeing it on my hand and my hand in Brody's troubled me. I quickly jerked it back and stood. As I started to walk past him, he grabbed my hand.

"It should've been mine."

Confused by the statement I asked, "What? What should've been yours?"

"The ring on your finger. It should be my ring. I should've been the one asking you to marry me. Not him."

"Well, maybe you'll still get your fuckin' chance." Jaxon's voice was gruff and tight.

"Jax." I was floored to see him there. I pulled away from Brody grasp and started toward the door where he was standing. "You're home? I thought you weren't gonna be here until Sunday."

"Sorry to disappoint ya, babe. Should've figured you'd be here with him." He was pissed. *Okay, pissed was an understatement.*

"What? What the hell is that supposed to mean Jaxon?" Brody stood and I knew what was coming. I turned to him. "Don't you say a fuckin' word Brody or I swear to God, I will slap you."

He clenched his fists and walked in the opposite direction to the gate, opened it and disappeared. Probably decided the front door would be an easier entry.

I looked back at Jaxon. "What *is* your problem? I haven't seen him since the night you let that skank dry hump you."

"Every time I turn around, he's with you. This is fuckin' bullshit Leila."

"Yeah, well, whose fault is that Jaxon?" As soon as it was out I wished I could take it back.

Jaxon's eyes narrowed. "Ya know what Lei…" His jaw tightened and he threw his hands up. "I'm out."

The door slammed shut so loudly it made me jump. I sat down, stunned. I wanted to run after him and beg him not to leave. I wanted to tell him I forgave him. I wanted him to hold me and tell me he loved me, but that all started with me going after him, and while I loved him, that wasn't going to happen.

He was the one who screwed this whole thing up, between the club hoochie and his overreacting about Brody, which was the one thing I told him would end up being a problem. I was right. He let Brody drive a wedge between us. No matter how many times I told Jax I loved him, and not Brody; that I wanted Jax, and *not* Brody. I warned Jax when he asked me to marry him that Brody would always be in our lives because of the baby. Jax promised me he could deal with it.

I stared at the fire until shouting and loud voices pulled me from my trance. I went back inside to find the living room empty and the front door standing open. The closer I got, the louder the shouts. In the front of the house on the sidewalk, Drew and Bobby were holding Jaxon back as Damon and Jasper were attempting the same with Brody.

Brody's nose was bleeding and his eye was swelling. Jaxon's lip was split and he was spitting blood. Unaware of my arrival, they were still cussin' at each other, grappling with their respective captors and looking wildly bloodthirsty.

"Shut. The. Fuck. Up!" I screamed at the brood of alpha males. "Are you kidding me?" They all stilled and looked in my direction. "I cannot believe you two. Y'all are acting like self-centered assholes. In case either of you have forgotten, since I haven't seen *either* of you in two weeks, I. Am. Pregnant. I don't need this shit." I shook my head, threw my hands up, turned around, then stomped inside. I slammed the door and contemplated locking it, but I didn't.

Jasper, Bobby, Drew and Johnny would all probably come back inside after Damon took Brody home and Jaxon left.

Grabbing a box of tissues from the downstairs bathroom, I took my fat, pregnant ass upstairs, whistling for Ruger. My cell phone was on vibrate, and each and every time it rang it lit the room up. Eventually there was a knock on the door.

"Sis, I hope you have clothes on because I'm comin' in." Drew opened the door and flipped the light switch on. "You okay kiddo?"

I looked down at the barrier of tissues surrounding me. "I will be. I'm sorry they ruined your night. I just can't believe they were out front fighting like that." My breath caught as I was sniffling. "What happened?"

"My best guess? Jax walked through the house out the front door, where Brody was, since he came through the side gate. They exchanged words, then blows." He didn't seem too bothered. "It was bound to happen. Those two have as much testosterone as a pride of male lions."

"What am I gonna do Drew?" I looked up through my tear soaked eyes. "Jax just said I'm out, then left. I don't even know what that means."

"What can I do? You want me to go drag Jaxon's dumbass back over here?"

"No." I sighed deeply. "You can't fix this one big brother, I wish you could though. I don't even know if I can."

"I'll try to talk to Brody and see if I can get him to back off a little bit, okay?" Drew offered.

"Thanks Drew."

Jasper appeared in the doorway. "Lei, you need anything?"

"No Jas, I'm okay, thanks. Well, I'm not okay, but you know what I mean."

"You sure? I could always lock 'em up," he teased and I grinned back.

"Nah, not right now, but can I reserve that right for a later time, just in case?" I smiled slightly as I teased.

"Sure can honey. Consider it reserved."

"Thanks. I'm gonna go to sleep y'all. I need to rest after the street brawl between my fiancé and baby daddy." I gathered the tissue and dumped them in the trash can next to the bed.

"Okay, but don't forget dinner Sunday," Jasper reminded. "Donna's makin' homemade chicken n' dumplins."

"Ooh, that's my favorite." I made the effort to sound excited.

"That's why she's makin' it. Get some rest, honey. See ya Sunday." Jasper walked over and kissed the top of my head before leaving.

"I'll be downstairs if you need anything." Drew tipped his head in the direction of the door.

"Thanks Drew. Love you."

"Love you too kiddo." He turned and left, shutting off the light in his wake and sending the room and myself back into darkness. Literally and figuratively.

My cell buzzed and lit up the room again. Reluctantly, I picked it up from the bedside table. I had six missed calls, four from Jaxon and two from Brody. There were three unread text messages, all from Jaxon. Two voicemails...*And a partridge in a pear tree.*

Text 1: *pls call me bck*

Text 2: *babe im sorry. pls call me. we need to talk*

Text 3: *Lei, I love you. I'm sorry I blew up tonite, I'm guessin u need time to think & that's why ur not callin me back.*

The voicemail from Brody came first. Calmly, he apologized for his part in the fight and for stressing me out, pregnant or not. He also wanted to ask if we could sit down, over dinner, and talk about everything. So in the wake of the colossal clusterfucker that became this night, he asked me out. Again.

Who does that? Oh, wait. Brody. He does that.

Jaxon's voicemail was more frantic. He must have left it as he walked home, trying to explain that Brody was goading him on and kept saying that he was gonna win me back. Admitting he fucked up and he didn't deserve me, Jaxon said he didn't want to lose me, he wanted nothing more in life than to fix us. He said he loved me like six different times in the rambling mess of a voicemail, but then he started back in on Brody, saying he was always there when we had a fight and the only reason we fight. *He must've forgotten the fights about club business and the skank ho.* He said he was sorry he left the way he did, and begged me to call him tonight instead of sitting and letting this stew.

I replayed his voicemail over and over. After the second time not even listening to the words, just his voice, I drifted off.

Chapter Seventeen

~Leila~

I woke the next morning to the awful—pregnancy—stench of coffee and the delicious smell of donuts. Blinking my eyes slowly, I saw my door open wide and heard hushed voices resonating from below. I was so warm and comfy in bed under the plush down comforter, but the potential reward of donuts won out.

I used the bathroom, brushed my teeth and washed my face. I rubbed my belly butter onto my enlarged abdomen and swollen boobs before putting on a pair of charcoal maternity leggings and threw on a sports bra. No way was I lugging these puppies around without help. Before pregnancy I was a 34D, and now...well, I didn't know exactly. Was cantaloupe a bra size?

I pulled on one of the two tees that I stole from Jaxon's drawer when I grabbed my scrubs. It was an old, soft, black Harley T-shirt that hit me about midthigh, even with the baby bump. Tucking my chin down, I brought the fabric to my nose and inhaled deeply. I loved the way he smelled. Polo Blue, with a hint of leather and musk.

I shuffled down the stairs and saw Bobby and Jaxon sitting around the bar, while Drew was standing on the other side. Drew was the first to notice my arrival, then the guys spun in their barstools.

"Mornin' sis. You wanna donut?"

"Hey baby." Jax, his lip swollen and slightly purple, rose and pulled me into his arms.

Still groggy, I mumbled to Drew, "Yeah, thanks." I wrapped my arms around Jax, pressing my belly to him just as the baby kicked.

Jax released me and slid his hands to the sides of my stomach. "Well, good mornin' to you too princess."

"Mornin' Lei, you get some sleep after the hectic night?" Bobby took the plate Drew passed with my donut and sat it next to him, where Jax had been sitting.

"Some. Little miss thing here"—I touched my belly—"decided to practice her jumping on my bladder, which meant I was up every two hours."

I sat down at the bar and took a bite of my glazed donut. Bobby and Drew exchanged a series of looks, then Bobby stood from the stool.

"Uh, I'm gonna run. Drew, thanks for the couch. Jax"—he noded at him—"thanks for the coffee and donuts. Oh, and for the, uh, show last night." Bobby snickered as he grabbed his coat and slipped on his shoes. He came back over to me, kissed my temple and whispered in my ear, "Go easy on him Lei. He loves you and Brody doesn't make shit easy."

Bobby dipped his head to Drew. "Later bro."

"Hey Bob, wait up." Drew rounded the peninsula and walked with Bobby over to the door. They spoke quietly to each other, then Bobby left. "I'm gonna grab Ruger and head down to the Battery for a run."

Drew disappeared, leaving me sitting at the bar and Jax leaning on the end of the tall counter. I drew in a deep breath as I finished my donut. We needed to talk, but I just didn't have the energy yet.

"You want another donut baby?" Jax took my plate into the kitchen.

"Nah, I really shouldn't have eaten that one, but you know how I love donuts. I don't need to gain sixty pounds while I'm pregnant."

"Lei, babe, you look fuckin' amazing. If you wanna eat a dozen donuts, then eat them. You're pregnant. You should allow yourself to eat whatever you want. And stop worryin' about your weight. You need to gain more. Dr. Rogers told you at our last appointment she wanted you to put a little more weight on." He dropped my plate into the sink and rinsed it.

"Well, I have. I got on the scale the other night and I was one hundred and forty-nine pounds. One hundred and forty-nine, Jaxon. That's twenty-five pounds more than I used to weigh. I feel like a freakin' whale. My feet hurt, my back hurts and I don't think adding more fat to the problem will help."

"Babe." He came around and pulled me off the stool and to the couch. "You're not fat. You're as gorgeous now as you were a year ago." He pulled my feet into his lap and started massaging at my heel.

"Is that why you're out getting lap dances? Because I'm so hot."

Jax stopped rubbing and winced. He sucked in a huge breath, clearly getting ready to speak, then stopped.

Drew walked through with Ruger on the leather lead. "See y'all in a little while."

I attempted to pull my feet out of Jaxon's lap. I was successful with one, not so much with the other. He held it in his calloused hands like it was his lifeline.

"Listen, I can say this until I'm blue in the face and the fuckin' cows come home. I fucked up. I should've made her stop. I should've told the boys why I was there. They wouldn't have sent her over if they knew. I should've stayed home with you. I wish I could go back and change it all, but I can't." He started rubbing the arch of my foot. "What I can do is apologize. Again. And just wait for you to forgive me."

"That's the problem Jaxon. I don't know how to. It's not that I don't want to, because I do, but every time I close my eyes, I see you with her. I see her grinding on you. You kissing her. Pulling her hair, the same way you do mine." I snatched my foot away and attempted to stand up. Jax jumped up and helped me. "Maybe that's what hurts the most, you used to do those things with me."

I walked to the bathroom leaving him slack-jawed in the living room. I peed, washed my hands, then blew my nose. Grabbing a few tissues, I returned to Jax.

"I pulled her hair to get her mouth off me, not to shove her tits in my face. I've told you that." I could see he was getting perturbed. "What do you want me to do, Leila?"

That was the problem. I didn't know what I wanted him to do. Even after two weeks of being apart, I still didn't know.

"I don't know Jaxon." I looked at him, then turned my gaze to my belly and whispered, "I don't know."

Just then the silence was severed by my phone ringing upstairs.

"Shit." I tried to scoot myself to the edge of the chaise to go get my phone.

"I'll get it." Jax bounded up the stairs. I heard him faintly.

"What do you want...Well, she's busy motherfucker...No, I won't fuckin' get her...Yeah, well fuck you too."

I stopped at the bottom of the stairs to see him coming back down them. "Who was that?" I asked even though I knew.

He didn't say a word as he clomped down the stairs, holding out the phone to me. His demeanor had changed completely. He was bristly and tense. His eyes dark, jaw tight and hands clenched.

"Jaxon who was on the phone?" I asked softer this time.

He stopped and his eyes settled on mine. The look alone made me tremble. "Let's not play this game. You know who it was."

"Brody?" I asked to be sure.

"Always in the fuckin' middle." He walked over to the kitchen and grabbed his keys off the counter.

"You're leaving? Now?"

"What do you think?"

"I think if you wanted to fix this, then leaving isn't the answer Jax. You're letting him do this. You." I was pissed. "You promised me on Valentine's Day, when you proposed, you wouldn't let him do this to us. And the first time things get rough you use him as an excuse."

"An excuse? A fucking excuse?" he shouted.

I screamed back, not backing down. "Yes. He didn't get a fuckin' lap dance in my face. That was you. You. You did this. Not him. He was just here to pick up the pieces." I started to calm down. "Just like you did when he fucked up...Oh my God, that's it." It suddenly dawned on me. "That's your problem. You think that since you picked up the pieces and we ended up together, that's gonna happen now. Right? That I'm gonna choose him over you."

He hung his head and stared at his heavy black boots and whispered, "Yeah. It's the exact same thing Leila."

"Wow...what you must think of me, to think that shit." I dropped to the couch with the weight of his words. "I think you need to leave Jaxon, because if you really think that I could jump from your bed back to his after what he did to me, then you don't know me at all."

A tear fell when I looked down at my ring as I slid it off my finger. I looked at the brilliant diamonds, then stood. I walked over to Jaxon, took his hand, placed it in his palm and closed his fingers around it. "Goodbye Jaxon."

I walked past him to the bathroom, shut the door and slid my back down the wall until my butt hit the ground.

Then I cried.

Harder than I ever had.

Harder than when Brody pulled his shit and even harder than when my mom died.

I felt like I was losing a part of my soul. Like someone reached into my chest and tore half of my heart out. I felt like I was dying as I sobbed hysterically on the floor of that bathroom.

*****

~Jaxon~

I kept looking down at the engagement ring I gave her. The one she just handed back to me. I listened to her crying in the bathroom as I stood on the other side of the door. The sound tortured me. I wanted to bust down the door and hold her. Promise to never hurt her again. Promise to never let that fucker come between us again. And promise to hold her forever.

But instead pride overruled good sense. And love.

I walked over to the dining room and carefully sat the ring in the middle of the table. As I opened the door, I looked back toward the bathroom door. "I love you baby." With that whisper, I shut the door and walked back down the street to our house.

As I reached our place, I sat down on the front steps and remembered all of the times I watched her walk past to and from work. The conversations we had at the sidewalk. Then I stood and walked inside. Everywhere I looked, there was a memory of her or us. A piece of her. I trudged up the steps to the second floor. Opened the nursery door and walked over to the pink upholstered rocking chair. I sat down and looked around the room where our daughter will be, or would've been raised.

And for the first time in my adult life I cried.

Chapter Eighteen

~*Leila*~

It had been a week since I tried to give Jaxon his ring back. When I had finally emerged from the bathroom and I saw my ring on the table, my heart knocked against my ribs—he wouldn't take it back. Perhaps there was hope for us after all.

Barb told me Viper—apparently, they were more of an item than she let on—said that he, Jax and a few other brothers had to do something for the Semper Fi Foundation. I tried not to let the fact that he hadn't called or texted bother me. Barb hadn't heard from Viper either.

It was Monday morning and I was on my way for a routine checkup with Dr. Rogers. This would be the first appointment that I went alone. Jaxon was...well, not in my life right now and I had to own that part of it was my doing. When I called Brody back, I forget to remind him of the appointment and I was sure he didn't remember.

Once in the waiting room, I pulled my iPad out and started to read about my latest book boyfriend. When the door squeaked open, I looked up to see Brody strutting over in a custom tailored suit. He unbuttoned his jacket and dropped down in the chair next to me. "Hey babe, how are you feeling?"

"Uh, fine. I didn't think you were coming. I forgot to remind you. How did you know?" I closed the cover on my tablet.

"I had Sara put it on my schedule last month. Where's he at?"

His question shook me. I wasn't prepared to tell him, but since he's asked I guessed now was as good a time as any. "He's not here. And it looks like he won't be at anymore appointments either." I felt the burning in my nose and tears welling in my eyes and blinked a few times, hoping Brody wouldn't notice.

"Leila Matthews?" the nurse called out.

Saved by the bell.

Brody helped me up and trailed behind me as we were led down the hall to the exam room. The nurse took my vitals and told us Dr. Rogers would be in shortly. She exited, leaving the door partially open.

"Want to tell me what's going on Leila? Where is Jaxon?" Brody sat in the chair by the counter.

"Wow, I'm shocked. You *do* know his name."

Brody crossed his arms across his chest and groaned. "Sorry I asked. Obviously you don't want to talk about it."

I took in a long breath, then slowly blew it out. "Last Sunday we got into a fight after he answered my phone when you called. I took off my ring and gave it back to him." Brody's eyes widened in disbelief. "When I came out of the bathroom it was sitting on the dining room table."

"So is that why you're still wearing it?" he said through gritted teeth.

"I love him Brody. I'm sorry if that hurts you. Giving him the ring back was impulsive and I shouldn't have done it. Knowing me as well as he does, he knew I wasn't thinking clearly, that I did it in the heat of the moment." I brushed a few tears from my cheeks. "He hasn't called me all week, but I know he's outta town on business for the charity. I'm presuming that's why."

Brody leaned forward, rested his elbows on his knees and clasp his hands together. "I'm not going to lie. I don't like him. I think you deserve better than he can give you. You deserve to be treated like a princess. To travel the world the way you want to. To stay at home and raise our little girl if you want to. Or hire a nanny and work the job you so love, but you deserve the chance to make that decision."

"Brody—" I was cut short by the quick knock and the door being pushed open.

"Leila, how are you dear? Any issues since the last visit?" Dr. Rogers asked as she set her tablet on the counter.

I plastered a smile across my face. "Good, can't complain."

Brody cleared his throat and glared at me like he was trying to shoot lightning bolts at me out his eyes. He nodded from me to the doctor. I gave him an evil glare and quickly shook my head, silently responding with *keep your damn mouth shut.*

"Well, since she's not going to say it, I will," Brody and his big mouth blurted out.

"Brody," I warned him.

"No, Lei. She's your doctor. She needs to know and if you're not gonna tell her, I will. That's my daughter in there. And, like it or not, I still love you." He turned to Dr. Rogers. "She's been having contractions for the last week. She thinks they are Braxton-Hicks, but according to the books I've read they shouldn't be painful. And they are." He trained his gaze back to me.

"Asshole," I sniped quietly.

"Okay. Leila, is this true?" she asked

Keeping my villainous look on Brody, I answered, "Yes, but I'm fine."

"How long have they been happening? And how long do they last?" she asked as she tapped away on the tablet.

"Well, the ones that are really painful, usually only last a minute or so. I guess they started about a week and a half, maybe two weeks ago, but really, it's nothing. They aren't regular and I don't even have that many a day," I explained as she nodded her head and continued to take notes.

"I'm going to step out and I'd like you to undress from the waist down. I want to check your cervix." She pulled a sheet out of the cabinet and handed it to me. "Open the door when you're ready."

I stood and looked at Brody with contempt. "This is all your fault. Turn around," I ordered.

"Seriously, Lei? I've definitely seen you naked." He motioned to my belly.

"Get out. Wait outside the door." I pointed to the exit. "I'm serious Brody. We aren't together anymore. And Jaxon would shit a baby goat if he knew you were in here while I changed. Go!"

Shaking his head and grumbling, he vacated the room. I undressed and folded my clothes and sat them neatly on the counter, wrapped the sheet around me and cracked the door. Brody came in first and sat down.

"I hope you know I plan to be in the room when you deliver," Brody informed me.

"Well, I hope so. It's not every day you have a child. I'll be really pissed if you miss it."

"Don't worry, I've made sure Sara knows not to schedule anything out of town after the first week of April." He paused and got this look on his face. "Don't take this the wrong way, but I can see your ass."

"Huh." I looked to my side. "Oh shit. Sorry." I tried to reach back and wrap the sheet around a little more. Dr. Rogers reentered the room and had me lay down. She washed her hands and put on a sterile glove.

"Feet up," she directed and helped put my feet in the stirrups attached to the table. "Little pressure."

"Uh, Lei, you want me to leave?" Brody's eyes widened.

I chuckled a little. "Nah, I'm good."

Dr. Rogers pulled back, patted my knee indicating I could sit up as she pulled her glove off. "So you're not gonna like it, but I need to send you over to—" I cut her off.

"Do not finish that sentence if it ends with hospital," I said with a groan.

"Sorry Leila. We need to make sure you're not in preterm labor. Given the fact that you've had a placenta previa, bleeding and you've been having contractions, it's a real possibility."

"Damn it." I exhaled loudly. "Can I at least go home first and—" This time Dr. Rogers interrupted me.

"Nope, afraid not." She turned to Brody. "Dad, can you make sure she gets there safely?"

"Of course," Brody agreed. "Isn't it too early for her to have the baby?"

"She's far enough along that it shouldn't be a problem if she did happen to deliver now. I hope that's not the case, though." She turned and looked at me. "You're almost thirty four weeks, but the baby would probably need to stay in the NICU for a week or two depending on her weight."

"Okay, but I'd really like to wait as long as possible. Another five or six weeks would be good."

"I understand that Leila, but sometimes we don't have a say in it," she said with sympathy. "I'll let you get dressed. I'm gonna call over to the L and D floor and let them know you're coming in for observation. Best case scenario, you'll be home later tonight."

"Okay." I rolled my eyes.

Dr. Rogers and Brody exited the room, leaving me alone to dress. I put my clothes back on, texted Barb and tried to call Jaxon. It went straight to voicemail and I left a message asking him to call me. I didn't want him to worry, so I didn't tell him what was going on. Barb texted me saying she'd meet me at my house.

Opening the door I almost walked into Brody. "Ready?" he asked.

"Yeah, can we talk out front first?"

"Sure." We left the office and stopped by the front doors. "What's up?"

"Don't get pissed but I'm going home first." He started shaking his head. "Wait, let me explain. I have to drop off my car, get my overnight bag just in case and get some things. Please don't fight me on this Brody or so help me God, I will ban you from my room."

"That's stooping pretty low, babe." He understood I wasn't playing and yielded. "Fine, but you have fifteen minutes from the time we get there, to the time I drag you out."

I grunted. "I'll see you at my place. Barb is meeting us there."

Chapter Nineteen

~Leila~

Barb was waiting inside with Drew when I got back to the condo. She already had taken Ruger out and made arrangements with Drew to take care of him.

"I just need to grab my bag, tablet, phone charger and I'll be ready to go," I said to Barb as there was a knock on the front door. "Can you grab that? It'll be Brody. He was at the doctor's appointment with me."

"I got it." Drew tossed aside the TV remote and walked to the door. "Hey B! Hear you might be a dad today."

"Honestly Drew, I hope not. As eager as I am to meet her, I hope she stays in there a few more weeks." He looked over to me.

"You and me both," I said climbing the stairs. I grabbed the overnight bag Jax packed for me a few weeks ago and threw in my tablet, chargers and my toothbrush and toothpaste.

As I came down the stairs, I heard Barb and Brody squabbling over who got to drive me to the hospital. "Okay, you two stop bickering like an old married couple. Brody, I called Barb to come pick me up. I'm sorry I should have told you to save you the trip, but I wasn't really thinking."

"It's not like it's that far out of the way," he grumbled. "I get it. Really. You don't want to upset Jax. Even though he's not here."

"Listen, I don't wanna sound like a bitch, but I'm probably gonna. If you feel the need to be continually passive aggressive about Jax, then maybe you should stay here with Drew." He started to say something, but I threw up my hand and didn't let him. "I'm quite capable of taking care of myself and our daughter. I've been doing so since September." His lips became a thin line. "And don't worry, I'll be sure to call you before I actually deliver. I wouldn't dream of depriving you of seeing the daughter you didn't want."

I swiveled my head over to Barb who was standing with Drew, both wide-eyed in disbelief. "You ready?"

"Uh, yeah?" Barb picked up her purse and keys, then gave Brody a compassionate smile. She whispered something to Drew that I couldn't make out, then followed me to the front door. I didn't look back to see what Brody was doing. *Frankly, I don't give two shits right now.*

Once we were in Barb's Jeep she turned to me. "I don't know about Brody, but you scared the shit out of me back there. What was that about?"

"I've warned him for weeks to lay off Jaxon. And I'm stressed out of my mind right now. I need support, not him being an asshat." I clicked my seat belt into place and adjusted it to fit under my belly with a loud huff.

She pulled onto East Bay Street and quietly asked, "Have you talked to Jax today?"

"I called, but no answer. I left a message, but I wasn't specific. Not the kind of thing I would want hear on a voicemail."

"I'll try Cole once we get to the hospital and get you settled in, okay?" she offered.

"Thanks Barb." I looked over at her. "I don't know what I'd do without you."

"Back at ya beotch. Now, let's get you to the hospital."

A few minutes later we walked in the front doors of the hospital and checked in. After completing registration, we were sent upstairs to the fifth floor. It took about thirty minutes to get a room assigned and another fifteen before the nurse came in to get the monitors hooked up. Barb being Barb, beat her to it and had everything set up and already recording.

"Hi, Ms. Matthews, my name is Lucinda. Uh, did another nurse come in and admit you?" the nurse asked, visibly baffled.

Barb laughed quietly and raised her hand. "Me, it was me. I hooked up the TOCO, but that's all."

"We are both RNs over at Shock Trauma, not just two crazy chicks that stayed at a Holiday Inn," I joked.

"Oh." She laughed. "That's cool. I bet that's a stressful place to work."

Great, she's probably thinking the same thing I think when we have nurses or doctors as patients. Pain in the ass.

"Don't worry, I'll try my best to be a good patient, but I make no promises," I warned as I shook my head.

"You'll be fine." She looked over at the computer screen and went through my medical history, allergies and birth plan.

Twenty minutes later, I was in an ugly blue gown, channel surfing while Barb was on the phone with Viper trying to relay information to give to Jaxon.

"According to Cole, he should be home later today. He had some meetings for that charity he's a part of, after they finished the run in Tennessee." Barb lay down next to me in the bed. "Anything good on TV?"

"Nah, just a bunch of daytime crap."

"Have you decided on a name yet for my goddaughter?"

"Not really. Jax and I had it narrowed down, but nothing set in stone." I yawned.

Barb climbed out of the bed. "You get some sleep and I'm gonna run to the cafeteria and get a quick bite to eat. You want anything?"

"Hmm." I knitted my brow. "Actually, yeah. I'm starving and I'm sure I missed lunch here since it's almost one thirty. Can you get me a cheeseburger and fries?"

"Of course my love." She looked over at the electronic fetal monitor and picked up the trace print out. "Hey, uh, you feelin' anything Lei?"

"Yeah, just a little cramping in my back. Why?" I tried looking over her shoulder.

"Huh?" She hesitated. "Oh, uh, just a few small contractions." She said it like it was insignificant.

"How many is a few Barb? Let me see." I pulled on her shoulder.

She turned and held the strip of paper out for me to see. "Only four over the last hour or so. No biggie." She dropped the paper and headed for the door. "I'll be back shortly. Try to get some rest."

"'Kay." I reclined the head of the bed, raised the foot and before too long, I dozed off.

When I woke I was lying on my side surrounded by fluffy pillows. Lifting my head, I looked around the dimly lit room to see Brody sitting in the oversized recliner with his tablet in his lap. *Figures, he's working.*

"Where's Barb?"

He bolted up. "Shit Lei, you startled me."

"Sorry. Barb?"

"She'll be back in a little while. She was gonna run and make some calls." He walked over to the side of my bed. "She left you a burger and fries, but I'm sure it's cold by now. You want me to have the nurse heat it up?"

"Yeah, would you?" I looked back to the pillows. "You do this?"

"What? The pillows?" I nodded. "Yeah. Well, I called Jane and she brought them over. I remember how much you loved the pillow on our, uh, my bed. Thought you'd like to be comfortable, seeing as you have to stay here."

"That was sweet Brody, thanks." I sat up and adjusted the bed. "Did Jane leave?" I wondered if she was still in the building. I wanted to see her.

"Yeah, she dropped them off about three o'clock." He picked up the wrapped plate. "I'll be right back."

"All right." I swung my feet around, slid them into my fuzzy pink slippers, disconnected the TOCO cords. Thankfully, Barb already put my stuff in here, so I didn't have to deal with that.

"Leila?" Brody called from outside of the bathroom door. "You okay?"

I pulled the door open with my toothbrush hanging out my mouth. "Fine."

"I set your food down on the tray. I have to run out and make a couple of phone calls. You need anything before I go?" he asked, swiping his finger up and down the screen of his phone.

"Nope." I spit the mouthful of toothpaste suds into the sink and wiped my mouth off with the fluffy gray towel. *What the...*"Hey, uh, Brody, did Jane bring towels too?"

"Oh, yeah. Those other things were scratchy and stiff. I've seen sandpaper less abrasive. I didn't think you'd mind." He looked up from his phone momentarily.

"No, I don't, but you don't need to do all of this. I'm not staying. They're only monitoring me," I informed him as I swayed back over to the bed.

"Right, we'll see what they say. I happened to see Dr. Rogers in the hallway. She said she'd be in to see you in a few minutes." He went back to his phone with a wicked scowl crossing his face.

"Damn it. Listen babe, I gotta call Sara, but I'm gonna be in the hall. I'll come back once I see the doctor coming in."

"Take your time. I'll fill you in when ya get back." I didn't need him sitting here with me holding my hand. I did, however, want Jaxon there. I couldn't believe he hadn't called me back or shown up.

"Okay, thanks. Be right back." Brody crossed the room in four long strides and left the door open on his way out.

I took a few bites of food and picked the tablet up off the bedside table and began reading. I needed to lose touch with reality for a little while.

Well, with my reality.

Chapter Twenty

~Leila~

Thirty minutes later there was a quiet knock followed by Dr. Rogers breezing into the room. "Hey Leila. How are things goin' in here?"

"Good, just catching up on some reading."

"I'm glad you're relaxing. Let me just check the print out and"— she lifted the monitor trace from the EFM—"then we can talk." She looked from the beginning of the recording to now. Concern swept across her face, but it was gone as fast as it appeared. "So have you been feeling anything?"

"Not really. A few Braxton-Hicks, but nothing painful. Why? What's it show?" I was starting to worry. Barb only said she saw a few minor contractions.

"Well, you have been having contractions. Nothing too many like you said, but contractions none the less." She dropped the unraveled scroll of paper. I watched as it fell weightlessly to the hardwood floor, kind of like my hope of getting out of here. "The good news is they are about twenty to twenty-five minutes apart and haven't changed all day." She swiped the screen of her tablet, tapped a few times, then began to type. "We can do one of two things. First option, get you up and have you start walking and see if your body wants to deliver. The second option is giving you magnesium sulfate and trying to stop the contractions. We can also give you dexamethasone to speed up lung development."

"Uh, okay. Can I have a little while to think about this and talk it over?" I didn't want to make this decision right this second and I needed to talk to Jax. But, I couldn't talk it over with Jax because he wasn't returning my calls or text.

"Of course. I'm going to finish my rounds and then I'll stop back in about an hour or so." She locked the tablet, cradled it under her arm and patted my leg on her way out the door.

I picked my phone up from the bed and called Jaxon. *Again.* And got voicemail. *Again.* I really didn't want to leave this in a message, but I was out of options.

"Jax, it's me. Listen, I didn't want to do this over voicemail, but I don't have a whole lot of choices right now. I'm in the hospital and I guess you could say I'm sort of in labor, well preterm labor. The doctor just left and I have to decide in the next hour if I want to get up and walk the halls to see if my body wants to have the baby now or if I want to lie in bed, get medicine to stop the contractions and get medicine to help speed up her lung development. I really need you here. I wouldn't admit this to anyone else but…" I fought back tears to whisper, "I'm scared. I don't…just…call me. Please."

I hung up the phone and swore to myself that was the last message I would leave. Maybe he really was done. The thought of it really being over was unbearable. The physical pain in my chest was a sick reminder of his absence. I didn't want to do this without him. He had become my rock and my soft place to land. We made all of these plans for our daughter. I didn't want to believe that he was choosing to walk away from us, especially after everything I told him about my dad.

My pity party was interrupted when I heard Brody outside the door.

"So what's the verdict?" He looked up from his phone. "Aw babe, you're crying. What's wrong? Is something wrong with the baby?" He was at my side in a flash, apprehension darkening his beautiful blue eyes.

"The baby is fine, I'm fine. I just"—I wiped my face with my index fingers and took a deep breath—"left a message for Jax."

Grimacing, he asked, "What did the doctor say?" He sat down on the foot of the bed.

"She's giving me two choices." I told him what she said.

"So that's why you called him." I nodded. He quieted and I waited for the spiteful comments about Jaxon to start, but they didn't. "I'd hope you were gonna include me in this decision, seeing as she's my daughter too." Surprisingly, he sounded nervous.

"Of course I am Brody. I didn't have any intention of excluding you in any way. I hope you know that." His shoulders relaxed. "It's just...I mean Jax...ugh. I don't know. I'm scared Brody and he always"—I shrugged—"knows exactly what to say to me."

"What would he say?" he asked quietly.

"He would say, 'Babe, it's gonna be fine. I gotcha. I won't let anything happen to either of my girls.'"

"God, I hope you don't ever impersonate me," he mocked.

I smiled. "It's not that bad." He cocked his head and winked. "Oh come on. It's what he'd say. Don't look at me like that."

Brody sat on the end of the bed shaking his head. "Okay. Let's talk about what you want to do. What are you thinking?"

"She's not ready yet Brody. I need her to stay here." I wrapped my arms around my belly. "I'm not ready to share her with the rest of the world yet."

"Babe, I get that. I want her to wait another month or so too," he agreed. "So, we tell the doctor to give you the medicine to stop the contractions and the other to speed up her development," he said as he held my hand.

"Did Barb say when she'd be back?" I picked my phone up. "I really thought she'd be back by now."

He looked down at his watch. "Huh, she said she'd be back around six and it's almost quarter of seven. Why don't you call her and see where she's at?"

"Maybe after Dr. Rogers comes back in." I wondered what was keeping Barb. It wasn't like her to be late. Then again, I was asleep when she left; she might've thought I needed to sleep, but still she would've called. I took a few more bites of the burger and looked around for a drink. "Hey, did she bring me a drink?"

"I don't think so, just the food. You thirsty? There is wat—"

"I'd rather grab a soda from the nurse at the station." I swung my legs over the side of the bed and stood up. Before I could disconnect the monitors, Brody was at my side taking the wires out of my hand.

"Sit down." He swung his head toward the bed. "Why must you be so damn stubborn? I'm right here," he huffed. "I can go ask for a soda. Lei. You need to start letting me help you. You don't have to do everything alone." He helped me back into bed and disappeared out the door.

I am doing everything alone. Jax isn't here, so I am alone.

Sure, Brody was here now, but it was only a matter of time before work called or he got freaked out again and ran for the hills.

"Here, I got you a ginger ale." He carried in the can of soda and a white Styrofoam cup.

"Thank you. Did you see Dr. Rogers out there?"

"Nah, it's pretty quiet right now. Have any more contractions?"

"Well, according to the monitor, yes, but I don't really feel them. I mean, I've got some cramps in my back, but nothing I can't handle." Just as I bragged I was hit with a pretty decent contraction.

"Ahhhh," I groaned and pushed my palm into my side. I turned away from Brody and took a few slow deep breaths.

"Uh, what can I do Lei?" he asked. "I don't know what to do."

It lasted about fifty seconds and wasn't too bad. It definitely caught me off guard, but I'd be prepared for the next one.

"You okay now?" I rolled back to see him looking at the monitor. "So that spike on the line was the contraction?" He pointed to the EFM screen.

"Yep. Sorry, that one surprised me. None of the others hurt." I rolled onto my back and sat up a little. "Just some back cramps."

Brody dropped the handrail at the head of the bed. "Scoot up."

"Huh?"

"Slide your ass to the middle of the bed." He pointed to where he wanted me to move. Begrudgingly, I obeyed and sat cross-legged on the bed. He slid in behind me and started kneading and rubbing my lower back and hips.

"Ooh, oh God that feels good," I moaned in relief. "Damn, that's it. Little higher…ahh, right there. I swear she has her foot between my ribs."

I grabbed a couple of the fluffy down pillows Jane had dropped off and hugged them, rolling forward to give Brody better access to my lower back.

While he was massaging the tension away, Dr. Rogers strolled in. "Everything okay?"

"Yeah, she just had a bit of a contraction," Brody explained as he stood up from the bed.

"Hey." I whipped my head around. "Why'd you stop? That felt good."

"Leila, have you had a chance to talk everything over and make a decision?" She laid the tablet down on the counter and pulled up the stool.

"Yeah. I want to try the medicines. We want to give her as much time in there as possible." I looked over to Brody who gave me a supportive nod.

"Sounds good. You do understand this is not a guarantee? You could continue to progress in your labor." She pulled the tablet into her lap and started typing.

"Yeah, I understand." I nodded slowly.

"So, we will do the initial dose of magnesium sulfate, then set up the maintenance dose to be given once an hour. The nurse will come in and give the IM injection of the dexamethasone and then again in twelve hours. I'll check back on you in the morning." She continued typing, then looked up at Brody and me. "Any questions?"

"How long will she need to stay here?" Brody asked as if he was reading my mind.

"At least until tomorrow afternoon. That's *if* the medicine works. Best case scenario, it stops them completely by tomorrow morning. Then we'll monitor you for a few more hours. If you have no more contractions, then you go home." She set the tablet down and continued explaining. "Worst case, the medicine only slows down labor, allowing the dex time to work on the baby's lungs. Some cases, this just prolongs the inevitable. If that is the case, then I would like to keep you on the magnesium sulfate until Wednesday or Thursday and give the dex at least forty-eight hours to be as effective as possible."

"All right, let's get this show on the road," I said wanting to stop labor from progressing. "Thank you Dr. Rogers."

"My pleasure Leila. The nurse will be in shortly to start the medicine and give you the IM injection. I will also write an order for Ambien, since that is safe for you to take, just in case you have trouble sleeping and Stadol, the drug of choice for labor pain, in case it gets too bad." She patted my leg. "Try to get some rest. I'll see you in the morning."

Brody stopped her before she could leave the room. "It won't be a problem for me to stay here tonight, right?"

I started to protest, but Dr. Rogers answered too quickly. "Not a problem, you're more than welcome to stay Dad. The recliner pulls out to a small, yet uncomfortable bed." She chuckled. "Have a good night."

"Brody, you don't need to stay. I'll be fine. Nothing is going to happen tonight." He wheeled the stool over to me and sat down.

"Lei, I'm not leaving you here alone. I'll just sleep on the recliner. It'll be fine." He took my hand in his. "I know I'm not the guy you want here, but—" I cocked my head and start to speak. "I know what you're gonna say. And you're right. I totally screwed this up from the moment you gave me this precious gift. I will never, ever, be able to tell you how much I regret what I did and what I put you through." He looked down at my hand in his.

"I'm incredibly grateful you've given me a second chance to be a father to this little girl." He gently slid his hand across my abdomen. "And for what it's worth, I'm genuinely sorry Jaxon isn't here for you. I hate to see you hurting. I hate more that I hurt you the way I did. I hope that I'll continue to have the chance to prove to you that you can trust me." He reached up with his thumb and swiped the tears from under my eyes.

"I do appreciate everything you're trying to do Brody. The little things that are really thoughtful show me that you care and it tells me you're trying." I blew a deep breath out. "And please don't take this the wrong way. As much as I love the attentive and thoughtful gestures, I need you to understand that doesn't mean we are going to get back together. And I'm *so* not saying that to hurt you. I swear. I just want us to be on the same page." Tears streamed down my face. It really hurt to say those things to him, especially since I had once thought I was completely and totally head over feet in love with this man.

"Please don't cry, Lei. I understand that's what you want. I promise not to push anything, other than being a supportive father." He smiled softly and nodded slightly. "Same page."

"Ahhhhhh." I leaned my head back and focused on a spot on the ceiling. I squinted my eyes as I winced in pain and concentrated on my breathing. Slow, deep inhale in through the nose. Slowly blow out through my mouth.

He grabbed my hand. "Squeeze my hand if you need to."

"I'm fine," I managed to get out.

"Babe, you're in labor. You don't have to pretend to be tough for me. I imagine it's painful." He stood and lightly ran his hands up and down my upper arm. "You don't have to be strong all of the time. Let me take care of you, for a little while." He gave my hand a slight squeeze and continued to rub my arm.

"Whew, it's easing off now."

"Did you take Lamaze classes?" He sat back down, but didn't release my hand.

"No. Jax and I were supposed to start them next week." I looked down, slipped my hand away and turned to my side.

"Well, if he doesn't join you, I'd like the opportunity to go with you." I looked up at him. "You know, so I could at least be of some help during delivery. Or maybe just find out how to survive without pissing you off or losing my balls."

I laughed. I forgot how Brody could make me laugh.

Chapter Twenty-One

~Leila~

A little while later the nurse came in and gave me the IM injection and started the magnesium sulfate treatment. She prepared us for the side effects. I prayed it wouldn't be a problem.

Apparently, I wasn't loud enough or God wasn't listening when I was talking, because I continued to have decent contractions every twenty-five minutes and to top it off I was puking my guts up.

As soon as I came down from a contraction, Brody had the wet washcloth and a trash can ready. It had been an hour since I started getting sick and he hung in like a champ. He didn't once hesitate to pull my hair back, get me a drink, wipe vomit off my face or just rub my back and tell me it would be okay.

Barb strolled into the room about ten seconds into the current contraction. "Holy shit Lei. They got worse?" She looked to Brody, since I was somewhat engaged at the moment.

"Yeah, started about—"

"Ooooh. This one's actually pretty painful." I tried to breathe through it, but damn if that shit didn't hurt.

"Grab my hand babe." He reached for my hand and rubbed my back. "Try to breathe."

"I *am* breathing," I bit back.

Barb jumped in. "No, you're holding your breath." I glared at her. "Don't look at me like that, girlfriend."

I continued to labor on my side and focused on a spot on the handrail. As it eased off I started to feel nauseous again. Without having to say a word or even move, Brody was in front of me with the pink basin, helping me sit up. I started dry heaving again as Brody rubbed the heel of his palm up and down my spine.

After it passed, Brody told Barb what had been happening.

"Did they give you Zofran?" she asked, standing at the foot of the bed.

"No," I grumbled as the wave of nausea passed.

"I'm going to get Zofran." She marched out of the room.

I looked to Brody with pleading eyes. He knew what I was thinking, yet again. "Nope, I'm not stopping her. She's right, you need something to help ease the dry heaves."

"I'll be—" I was cut off by another violent retch. "Ugh. This fuckin' sucks."

"I'm sorry babe, I wish I could do something to make it stop."

"It's okay. I appreciate you just bein' here." *Even though Jax isn't and that's who I really want right now.*

Barb strolled in with my nurse, Lucinda, five minutes later. "I come bearing gifts," Barb squealed.

"Okay. Maybe I'll be able to get some sleep if I can't feel the contractions." I was hopeful but realistic. If the medicine didn't work then I could be in for a long night.

"Okay," Lucinda said after she'd gone through the information drill, "I'm gonna push Zofran first, then I will flush and then push the Stadol." She swabbed the port on the IV line with an alcohol pad, then administered the medicines. "You know the Stadol will make you drowsy and you'll need help to get to the bathroom." She looked at Barb and Brody. "Don't let her go in alone."

They both nodded in agreement.

Two minutes after Lucinda left, I said, "Whoa," then leaned back in the bed and giggled. "This shit's heavy duty."

"Oh, this is gonna be fun." Barb smiled deviously and looked over the bed to Brody. "Haven't seen her on narcotics yet, have ya?"

"Uh, no…Why?" he questioned.

"She's a fuckin' hoot on drugs. Her brain to mouth filter is totally nonexistent. It's g-r-e-a-t," she whisper-yelled.

"Yo beotch, you talkin' 'bout me?" I pointed at Barb, my words slurring.

"Sure am. Just tellin' Brody how funny you are when you get drugs." She laughed. "Wanna watch TV?"

"Nope." I popped my "p." "Did ya hear from my asshat of a fiancé yet?"

"Nah, not yet, but I'm sure he'll call soon."

"I've left him four messages, Barb. I think when he said he was"—I threw my hands up and pulled out the air quotes—"out he actually meant he was out and not comin' back."

"I think you need to just wait for him to call you. Don't jump to any conclusions," she warned.

"Um, I'm gonna run out for just a little. I need to make some phone calls." Brody scrolled through his phone. "I just want to make sure Sara clears my schedule and knows what's going on."

"Fine," I muttered. As soon as I thought he was out of the room, I looked at Barb. "Great, now I've run him off too. Ugh, what is wrong with me Barb?"

She pushed me over on the bed and crawled in next to me. "There is—"

Brody barged back in the room. "First of all, you didn't run me off. I thought you'd like to talk to Barb alone. Secondly, there is absolutely nothing wrong with you." His eyes were dark as he strode right up to me. "You're not getting this…I'm not leaving you. Made that mistake once. Not doing it again, regardless of what you may think. Now, I have to call Sara. I'll be back in ten minutes. Do you want anything from the cafeteria?"

"Uh, no?" It came out sounding more like a question than an answer. His little rant caught me completely off guard.

"Okay, I'll see you soon then."

Barb elbowed me. "Fuck girl. I love Jaxon and all, but that was seriously hot."

"Dear God, help me. What in the Sam Hill is going on with the men in my life?" I groaned loudly. "First, Brody bails when I find out I'm going to have a baby. And now Jaxon is bailing as I'm having the baby. FML."

"Simmer down. You don't know what's goin' on with Jax."

"Fuck." I huffed. "I gotta pee." I felt like I drank a fifth of Captain Morgan. "Come on bitch, help me get my fat ass outta this bed."

Barb laughed. "Well, since you asked so nicely…come on lil' momma." She pulled my arm over her shoulder. "Go slow, that Stadol will kick ya ass like Bruce Lee."

Sure as shit, it did too. As I stood up the room began to sway back and forth like I was waltzing. "Damn, I feel like that time we went to the Bahamas and drank Mai Tais poolside for like six straight hours."

"Oh, I remember that. Good day." She giggled.

Barb slid the IV pole into the bathroom after she disconnected the monitor wires for the EFM. Once I was on my feet and got my bearings I was fine. Okay, maybe fine was too strong a word. I was safe to walk alone. Barb leaned against the door while I used the toilet. It wasn't as if she hadn't been in the bathroom with me while I peed a hundred and twenty times before. Plus she was a nurse; nothing fazed her anymore.

She helped me back to bed and we flipped through the channels. It was a little after 8:00 p.m. and I was surprised she didn't get kicked out since visiting hours were almost over.

"Whatcha wanna watch? *NCIS* is on." We both loved that show.

"Yeah, that's fine. Can't promise I'm gonna make it very long. That medicine put me on my ass." I said with a giggle.

"Cool." She found the channel, then set the remote on the side of the bed. "Uh, Lei, where the hell did all these pillows come from?"

"Huh? Oh. Brody called Jane and she brought them down. He remembered how much I loved them and he said he wanted me to be comfortable." I shrugged.

"Gotcha." Her phone started buzzing and she pulled it up to her ear. "Hello? Oh hey Drew." My heart dropped; I love my brother, but that wasn't the name I wanted to hear. "Nah, she's gonna have to stay tonight at least. I'd let her talk but she just got pain meds and is starting to nod off. I'll call you back a little later and fill ya in...I will...'Kay, g'night.

"Drew said to tell you to take it easy and sleep when you can. He's gonna come over in the morning and he said he loves ya," she said, relaying his message.

I yawned and stretched. "Hey Barb"—my voice warbled—"can you look and see how long it's been since my last contraction? I feel like I should've had one by now." I looked over to the EFM.

"It looks like the medicine is working. It's been thirty-five minutes since the last one, which means you may have one soon."

"Oh, thank God." My shoulders sagged in relief. "I can't tell you how happy I am to hear that."

Barb's phone chirped. "That's Cole." She read the message, then looked up and I could tell I wasn't going to like what I heard. "He talked to Jaxon and told him what was going on. Jax asked if Brody was here and Cole told him he was. Jax got pissed and started drinkin' the second he got to the club. Cole doesn't think Jax is gonna come up here." Her hazel eyes settled on mine. "Oh Lei, honey, I'm so sorry."

I tried so hard not to cry. I bit my cheek until the metallic taste filled my mouth. It didn't help. The tears rolled down my face. I didn't make any noise, wipe my face or acknowledge the tears dripping from my nose and chin. Thank God for Stadol. It helped numb the emotional pain Jax just dealt by his intentional absence.

As if the universe wasn't cruel enough, in walked Brody. He looked gorgeous in his black Armani custom tailored suit, with the jacket slung over his shoulder. His second day stubble added to his sexy face, as if the devastatingly blue eyes weren't enough. He ambled in while messing with his phone. He was fully in the room when he finally looked up.

"Hey, I just sp—" His eyes trained on my tear-soaked face. "What happened?"

I knew he was there and I heard him ask the question but I just stared at the end of the bed. Tears continued to spill and roll down my face onto my gown.

"Cole just texted me, Jax knows she's here but he's not coming," Barb explained as she climbed down from her cozy little spot next to me.

"What. The. Fuck?"

Barb's eyes cut to me, then back to him. "Jax asked if you were here and Cole confirmed you were, so Jax isn't coming. Said you were here so she didn't need him."

Brody looked at me as he walked away from Barb and resumed his spot on the stool at the head of the bed. "Babe, look at me." I just blinked at my feet. "Leila, look at me. Tell me right now and I will go. I promise. If you want him here, then I will leave. I love you enough to give you whatever it is you want right now. Even if that's him."

That got my attention. I looked into his baby blue eyes and knew he meant every word. He would get up and walk out, against every desire he had, to give me what I wanted. He would put my needs and wants above his own.

"Babe, I'm gonna go. Barb, can you please stay here with her tonight?" He looked from me to her standing across the bed from him.

"Yeah," she agreed quietly and nodded.

As he stood to leave I reached out and grabbed his hand. "Don't leave," I murmured, "please."

"Leila, I'm the reason you're miserable right now." He sat back down and held my hand.

"Well, yeah, you're the one who got me pregnant." I shrugged.

"I'm being serious Lei. If I wasn't here, then he'd be here." He pulled his hand out mine and paced the room.

"If you're gonna play the 'what if' game, maybe you should start with if you wouldn't have run out on me." All of a sudden, I felt awake and clear. Brody stopped dead in his tracks. "Shit. Brody, I'm sorry. I shouldn't have said that."

He dropped to the recliner and held his head in his hands.

"You are here now, that's what matters. You said you'd be here and you are. Which is more than I can say for Jaxon." I dropped my head back to the pillow and closed my eyes. Clarity gone. My head was spinning and I felt awful for shit-shooting Brody after he'd been a trooper all day.

"Please stay. With me. With us." His eyes found mine as he lifted his head. "We need you he...he...here." My whispered words turned into a loud groan as I was overtaken by a contraction. I gripped the handrail and took slow, deep breaths.

Brody was on his feet and holding my hand. "You're doing good babe, just keep breathing."

"You're almost to the peak Lei...just a few more seconds and it will start coming down," Barb said rubbing my arm.

"I'm okay," I gritted out through clenched teeth as I squeezed my eyes shut. "'S not that...bad." And I wasn't lying, the pain wasn't as bad as before. The Stadol definitely helped.

"Comin' down." Barb gave my forearm a reassuring squeeze. "Hmm, that's good. That one didn't last as long."

"That's good news babe, the medicine is working." Brody's whole body seemed to settle as he let a deep exhale go. "You should try to take a little nap," he suggested as he stood and picked up his phone.

"You're not gonna leave, right?" I asked.

"I just need to make a quick call and I will be right back. Promise," he assured me as he advanced toward the door.

Barb picked up her phone and purse. "Listen, I'm gonna go, but if you need anything, you call me. I want you to try to get some sleep. Let go of the stress for a little and let the medicine do its job. Right now, it's about her, not him."

"All right," I replied.

"Love ya bitch."

"Back atcha hooker," I called back.

I grabbed the remote and turned on the end of *NCIS* as I tried to fall asleep. I started to wonder if Brody was going to come back. *God knows if I was him, I would've run for the hills.* I was such a bitch earlier. Here he was trying to be sweet and thoughtful, bringing me pillows and soft Egyptian cotton towels, and I threw in his face, yet again, that he walked out on me. *Well, he did.*

I turned out all of the lights and looked over to the recliner. Sitting on the cushion was one of the fluffy pillows and a few blankets for Brody. That was my last thought before I fell asleep.

Chapter Twenty-Two

~Leila~

Three more contractions woke me up between 11:00 p.m. and 5:00 a.m. They were getting further and further apart, just as the medicine intended. After the 5:00 a.m. contraction, I got up and used the bathroom. I was careful to turn the light on after I closed the door, as not to wake Brody. He was up with me for every contraction, except for the most recent. I knew he had to be exhausted.

I washed and shampooed my hair, then dried off with the soft, cottony towel. As I combed out my damp hair, I heard Brody holler my name. I opened the bathroom door to see him throwing the blankets off himself in a panic. "Brody, are you okay?"

His eyes were wide with terror. "Oh God, you're here. You're okay." He seemed to relax slightly.

"Of course, I'm here." I tightened my grip on the towel and walked over to him, sitting down next to him on the recliner bed. "What's wrong?"

He grabbed my hand. "I had the worst dream, and it seemed so real. The medicine didn't work and you had the baby, but something happened and you started bleeding. And the baby was so small, God Lei, she was so tiny." Tears welled in his eyes. "They couldn't stop the bleeding and they tried surgery, but then Dr. Rogers came out shaking her head and I knew I lost you. I was holding our daughter thinking I couldn't raise her without you." He wrapped his arms around me and pulled me to him. "It was so real," he whispered against my hair. "I can't lose you. I love you Leila. I need you. Our daughter needs you. Please don't leave me. Please," he begged.

"Brody, I'm okay. I'm not going to die. Look at me." I pulled back and seized his hand, placing it on my belly. "She's right here and the meds are working. Brody, it's okay. We're fine."

He looked down at his hand, then his eyes found mine. They searched like he was looking for my soul. Our daughter decided at that very second to wallop the hell out of my side.

"Ouch." I placed my hand over his.

"I guess that was you reassuring Daddy that you're okay, huh princess?" He looked at our hands as he talked to our daughter.

I was suddenly aware of the fact that I was damn near naked, sitting on a bed with someone who wasn't my fiancé. I stood up, gripping the top of the towel above my breast. "I'm gonna get dressed and reconnected." I didn't want to lead Brody on or give him any false hopes. I crossed the room, entered the bathroom and resumed my morning ritual.

As I was brushing my teeth I heard Brody raise his voice at someone.

"—course I stayed here last night. She was in labor you dick. I wasn't gonna leave her here alone and scared. Not like you did."

"Fuck you." It was then I realized Jaxon was there. I scrambled to put my clothes on thanking God Jaxon hadn't walked in ten minutes earlier.

"Tell me, how do you look at yourself in the fucking mirror? Knowing she called you crying and fucking begged and pleaded for you to be here with her. While she was scared and in pain," Brody seethed.

"I could ask you the same fuckin' thing," Jax spit right back.

"Except the difference is, she wasn't in labor. She wasn't in pain. She wasn't crying because she was afraid her child was gonna be born too early." He paused. "I was stupid and I ran because I was scared. What's your excuse?"

I finally had my bra, panties, shirt and yoga pants on and I flung the door open. My eyes settled on Jaxon first. He was wearing a pair of well-worn Levi's hanging low on his hips, a white Henley that was almost too small for his thick arms. As he turned his attention to me, I saw that a few days worth of scruff covered his beautiful face.

"Stop. Both of you. I don't need this shit right now. Get over yourselves for five goddamned minutes." I started to climb into the bed and Brody tried to get past Jaxon to help me, but Jaxon blocked him and helped me himself.

I was well past due for my next dose of Zofran and Stadol; I was starting to feel nauseous again. If the contractions stayed the same time apart, I would be having another one shortly.

"Brody, can you please go see if the nurse can bring me in my meds? I'm not feelin' good again." I smiled sweetly as he stood at the end of the bed.

He glared back and forth between Jaxon and me before huffing, "Yeah, I'll be back in a few minutes."

I turned to Jaxon. "So you finally decided to show up?"

"Doesn't exactly look like I was needed here anyway." He dropped his eyes to my left hand. "Jesus Lei, we aren't even apart and you've already taken your engagement ring off."

"Actually, Jaxon, I just got out of the shower." I got up, grabbed the front of his shirt, turned and pulled him to the doorway of the small bathroom before letting go. I picked up my ring that was sitting in the middle of my watch on the Formica countertop, near my toothbrush and comb, and held it up for him to see. "Before I overheard you two asshats out here thumping your chests, I was doing bathroom stuff. Then, 'cause you both can't be normal, civilized people, I threw on my clothes and ran out here. So forgive me, I was worried about you two punching each other in the face again and forgot my ring." I slipped on the ring, grabbed my watch and slid it on my wrist.

"Shit, babe, I'm sorry. I shouldn't have assumed anything. Just that he's here. Again."

"Yeah, he was here when you weren't. I called you and texted you and called you. You didn't come to the doctor's appointment or you would've known. I was alone. And for the record, Barb brought me to the hospital because I knew you'd have a fuckin' baby goat if Brody drove me." I cut him off before he could say anything. "He stayed because he knew I was terrified, in preterm labor and violently ill."

"I'm sorry I didn't call you back." He backed up and sat down on the chair as I hooked myself back up to the IV and EFM.

"You're sorry you didn't call? But you're not sorry you didn't come?" As I said it, it was a realization. He wasn't sorry he wasn't here for me.

"That's not what I meant." He was visibly frustrated. "I am sorry that you were scared and not feeling good, but like I said, he was here."

"Barb conveyed Cole's message. Ya know, Brody offered to leave last night so you would come up here because he knew I wanted you here and that it was because of him you weren't here. He was willing to put my needs and wants above his own." I scowled at him as a wave of nausea hit me like a freight train. I swallowed hard and looked for the pink basin or trash can. "Can you please hand me that pink basin?"

"Yeah." He snatched it from the floor near the bedside table and handed it to me just in the nick of time. I hadn't eaten since last night, but I had been sipping ginger ale. After I finished throwing up Jaxon took the basin from me.

"Can you grab a washcloth from the bathroom or some tissues?"

"Yeah." He went to the bathroom and ran water over a washcloth, came back out and handed it to me.

"Thank you." I took the damp, folded washcloth and wiped my mouth.

Brody returned to the room. "You okay?" he asked me.

"Of course she's okay. Why wouldn't she be? You think I'd do something?" Jax cut his eyes at Brody.

"No, dickhead. She looks pale. The same way she looks after she gets sick." He looked back to me. "Are you feeling okay?"

"A little better now." I frowned. "I just got sick, again."

"Speaking of which, the nurse will be in with the medicines in a minute." He glanced at Jaxon, then quietly spoke. "Do you want me to leave for a while so you can talk?"

"Thanks Brody that would be good. Arghh." Pain racked my abdomen. I squeezed my eyes closed and groaned.

"Breathe Lei, you can't hold your breath. Slow deep breaths." Brody was by my side immediately. I rolled to face away from him and stared directly at Jaxon. Brody dropped the side rail and started massaging my back, just how I like it. "Good, you're doing good babe. Almost to the peak."

"Get your fuckin' hands off of her." Jax jumped up.

"Ehhhhhh. Shut up," I yelled as I hit the climax of the contraction. "Owwww. Oh, this one's really bad," I gritted out.

"Sorry baby. What can I do?" Jax looked on helplessly as he stroked my face.

"Grab the pink basin and the wet washcloth. She gets really sick after the contractions," Brody informed him.

"Uh, okay, but she just got sick?" he asked Brody.

"Yeah, it's the magnesium sulfate they're using to stop labor," he explained. I was shocked. They were speaking to each other like human beings and not two little boys fighting over a baseball card. "Doing good. You're at the peak and should feel it easing off now." Brody had become a pro overnight. He knew exactly what I needed to hear and when I needed silence.

True to form, I got sick again as soon as the worst part of the contraction was over. Jaxon held back my hair and handed me the washcloth. For a moment, we were *us* again. Quiet, Intimate. Close.

Brody cleared his throat. "I'm gonna run down to the cafeteria. You want anything Lei?"

"No thanks, I'm good right now." I turned and gave him a halfhearted smile.

Jaxon stood and began pacing the room.

"Why did you decide to come here this morning? Honestly," I asked as I eased back, trying to relax.

"You really have to ask me that?" He stopped and looked shocked.

We were interrupted by a knock and the nurse coming in. "Good morning, Leila. Brody said you weren't feeling well and were ready for your next dose of Zofran and possibly Stadol."

"Yeah, I started getting sick again and the last contraction was really uncomfortable." I pulled my arm out from under the covers, giving her access to the barcode on my wristband.

She laughed. "Uncomfortable is one way to describe labor honey. Let's see if we can't get you back to comfortable and maybe even sleeping again." She drew up the meds, then asked me my name and date of birth. "Okay, remember not to get up without help."

I smiled as the warmth of the pain medicine coursed through my veins. "I will."

She logged off the computer and left the room.

"As I was saying before the nurse came in, I can't believe you need to ask why I'm here," he said again.

Feeling no pain and my filter falling away, I started rambling. "Well, I wonder why I'd ask that? Hmm, maybe 'cause I begged you to come yesterday. And did you? Oh no, you couldn't stand to possibly be in the same room as Brody, even though you swore you could deal with all of this. As fucked up as it is, you said you'd deal. Well, when I needed you the most, you bailed. You promised, yet you weren't here. I was scared and crying and you still couldn't get over your own shit for my sake. So yes, I need to ask why you decided to show up today."

He was quiet, pensive. I waited. Finally he said, "I needed to see you and make sure you were okay. I hate the way we left things. I love you Lei. Both of you. I'm sorry I wasn't here yesterday. I was on a run and shit got messed up on the delivery—" He stopped himself from saying more. "I got your message and Viper called me and told me you were here with Brody, so I was pissed.

"Honestly, looking back, most of it probably wasn't about this, but about the club. I met up with the guys at the clubhouse and started drinking. I just couldn't deal with all of it at the same time last night."

"So in other words, the club's bullshit pissed you off and I pissed you off even further, so you got drunk?" I pursed my lips. "While I was sitting here trying to decide whether or not to have our daughter? Terrified that she might not make it because it's too soon? Questioning whether to take medicine that A, makes me violently ill and B, might slow down labor enough for the other medicine to speed up her lung development, so she would have better chances." He had the decency to look contrite. "While you were drinking, Brody was here helping me. He even offered to leave so you, who were being a big baby, could come up here and be with me."

The look on Jaxon's face said it all. He was surprised and totally caught off guard by my outburst. "I wasn't being a fuckin' baby. I was dealing with other shit—"

I cut him off. "Exactly! I was in labor. I still am, if you haven't noticed. Most men in your position would have rushed to the hospital, regardless of who was here." I was getting more hostile by the minute. "If you wanted to be here, then you should have shown up. You knew Brody was going to be around and in our lives because of our daughter. You told me you understood and would deal. I need you here, but I also want him here too." My tone softened. "I'm sorry if that hurts you, but he's her biological father Jax. I won't cut him out of her life. She deserves to have him. I want more for her than what I had."

"I'm sorry Lei—" He was interrupted by Brody coming back into the room with a large Starbucks coffee and a white Styrofoam cup.

"I got you another ginger ale, with extra ice." He sat down on the makeshift bed after handing me the soda.

Jax stood up. "Can we have five more minutes?"

Brody looked from him to me, then back. "That's up to Leila."

"Don't you have some work or something you need to do. Just give us five fuckin' minutes," Jax said coarsely.

"It's fine Brody," I huffed.

Brody got up with his coffee and stalked out the room.

"Now, you have me all to yourself again. What?"

"Put yourself in my position Lei."

"Sure, right after you do the same. You come lie in the bed and have your body feel like it's tearing in two, then you puke your brains out." I took a deep breath. "I understand this isn't easy Jaxon. It's not easy for me either, but you told me you could do this. Are you saying now you can't?" My heart pounded so hard I could hear it in my ears. The silence told me I didn't want to hear his answer.

"I don't know." He hung his head. "I guess…I need to get my head on straight."

"Well, it would be great if you could figure it out really quick. Our daughter could be here any time now, especially if the medicine doesn't work."

"I am sorry, Lei. I wish I could ignore him, but he's always here. He's arrogant and I see how he fuckin' looks at you." He clenched his fists. "It fuckin' kills me to see him touch you and for him to tell me what my woman needs."

"He wouldn't be touching me or telling you anything if you were here. You'd be massaging my back and you'd know I get sick after contractions. So stay."

He looked at his boots. "I can't. I'm sorry. I really am, but I just can't right now. I need some time to think." My words, my excuse, came back at me in spades. And it felt like a scalpel carefully wielded to inflict precise wounds. Tears dripped from my eyes as I stared down at my belly. "Don't cry babe." He tried to grab my hand, but I jerked it away.

"Please just go." I rolled away from him and faced the windows and recliner. I sniffled back a few tears.

"Babe," he rumbled, "I'm sorry. God. This is so fucked up. Lei, I love you. I really do. I'll text you later and check on you." I felt his weight on the bed, then he kissed the side of my head.

I didn't say a word as he left.

I did the only thing I could do.

I cried.

Chapter Twenty-Three

~Leila~

Brody came back in the room and sat down on the bed next to me. He didn't say a word, just rubbed my back and let me cry. We stayed like that long enough for another contraction to come around.

"Oooh, this one feels weird. It's like I can feel it, but I can't feel the pain. Does that make any sense?" I sat up in the bed with a cloud of pillows cocooning me.

"Well, considering you just got pain meds, it does make sense. Even if you don't," he teased.

I started to argue, but the PCT brought in my breakfast. "Good morning Ms. Matthews. I'm Lorrie, I'll be your patient care tech today. I saw dietary a few doors down and grabbed your tray since I knew you were awake." She sat the tray on the rolling table and slid it over to me as Brody stood and moved back over to the now folded up recliner. "Is there anything I can get ya?"

"Nah, I'm good right now, but thank you Lorrie." I adjusted the bed to accommodate the bedside tray table.

"Well, please buzz me if you need anything." She turned to Brody. "Can I get you anything sir? I see you've already been out for coffee. Musta been a long night." She chuckled quietly.

"Thank you, but I'm fine." Brody, ever the gentleman.

"Okay then, ring if you need anything."

"So now that you're a little calmer, do you want to talk about what happened or do you want to wait for Barb?" Brody asked from the recliner, his coffee in hand.

"Honest, I'm not really sure what's happening." I lifted the cover off of the pancakes and sausage. Thank God it wasn't eggs, there is nothing worse that hospital eggs. "He said he needed time to think.

I'm not sure if he can handle the situation. He hates that you're here, but I told him you were gonna be around. Shit…this is so fuckin' complicated." I dropped my head back to the pillow. "I just want a normal life. Is that too much to ask for?" I spoke to the ceiling like it had all of the magical answers to my ridiculous questions.

"Good morning." My nurse Lucinda knocked and entered the room. "I've got to give you the second IM injection of the dexamethasone and then Dr. Rogers should be in."

"Lei, I'm gonna step out in the hall." Brody stood as I rolled on my side and pulled my pants down, exposing the top half of my right butt cheek.

Lucinda was done before I knew it. Even though I was a nurse, I wasn't a big fan of intramuscular injections. She was good; I didn't even feel it.

"Okay, you're all set." She clicked on the mouse as she charted the injection.

A few minutes later Dr. Rogers came in and Brody followed. She was happy to see the contractions had tapered down to once an hour. She agreed to release me on one condition. I had to have someone with me at all times, which would be difficult at the condo. Drew worked crazy hours and was on call. Barb worked the next three nights. Jaxon…well, I didn't think that was an option right now.

I knew Brody would probably drop everything if I asked, but that would just add fuel to the fire with Jaxon. I made the decision to call him and ask anyway. That way, if he said no it wasn't like I just asked Brody. The ball would be in Jaxon's court.

"Brody, could you give me a few minutes?"

"Sure, I'll just run to the cafeteria and grab a quick bite to eat." He strolled out, taking his phone out of his pocket as he went.

I grabbed my phone and hit the direct dial for Jaxon's cell. He answered on the second ring. "Hey Lei, what's up?"

"Uh, Dr. Rogers said she'd discharge me today since my contractions have eased up, but I need someone with me at all times. Barb is working the next three days and Drew has crazy shift work and could be called out at any time. I was hopin' you might be able to stay with me. Actually, I would stay with you at our, err, your place, but I need someone with me at all times."

He was quiet but I could hear voices in the background. "Uh, I can't. I'm not in town. After I left you, Mark called and needed my help with some club shit. I'm halfway to North Carolina."

Really? "Hmm, that's funny. It sounds like you're surrounded by people, not pulled over on the side of the road talkin' to me."

"We just stopped to grab food and fill up. Mark was already on the road when we talked, so I met him here in St. Matthews."

Rejection ripped through my chest as hot tears slipped from my ducts. "Sorry, I bothered you Jaxon."

"Lei…babe. I'm sorry. If I was there you know I'd—" He started to tell me he'd be here or he'd take care of me but I didn't give him the chance. I didn't want to hear it, and I didn't believe it.

"I get it. The club comes first. It's perfectly clear, *Remi*. You don't need to explain yourself to me anymore."

As I pulled the phone from my ear I heard him say please, but I pressed end, then stared at the picture of us on the screen. I wiped the salty mess from my face and sent Barb and Drew a text filling them in. It was only a matter of seconds before Barb's face appeared on the phone as she called me back.

"That was fast," I answered.

"So what are you gonna do? You really shouldn't stay alone," she said groggily.

"I haven't talked to Brody yet, but I think I'm just gonna stay at the condo. Drew will be there and it's not like I'm far from the hospital. It'll be fine."

"Damn, you're such a stubborn bitch."

"Listen, I need to start figuring this shit out on my own. Contrary to what he promised me, it's clear Jaxon's first priority will always be the stupid club. I need to stop thinking I can rely on him. He's proven today that I can't."

Barb took a deep breath. "I'm sorry Leila. I wish I could smack some of the stupid outta him for ya."

"Me too honey, but it's better I find this out now, I guess."

"I think you two need to sit down and talk. I don't think he realizes you think it's over," she said quietly.

"No, I'm pretty sure with the way I left things, he got the picture. He's not here. He's made it clear where his priorities lie. He knows I'm in the hospital. He knows what's going on. Yet he chose club business over me. He didn't even try, Barb. I think that's what hurts the most. He didn't even try to help me figure out another way."

"Did you tell him that Brody was there and willing to take you home with him?" she asked.

"No way. Did you drink a big, steamy cup of stupid this morning? I still love the man and want to work things out. I don't want him in jail for chopping my baby daddy into tiny pieces."

"I knew it." I could hear her shit-eating grin through the phone.

It wasn't until I heard her statement that I realized what I had said. I still loved the man and wanted to work things out. *Did I? Could I forgive all of the craziness over the last few weeks?* "Brody is back. I'll call ya back later."

"So what's the plan? Is Barb staying with you?" he asked.

I sighed deeply. "No, she's gotta work the next three nights. Drew's working too. And Jaxon is…outta town." I pick my cuticles as I explained, then looked up to see the question on his face, but I didn't give him a chance to speak. "Don't ask, 'cause I'm not talking about him."

He threw his hands up in surrender. "Didn't say a word."

"You didn't need to Brody. It was written all over your face."

He looked a little too smug for my taste. "That's it. You'll stay with me." I started to object, but he steamrolled over me. "Shut it, Leila. I'm not done. I'll be there most of the time and if I'm not, Jane is always there. She can make sure you're eating right and not getting dehydrated and also take care of Ruger."

"Brody, I don't need a babysitter. I just need someone there in case the contractions get too close together. I'll be just fine at the condo. Drew will be there some and Barb only works at night."

"Drew's on call with the damn SWAT team Leila. And yeah, Barb works nights, but she also sleeps all day. Be sensible. You're coming home with me. End of discussion." He stood and walked out of the room. I heard him at the nurses' station telling Lucinda he would be taking me home, to get the discharge started.

"Geez, bossy much?" I grumbled. I forgot how domineering and intimidating he could be. The last few months he'd been at a disadvantage, trying to get back into my good graces. He had been agreeable and accommodating, but the second he saw an opening, he grabbed it with both hands and held on for dear life.

He strutted back into the room. "The nurse will be in shortly with paperwork and to disconnect you."

"Hang on, Brody I don't think this is a good idea. Jaxon will be past furious when he finds out." I swung my legs around and stood up.

"Sit down. I'll get your stuff together." He walked around and grabbed my overnight bag out of the small closet. "Jaxon isn't here. He couldn't be bothered to support and care for his fiancée. So I am taking the mother of *my* child home with me to take care of her. If he's pissed, then he'll only have himself to be pissed at. He had his chance. I know you called him," Brody growled.

"Thank you very much. I forgot he wasn't here. I forgot that he had prioritized work over me." *While I'm in labor.*

"You're. Welcome," he responded as he snatched my toiletries from the bathroom.

I could feel the fury vibrating against my nerve endings and running through my muscles. "Son of a bitch." I gripped the blankets, bracing as the contraction took hold over my abdomen.

Dropping everything, Brody rounded the bed and started sliding his hand up and down my back. "Breathe, babe. Slow, deep."

I controlled my breathing and rode out the contraction. Brody slid his hand along my cheek and tilted my head up to look at him.

"I'm sorry. I shouldn't have said those things. I just...I hate seeing you hurt. Especially knowing I hurt you like he's doing now. Jesus." He took his hand away to drag it over the back of his neck. "Lei, I'd give up everything I have if I could go back and do it over. I want to fix this."

"Can we not do this?" I paused. "Not right now. Later, I promise we'll talk, but just not right this minute. I can't."

"Sure babe, whatever you want."

Right at this moment, he'd probably give me anything I wanted.

Chapter Twenty-Four

~Leila~

We left the hospital about noon, which felt like a jailbreak. I was so happy to go anywhere but here. We stopped at the condo to grab some clothes, the ginormous body pillow and Ruger.

We arrived at Brody's around 2:00 p.m. As Brody shut the door, Jane practically leapt off the couch and ran to us.

"Oh praise Jesus, she's home. Oh, and where is my handsome boy?" she sang.

"I'm right here." Brody stepped around me grinning.

"Oh, not you. Where is my Ruger?" She knelt down and he trotted over to greet her with a warm, slobbery welcome. "Oh, there he is. There's my sweet boy. You wanna treat, good boy?"

"Hey, what the hell? What am I? Chopped liver?" Brody clutched at his heart. I smiled at their antics.

"I'll just put your bags in the bedroom." Brody started up the staircase.

"I'll follow you. I wanna lie down for a little while, I didn't get much sleep last night," I said as I climbed the steps behind him.

"I wouldn't doubt it," Jane agreed. "With all those people in and out of there and the contractions, I bet you're exhausted. You rest and I'll work on some dinner for later. How 'bout grilled chicken Caesar salads?"

"You don't have to make anything special for me Jane. I will eat anything you cook and love it. Besides, I know some people"—I tilted my head up the stairs—"don't really like salads."

"I heard that," Brody mumbled from above.

"Don't worry, I will whip something yummy up for us," she said as she turned toward the kitchen with one overzealous German Shepherd in tow.

As I climbed the stairs, I noticed Brody walking through the doorway to his room. There was no way he thought I was going to sleep in there with him. If he did, he certainly had smoked the bad crack today. I walked to the doorway and gave him a WTF look.

"What?" he asked sheepishly.

"Uh, why are you bringing my stuff in here? I thought I'd stay in the guest room down the hall, by the bathroom."

"Oh come on, I know you love my bed." He hesitated for a second. "Wait, that didn't come out right. It's not what you're thinking. I swear. I just meant that this bed"—he nodded to his left—"is more comfortable. Plus the bathroom is right there. I thought you'd like to take advantage of the tub and soak some to help you relax."

"That's all well and good Brody, but we aren't sleeping in the same bed. I'm not tryin' to be a bitch. It's just that Jax...I mean, I don't know..." My shoulders dropped. I could feel the emotions welling up in my throat.

"Hey, it's okay. I was planning on staying in the guest room and letting you have my room. I know I can be presumptuous, but you've made it perfectly clear where we stand. And I'm okay with that...for now. I had no ulterior motives when I asked you to stay here, other than taking care of the mother of my child." He set the bag down on the foot of the bed and crossed the room to me. "I simply want to help you. I know you're fiercely independent and you can do all of this on your own, but I'm here to tell you that you don't have to."

Still holding my pillow, I walked over to the bed and tossed the pillow into the middle. "I do appreciate you offering to let me stay here. I don't want you to go out of your way and I certainly don't want to put you out of your own bedroom. I can stay down the hall."

"Enough Lei, you'll be more comfortable in here and this conversation is over." He turned and walked toward the bathroom. "Besides, Jane already moved some of my things to the hall bathroom. Now, would you like me to—"

As he turned he was interrupted by my loud groan. "Shit." I planted my hands on the edge of the bed and bent over. "I forgot how much these damn things hurt without pain meds."

Brody darted to my side and started kneading my lumbar area. "Stop holding your breath. You need to breathe," he whispered.

I took several slow, deep breaths as the contraction started to ease off. I climbed up in the bed and snaked my ridiculous pillow around my body.

"Oh God, I forgot how freakin' comfy this bed is." I wiggled down into the bed. "Can you wake me—oh geez Pete. Here, gimme your hand."

Brody sat down next to me as I grabbed his hand and placed in on my belly near my ribs. "Feel that, it's not a kick. She's stretching. It's more like a rolling feeling."

"Oh whoa, that's crazy. What is that?" he asked as he stared at our hands.

"Her foot, I think. Here, watch." I pulled up my shirt, exposing the taut skin stretched over my swollen abdomen. "You can actually see her, it's so cool."

We waited and, of course, she was still. It's like she knew we were waiting for her to perform and she had stage fright. Just as I started to tell Brody to keep talking, he leaned down slightly.

"Hey sweet girl, are you sleeping in there? I know you want to push on Mommy's ribs again. You must be paying her back for getting squeezed so much, huh?"

Just as he finished she slid her foot across my side back up toward my ribs.

"Oh my God, that is so weird." Brody lightly touched his fingers to the gliding mass. I lay on my side watching him watch our daughter move inside of me. I was so tired I started to drift off as he continued to talk to her.

Sometime later I woke, feeling a large hand sliding up and down my arm.

"Lei, babe, wake up. It's almost six o'clock and Jane has dinner ready," Brody spoke quietly, knowing I hated to be woken up.

"Hmm." I blinked a few times trying to focus. It took me a minute to remember where I was. "Oh, okay. I, uh, just need to use the bathroom and then I'll be down."

Brody stood up and started toward the open door.

"Hey, wait, you said it's six o'clock? Hmm, that's weird. I don't remember waking up with any contractions." I scrunched my nose and wrinkled my brow trying to remember. I looked over toward the sitting area and noticed his laptop on the coffee table.

"That's because you didn't have any," he confirmed.

"Did you stay in here while I was sleeping?" I asked, looking back over to the sofa.

"Huh." He looked over his shoulder. "Uh, yeah. Not the entire time, but for a while. I had to make some calls, so I went downstairs to the office for those, but I was worried you'd wake up with a contraction and…uh, I don't know, need me."

"Oh," I said, surprised by his response.

I climbed down and went to the bathroom. Looking around, I finally found my purse and took out my cell. Only one text message from Drew telling me to call him tomorrow, that he was going to be working tonight. I don't know why I was disappointed that Jaxon hadn't called or texted me. I knew, before I picked up the phone, there wouldn't be anything there, but I still felt the empty pit in my stomach deepen.

We had dinner around the island in the kitchen. Caesar salads. Of course. Jane had told me Brody could stand to eat a few more salads and less steaks. She cleaned up after dinner while I retreated back to the bedroom and turned on the TV.

Around 8:00 Brody appeared in the doorway. "Do you want to watch a movie?"

"Sure, what did you have in mind?" I scooted up and tossed the remote over to the side of the bed I knew he slept on.

"I was thinking we should watch a baseball movie." He grabbed the remote. Brody had an expansive movie collection on his DVR.

"Uhh, really? Baseball, Brody?" I groaned.

"Trust me, 'kay?" He started pressing buttons until the movie appeared on the screen. I knew it as soon as the opening credits began.

"Oh my God, you remembered." I realized he actually listened when I talked about my favorite movies. "How about I go make us some popcorn?"

"I already put some in the microwave and Jane should be bringing it up any second." He settled into the bed next to me.

"Brody, I have to say I am really surprised that you remembered *For Love of The Game*. You were really drunk that night." I smiled as I recalled the evening.

"For the record, I wasn't that drunk. I still remember sitting up talking about all of your favorite movies, songs, foods and books. What I remember most about that night in Parrot Cay was afterward, making love to you on the beach under all of the stars." I blushed at his reminder.

"Knock, knock." Jane was in the doorway. "I have popcorn, beer and a bottle of water for you, my dear."

She handed me the large yellow melamine bowl full of buttery goodness and a bottle of Evian. Brody crawled over toward me and took the bottle of Miller Lite.

"Thanks Jane." He sat back down on his side as Ruger came trotting in.

"Yes, thank you. Jane, do you want to watch the movie with us? There is plenty of room up here," I asked, even though I knew she'd decline.

"Oh, no thank you, sweet girl. I have to get downstairs and watch *NCIS*. You know how much I love Gibbs." She smiled and laughed as she left the room.

Brody grabbed the large remote and dimmed the lights and turned up the Bose surround sound. Ruger curled into his bed and was whimpering in his sleep in no time.

I set the bowl of popcorn between us as we watched Kevin Costner flash back through his past as he attempted to pitch an extraordinary perfect game. We watched the movie until I had another contraction. It wasn't too bad and lasted about forty-five seconds. We went right back to watching the movie, without skipping a beat. I felt my eyes starting to get heavy, but tried to push through.

I woke to a dark room. I was lying on my side hugging my pillow. Two fluffy pillows were stuffed behind me to support my back and I was tucked in under the covers. In front of me, Brody was lying on top of the covers, hand in the popcorn bowl, remote on chest and his head resting uncomfortably on his own shoulder. That would hurt tomorrow if he stayed like that.

I was torn as to what to do. I should wake him up and send him to the guest room, but he had been with me at the hospital and I knew he didn't get any sleep. Besides, this bed was huge, and he was on top of the comforter. Lazy and full of justifications, I decided to roll over and go back to sleep.

The next morning, I woke up and was overly warm. It didn't take long to realize there was a thick arm draped over my side holding my belly. My eyes flew open. I looked down and saw Brody's hand resting right below my belly button. I noticed the pillows were at the foot of the bed and my C-shaped pregnancy pillow was on the floor on my side of the bed. Brody was tucked in, right against my back. I picked up his arm and tried to carefully slide out without waking him, but no such luck.

"Hey, what's going on?" he asked sleepily.

"Uh, well, I need to pee and you were spooning me." I climbed down and went to the bathroom. I brushed my teeth, washed my face and as I was drying my face I realized all my stuff was in here and put away where it used to be.

"Hey, Brody."

"Yeah?"

"Did you put my toiletries in here?" I opened drawers and cabinets finding things in there that I had not taken to the hospital.

"Uh." He stood in the doorway. "So, don't freak out or anything, but I never got rid of any of it."

Say what?

"You didn't get rid of it? But I came by and picked stuff up and Jane brought me the rest. *I thought.* Are you saying you kept all this?"

"Some of it, yeah. The other stuff I had Jane pick up yesterday before I got you home. I knew you wouldn't remember everything since you had packed in a rush and Jane remembered everything you used and liked." He walked over to me. "Don't be angry Lei. I was just trying to make this as easy as possible."

He dipped his head. "I probably should've gotten rid of the other stuff, but I couldn't bear to. Throwing it away would have made everything so final." He lifted his eyes to mine. "And even though I was a total asshole and walked away from you, deep in my heart I knew it wasn't over. That it would never be over."

God, why was he saying this to me now? He couldn't have figured this shit out seven months ago? It was everything I wanted to hear *back then.* I looked down at my unpainted toes as the tears cascaded down my cheeks and dripped on the limestone tile floor. "Brody, you can't say things like that to me."

He slipped his hand under my chin and raised it so I was looking into his cool blue eyes. "Baby."

It's all he said aloud, but his eyes said it all. They were filled with love and compassion and maybe an icy glimmer of desire. His hand was still holding my face when a contraction surprised me.

I hunched over, holding onto the vanity and whimpered. "Owww, damn."

Brody came around behind me and started massaging my lower back and hips. "You okay?"

"Yeah, gimme a minute." I turned toward the vanity and rested my head on my forearm. Brody dragged his fingertips gently up and down my spine as it eased off. I blew out one last breath before I righted myself. "I need to lie down. That one hurt."

"Should I call Dr. Rogers?" he asked, following me to the bed.

"No." I spun around quickly and gave him a vicious look. "No way. She'll make me come back and keep me locked up in that stupid hospital room. Let's just wait and see when the next one comes. It's been"—I looked over to the bedside table to the clock— "seven hours since the last one."

"Okay. We'll wait. It's probably nothing. You might just need to get hydrated and get some food in you." He walked into the massive closet. Massive, as in you could probably start a third world country in there. "Lie down and I will get dressed and get your breakfast."

For a change I did what he asked without arguing or griping. I was still exhausted and my body felt like it had been through a ringer. I lay down and quickly fell back to sleep.

Five hours later I stared at the clock as my stomach bubbled.

"Hey, you're awake," Brody said as he walked into the bedroom and handed me a bottle of water. "You hungry?"

"Nah, thanks for the water though. I had the worst dry mouth, it felt like my tongue was wearin' a fuzzy sweater." I pulled the down comforter up around me and was about to ask for the remote when I heard voices yelling in the hallway.

"You cannot go in there. You should have called first." I heard Jane admonish. It was followed by a shrill, evil voice. A voice I hoped I would never hear again.

"I don't need to call. Brody will always see me. You'd best remember that," Jenifer, Brody's bitch ex-girlfriend from hell, snarled.

"You've got to be fucking kidding me." He went to the door as it flew open. Standing there was the wicked bitch of the west. Ugh, I hated her. Bitch was too nice a word. I didn't think there was a word in any language that would do her nastiness justice.

"What are you doing here Jenifer?" Brody gritted out. "I told you last week I was busy and I didn't have time for a visit while you were in town. And, I've told you on plenty of occasions, I'm done. We're done."

I didn't think she noticed me quite yet.

"Oh, Brody love, I just wanted to come by for a few minutes and…catch up. I haven't seen you since last month…" And then she took notice of me. "Oh…what is she doing here? I thought you got rid of her?"

I grabbed the remote and thought about cranking up the volume. Then I had a better thought. "Brody, honey, can you please have her leave? Remember the doctor said to avoid any unneeded stress. Her face is giving me arrgghh. Son of a bitch!"

And cue an immense contraction.

"Ugh, what is her problem?" Her ugly face made an even uglier face.

"Lei, breathe baby. Slow, deep breaths, stop holding your breath, honey. You gotta breathe. Is this one worse than the last one?" Brody climbed onto the bed next to me.

I couldn't speak, moaning in pain, I nodded my head.

"Brody, why is she here?" Jenifer demanded coming toward the bed.

"Jenifer, I asked nicely once, the next time won't be." Brody turned to her briefly, then was back to me. "You should be almost done. Getting better?"

I took a few more deep cleansing breaths before I spoke. "Yeah, it's easing up now."

Jenifer stood there for a second. "I'll wait downstairs for you." She turned on her stilettos and left.

"Seriously Brody? You're fuckin' her again?" I said, disgusted and, surprisingly, feeling a twinge of jealously. *Where did that come from?*

He looked at me for a minute, studying my expression. "Why Leila? Would it bother you if I were? Does she make you jealous?"

I bit the inside of my cheek. "No, I just think you can do better than that silicone enhanced troll. And frankly, if she's in your life I'd like to know. I do not want my daughter around her."

He sat there with a shit-eating grin on his face. "Nah, I think you're a tad jealous."

"I'm serious, Brody, I don't like her. She's a bitch and you know it. You can do so much better than her."

He finally stopped grinning. "To answer your question, no, I am not sleeping with her. I ran into her and her parents when I was in New York in January. She told me she'd be coming down to her parents' beach house and asked to have dinner. I told her I'd be busy. I should've known she'd just drop by."

I just rolled my eyes. I couldn't be upset with him, even if he did choose Jenifer. He's not mine to be jealous over anymore.

"I'm going to go deal with her and see if Jane has lunch ready. She's making sandwiches, unless you'd rather something else?" He rose and started for the door.

"No, sandwiches are fine. And Brody"—he turned to face me—"I'm sorry. I shouldn't have said what I did. Who you decide to sleep with isn't my business. I just would appreciate in the future, when you have our daughter, that you not have women traipsing in and out of the house. And before you say anything, I've heard plenty of stories, so don't try to deny it."

He came back over to me. "I *did* have a reputation. Operative word, did. I promise, Lei, that's in the past. I have a daughter to think about. Things have changed and I'm not the same guy I was a year ago. You changed me."

With that, he turned and left before I could say anything else.

Chapter Twenty-Five

~Leila~

We settled into a routine. I slept. A lot. Walked the grounds, a little. Ate Jane's fabulous meals. And she and I watched *General Hospital* religiously. Brody went to work and was gone a good part of the day.

After that first night, he slept in the guest bedroom. He would stay with me in his room until I went to sleep. When I woke up in the middle of the night to use the bathroom he was gone. The contractions had eased up significantly. I was only having a few a day.

On Thursday Brody took me to the doctor for a check-up and Dr. Rogers was pleased with how I was progressing. Drew came over and hung out with me for the rest of that afternoon. We finally had some time to sit and talk. He tried to give me advice, but, as he put it, he was at a loss.

On Saturday, Brody dropped me off at the condo on his way to work with the expectation that if anything should happen, Drew would call him immediately.

Drew and I spent most of the day just hanging out watching TV. It felt almost normal, which was more than I could say for my jack-in-the-box emotions. Brody's behavior was perfect. Jaxon was absent. And I was a mess.

Saturday evening, when Brody returned from work, Jane and I were watching TV in the family room. He came in and told me to get ready to go out. He wouldn't tell me where we were going, just that I needed to wear comfy shoes.

Ha! What pregnant women in their thirty-fourth week didn't wear comfy shoes?

"You wanna take the Henney?" I asked as I grabbed my purse and followed him out to the garage.

"No way, that thing's not safe for you to ride in, we'll take the Mercedes. Besides, we'll need all of the room in the backseat for what I have in mind." He cut his eyes to me with a pants-dropping grin that stopped me dead in my tracks.

"What in the hell do you have planned?" I asked. He just kept grinning. "You're up to something, aren't you?"

"Who me? Never." He opened my door and helped me in.

"Who me? Never," I mocked, scrunching my face.

We drove toward Charleston. The sun had just started to set as we passed the outlets. My text message alert went off as we turned onto Rivers Avenue.

Jaxon. My stomach dropped and my pulse rate doubled. He was home and asked if we could get together and talk. I just stared at the screen.

"Who's that? You okay?" Brody glanced over as we were waiting at a red light.

"Huh…oh…uh, yeah. I'm fine. It's Jaxon, he wants to meet and talk. I'll text him and tell him I'll meet him tomorrow," I said as I was typing out the message.

He replied.

2moro works, if ur busy tonite. meet @ the condo around 12?

Was that his way of asking if I was out? Or did he go by the condo and knew I wasn't home? Did Drew tell him I was staying with Brody? *Shit, I should probably tell him.* This should go over about as well as a cat getting a bath.

2moro@12 works. I'm stayin @ Brody's so I'll have Jane bring me. & b4 u freak out, I had to stay there. I had no other choice. Barb & Drew are workin & u were busy with ur own things. And just so u know, we R stayin in separate rooms

I sat and worried about the text that would come in response to mine. I didn't have to wait long.

We can talk about everything 2moro. How r u feelin?

Okay, that was *not* what I was expecting. I softened.

I'm doing ok. I miss you tho. How r u?

"Lei, we're here." Brody's soft voice startled me. I looked up and saw we were parked in front of a mega baby superstore. I smiled. Brody always knew how to surprise me. My cell vibrated again.

I'm fine. I miss u2 but we'll talk 2moro. love u

I love u too Jaxon

I locked the phone, slipped into my purse and took off my seat belt as Brody opened my door. "Thanks B. This is just what I needed."

He slipped his hand in mine and pulled me toward the store. "Let's go get our girl some furniture and clothes."

Two hours later we left with a solid wood convertible crib, matching dresser with changing table top and night stand. Brody insisted on getting the gray oversized double rocker. Thankfully, that wasn't in stock and had to be delivered to the house, along with the dresser and nightstand. He also bought me a breast pump to keep at his place and a stockpile of storage bags.

As we walked around the store I couldn't help but think about Jaxon and the nursery we had created together, just like Brody and I were doing now. He would need all of his own stuff for when the baby was with him. After he spent a shit-ton of money on furniture, a bassinet, bedding, blankets, bottles, pacifiers, breastfeeding accessories, a stroller and car seat, he took me to dinner at a little Mexican restaurant.

I was quiet during dinner. My mind, however, wouldn't shut up. One second I was trying to figure out how to share a child with a demanding Brody, then I was worried about where I was going to put a crib in the condo. Then I would bounce to Jaxon. How was tomorrow's conversation going to go? Was he going to tell me he was done, beg for forgiveness or just pull more of the "it's Brody's fault" bullshit? Then I was back to Brody and what I was feeling for him. Which, of course, made me feel guilty and I would think about Jaxon again.

I was torturing myself and doing a damn good job of it.

Once we were back at Brody's house, he sent me up to rest while he and Jane unloaded the car. He brought the crib upstairs to the bedroom across the hall from his room, which he had emptied in preparation of the baby. It was a large room with a big walk-in closet and two beautiful bay windows. It was the smaller of the rooms in his house, but still about the size of the living room in my condo. This little girl would be as spoiled as a true princess.

Drifting asleep, I was startled by a loud curse and thud. I quickly—okay, maybe not your quickly, but my new quickly—scurried to the door and opened it. The baby's room door was open and there was Brody, sitting bare-chested and cross-legged with a half put together crib and several pages of directions scattered about.

"Stupid fucking directions, this shit doesn't even make sense," he cursed and muttered, until he looked up and saw me. "Don't Lei, I swear to God."

I tried not to laugh, covering my mouth with my hand to hide the smile that stretched across my face. "Can I help you with anything?"

"No. I am perfectly capable of putting my daughter's crib together. Just these damn directions are ass backward. They don't make any fucking sense, but I'll figure it out. Go back to sleep. I'm sorry I woke you." He picked up the directions and flipped it over studying it.

I turned and went back to his bedroom. Once safely on the other side of the closed door, I finally released the giggle I was holding in.

Sunday morning, I woke up later than I had planned, which left only an hour before I had to meet Jaxon. Scrambling as quickly as I could, I showered, got dressed and made my way downstairs.

"Jane, do you think you could drive me to my place? I'm supposed to meet Jaxon in thirty minutes," I asked as I opened the refrigerator and grabbed a bottle of water.

"Absolutely, let me grab my purse and I'll meet you out front."

Brody came strolling into the kitchen. "Jane, please take the Mercedes."

"Whatever you want my boy." She smiled sweetly and patted his shoulder as she passed by.

"See, that's his problem," I said to Jane. "You can't tell him 'whatever he wants.' He now expects me to say that too and that's not happening." I cocked my head and grinned.

"You know I always get my way…eventually."

I knew what he was implying. He still thought he would be able to win me back. I shook my head as he looked at me with his sinfully gorgeous, hooded blue eyes. That look did things to me still. A shiver rippled through my soul. That look made me think about what could have been if he had not walked away from me that September night in New York City. That look made me forget that I was going to be late.

Shit!

"I gotta run. I'll drive myself back, that way I have my car here. If I need to go anywhere I won't have to bother you or Jane." I walked past him at the large granite island. As I did, he grabbed my hand.

"No, call me. Either Jane or I will come get you. I don't want you driving in case you have a contraction."

"I will be fine. There's no sense in either of you having to come all the way back to town. I won't be a burden while I am staying here. I'm perfectly capable of driving myself around." I dropped his hand and walked to the garage.

"Leila, stop. You're not a burden or a bother. You're the mother of my child for Christ's sake. I'm going to make sure you are taken care of, whether you like it or not," he insisted. "Besides, Jane was just talking about going to King Street to do some shopping, so she can swing back by on her way home. No big deal."

Jane chimed in, "It's true, I did want to go to the Open Market. I'll probably be there for a couple of hours, so you may have to wait a little while for me."

"Are you sure?" I felt bad asking her to take me, let alone pick me back up.

"Of course, my sweet girl." She tilted her head.

"Okay, that'll give me some time to pack more clothes."

With that settled, we got in the SUV and drove downtown. I texted Jax to let him know I might be a minute or two late.

We pulled up in front of the condo at noon. I didn't see Jaxon's bike. I unlocked the front door and just as I pushed the door open I heard the rumble of the Shadow Rocket. The sound gave me butterflies in my stomach and set my nerves aflame. I knew I missed him, but seeing him pull up hit me like a Mack truck. Immediately, like the wuss I was, I teared up.

Jaxon turned the key, killing the engine and swung his large jean-clad leg over the bike. He looked so mouth wateringly delicious I wanted to maul him right there on the sidewalk. Then the memories of the past month flooded my mind. My smile fell slightly.

As he walked over to me, I stared, taking him in, all of him. He was truly magnificent. His wide shoulders tapered to his trim waist and in his tight black T-shirt I could almost make out his tightly cut abs. He ran his hands through his unruly blond hair. It had gotten longer in the last month and it looked like he hadn't shaved in a week; he was sporting a sexy, blond scruffy beard.

"Hey," was all I managed and that was barely audible.

"Hey baby." He pulled me to him and wrapped me up in his arms and whispered in my ear. "God, I've missed you so much Leila."

He almost never called me by my first name. I mean, sure he called me Lei or baby girl, princess or babe, but the only time he called me Leila was when shit got serious. Hearing it now caused my stomach to churn.

"I missed you too Jaxon. Let's go inside so we can talk. Drew's not home. We have the place to ourselves." We sat on the sectional in the living room. I wasn't sure even where to start. Thankfully, he started first.

With a deep sigh, he reached for my hand, taking notice of my engagement ring. "I wasn't sure if you'd still be wearing this after how badly I fucked up."

I didn't know what to say so I just shrugged.

"The last few weeks have been really rough. Between not seein' you, knowin' you were probably with him and all the shit that's goin' down with the club. It's completely fucked my head up. I hate how we left things in the hospital. You needed to know if I could deal with our situation, and at the time, I wasn't sure if I could. I've had enough distance, open road and time to know, for sure, that I can." He rubbed his thumb across my knuckles. "I want us back Lei. I know I really fucked up and I hate that I hurt you, but I don't think I'd have been able to come to the realization that I did without putting distance between us. When I'm alone with you I feel like I could deal with anything, but then when he's around you, I just lose it. I hate the way he looks at you. He's still in love with you."

"I'm not going to sit here and tell you he's not, because I know he is, but you have to trust me. I love you. I'm *in* love with you. I'm wearing your ring on my finger." I wiped a stray tear from my cheek. "And I have missed you, I can't deny that, but when I needed you the most you weren't there. Regardless of who was there, you should've been there, holdin' my hand, helpin' me make the decisions and bein' my rock. You allowed him to come between us. You chose to ride off on your bike and stay gone from my world for weeks. I'm really glad you know now that you want us to work this out, but what I can't seem to get over is how easy it was for you to just walk away from me."

No more tears. I had my life to get straight and hormones be damned, I needed to say my piece.

"Now you say you're ready to deal with all of this and that you can deal with Brody being in our lives, but you said this before. Then, when push came to shove you bailed. What's different this time? Why should I believe you? What makes you so sure you won't get fed up again and roll?"

"I understand you're skeptical. I get it babe. I'd be too, but before, I'd never been without you. I didn't know what it felt like to go to sleep without you or waking up alone in our bed. Walking down the hall and not hear you singing in the shower. I've had to live without you for weeks. It's like that saying, you don't know what you have until it's gone. I'll find a way to deal with Brody, but I think the three of us need to sit down and set some boundaries and get on the same page. He needs to know we're together and that he lost his shot."

I groaned. "He already knows all of this, but he doesn't trust you. He didn't trust you before you left me high and dry and he *really* doesn't trust you now."

"I don't care if he trusts me. What I need to know is if you trust me? Can you trust me again? Can you forgive me for screwing up?" Anguish. Expectation. Fear. It was all there, written on his face. "I love you babe. I'll spend the rest of my days trying to make this up to you."

I sat there trying to figure out if I could forgive his deplorable actions with that slut at the club and if I could pardon him for deserting me. I really wasn't sure. He watched me with hope and desperation shining in his jade eyes. He was searching my face for any sign of what I would do. He'd be staring for quite a while for that answer, because I didn't have it. I couldn't tell him what he wanted to hear because I was so confused. He wanted a second chance, but so did Brody. If I could forgive Jaxon, why couldn't I do the same for Brody?

Brody has asked for forgiveness and, slowly, I have forgiven him. I hadn't forgotten what he did, but I realized, I had forgiven him. Essentially they both did the same thing; they left me. The reasons were neither here nor there at this point. Why should Jaxon get a second chance if Brody didn't?

All of these questions swirled in my head as my little girl decided to kick the crap out of my bladder. "I've gotta pee."

I got up and walked toward the bathroom as confusion spread across Jaxon's face. "You gotta pee? Can't it wait a few minutes babe?"

I stopped, spun on my heel and gave him my best are-you-kidding-me face. I looked down to my round belly and back up to him. "Uhh, just a little pregnant here. And she's bouncin' on my bladder like she's Tigger. So, to answer your question, no. I can't wait."

When I returned to the living room, Jaxon was holding the most recent ultrasound picture that I left on the dining room table last week.

"It's amazin' how much I can actually see on this thing now. It used to just be gray and black fuzz with flecks of white thrown in there, but now I can see her face, tiny little fingers and her belly." His eyes shined with tears as he looked down at my stomach. "I can't believe I have missed so much. She's gotten so big."

"You have missed a lot. Four weeks' worth of kicks, stretches, hiccups, middle of the night potty breaks and my new crazy cravings."

"I'm sorry babe."

"You should be." I looked away and walked to the kitchen. I needed the distance. I didn't trust my hormones around him, plus he smelled so damn good. His scent flooded my nostrils, making me reminisce about our mornings together. I loved that smell, but now was not the time to start thinking about him in the shower. His broad, muscular frame as the water rained down over him. Sliding down his tongue worthy abs and the V of his obliques.

Jax stood and watched as I frowned, then shook my head. "You okay?" he asked.

"Huh?" I snapped out of my tormented daydream. "Oh, yeah. I'm fine. Sorry, I was just thinking."

"Why don't we sit and finish our conversation?"

I attempted to sit down gracefully, which was an epic fail. Halfway down I lost my balance and plopped onto the couch. "Ugh, I am so over this pregnancy. I am ready for her to be here."

"Then why take the medicine to stop labor?" Jax asked.

"She's not ready yet." I rubbed my belly.

Jax placed his hand over mine and slipped his fingers between mine. "Okay, so back to us. Can we get back to where we were before I lost my mind? Can you forgive me and take me back?"

I looked down at our hands interlaced together, hating myself for what I was going to do next.

Chapter Twenty-Six

~Leila~

Our hands fit together like a puzzle. He sat there, waiting for my answer with a look that didn't fit Jaxon. He didn't do nervous.

"Listen Jax." I brought my eyes to his as the hope seeped out of them. "I love you, please don't ever doubt how I feel about you. I honestly wish I could tell you what you want to hear and what I want to say, but I can't. Yet. Everything's not straight in my head." I took a deep breath. "I'm tryin' to comprehend how I forgive you what I couldn't forgive Brody. You left me just like he did. Don't you remember what a mess I was? That's exactly what you did to me, but it was so much worse." I could see his frustration setting in. "Don't Jax. This isn't about me wanting or loving Brody. I know where you think this is going, but it's not. Well, I don't think it is."

"Wait, you said it's not about you wanting or loving Brody. You want him? You still love him?" Frustration was gone, replaced with rage and disappointment.

"God, men are such pains in the ass," I said with a groan as I looked up at the heavens above. "No. I just said it's *not* about that. Meaning it has nothing to do with the situation because I don't want him like I want you."

As if someone flipped an emotional switch, the sweet, loving Jaxon was back. "Oh"

"If I'm completely honest, which I want to be, I do think there is a part of me that still does have feelings for him."

Flip…the anger returned.

"He's been taking care of me for the last few weeks. Making sure I have everything I need and he's been really supportive. I thought you abandoned me. And as the days went by, the feelings I used to have for him started to resurface. I know you don't want to hear this, but you need to understand where I'm at in my head."

He watched me with a knitted brow and tight eyes. I knew this was going to be painful, but I needed to be completely forthcoming with my feelings.

"It wasn't like I wanted to start forgiving him or remembering the way things used to be, but it's hard not to. I was in love with him. He fathered my child, Jaxon. And staying with him for the last week…I don't know. It felt like it used to. Well, without the physical aspect."

"Well, I'm glad to know you didn't let him—" He stopped himself before he finished that thought. "I'm glad he didn't touch you. He didn't, did he?"

Well, shit, how did I answer that? If I said no I'd be lying. I woke up with him cuddled up behind me, but if I said yes, I was pretty sure Jaxon would shit a baby goat right here, right now.

Ughhhhh, damn you conscience.

"Uhh, not really." I decided on noncommittal and vague.

He sat up and leaned back slightly. "What the fuck does not really mean Leila?"

I slouched my shoulders and rested my head on the back of the couch. "He held me once, uh, okay twice, but it wasn't in the way you think. It wasn't sexual at all."

"Oh really, then how the fuck was it Lei?" The vein in his forehead was pulsating like a strobe light at a rave.

"Chill out Jaxon. It's not like it seems. The first time was at the hospital after you left me. He had a nightmare that I died and the baby was in danger. He hugged me."

He seemed to soften a little at that, but then his eyebrows rose. "And the other time?"

Well, fuck…Let the shit-show begin. "We were watching a movie in his bed, since I was still having contractions." He groaned. "We both fell asleep since we didn't get a lot of sleep the night before because we were at the hospital and I was having contractions all night. And when I woke up Brody was curled up behind me. Wait. Stop. Don't freak out. He was on top of the blankets and I was under them. It's not a big deal. You and I slept like that a few times when we were just friends."

He stood up and paced. "Yeah, we did. And I wanted to fuck you then. Just like he wants to fuck you now," he roared.

"You're being ridiculous."

"Oh yeah, put yourself in my place Lei." He glared at me.

Oh no, you did not just say that shit to me.

"What the fuck did you just say to me?" I asked with my head cocked angrily to the side. "Myself in your place? Hmm." I paused for dramatics. "Now that you mention it, I'm pretty sure my place was far worse on Valentine's Day, just hours after you asked me to marry you. Picture this Remi," I sneered. "Close your eyes and imagine watching me kiss Brody. Imagine me rubbing my tits all over his face and grinding up and down on his cock."

He stopped pacing and hung his head before sitting back down on the chaise. "That's different," he said quietly.

"Really, how? She fucked you in the past and clearly was trying for the same thing then. Please, explain to me how it's different Remi?"

"Stop. I told you I don't want you calling me that Leila. And it's different because I didn't lay down with her—"

"No, you just let her give you a lap dance. Sorry, I think that's worse. And since I'm the pregnant, hormonal mess that *you* walked out on…"

We were both quietly brooding and I knew the next move was mine. I sat forward and reached for his hand. "Jaxon, I do love you. I do want to find a way to work things out, but I need time. I need to figure everything out in my head. I need to be sure I can get past all of the things you've done in the last month. And I hate to say it, but I need to be sure that the feelings I have for Brody aren't more than I think they are."

Jax took a long, deep breath. "I agree. I want you to be sure you don't have feelings for him, other than him being the father. I'm tryin' to be reasonable, but fuck…it's a bitch."

I could see how torn up he was about not controlling the situation. The Jaxon I knew wanted to thump his chest and claim me as his, but he knew that approach wasn't going to work this time.

"Where are you gonna stay while you're thinking?"

"I'm gonna go back and stay at Brody's. Ruger's already there and Jane is home all day. She has been wonderful, she's so sweet and has taken great care of me. I've really been missing my mom lately and she reminds me of her." Jax sighed as I continued. "Brody's been really good to me and he's only slept in his room with me that once. He's at work all day and half the night, so you don't have to worry about that."

"So what's gonna happen? You're gonna go back and live with him while I'm at our house doing what...waiting?"

"We both know you'll be at the clubhouse or out on runs. So don't try to guilt me into feeling bad and implying you're gonna be sitting around waiting on my decision. I don't appreciate that Jax."

"We both don't know that. I told Mark I needed some time to make things right with you. Although, it seems I've fucked them up beyond what I realized."

"What the hell did you think was gonna happen here Jaxon? That you'd come over and tell me you were done being a twatwaffle and I'd throw my arms open and run to you, like you did nothing wrong? Like this whole seriously fucked up situation didn't start off because you let that cock-juggling cum-dumpster give you a fuckin' lap dance, kiss you and rub her silicone-filled, fake-ass tits all up in your face." I was now standing, waving my hands about like a stark-raving lunatic.

"Well, I sure as shit didn't expect you to tell me you may still have feelings for that fucktard ex of yours. You fuckin' blindsided me with that shit." He stood up, fisting his hands.

Just when I thought things couldn't get any worse, they did. Because again, that was just my luck.

My phone started blaring my ringtone for Brody. Unfortunately, Jaxon knew this too.

"Jesus, I can't have you to myself for an hour without him interfering," he muttered under his breath.

"I heard that," I said as I grabbed my phone and swiped my thumb across the screen. "Hey B, what's up?"

"Hey babe, I just wanted to let you know that I have a meeting this afternoon and it will probably be later than normal when I get home, so I didn't want you waiting for me for dinner. I would have told Jane, but I didn't want to bother her while she was out. Plus, I wanted to see how things were going with you. You okay?"

"Fine. I'll let Jane know when she gets here. Thanks for letting me know about dinner. Things here are fine. I'll see you later at your place, okay?"

"'Kay, sounds good. Let me know if you need anything, all right?"

"I will Brody, see ya." I turned and saw Jaxon calmly sitting on the chaise with his elbows resting on his knees.

"Bye Lei."

"So what did he want this time?" Jaxon questioned.

"He's got a late meeting and wanted to let me know so Jane and I didn't wait for him to eat dinner. He knows how this hungry little peanut"—I talked down to my belly—"makes me cranky when she wants to eat."

"Shit, I didn't even think about it being lunchtime Lei. I'm sorry. Are you hungry? Do you wanna go get lunch?"

"Actually, now that you mention it, I am a little hungry. You want to walk down to the deli?" I asked as I remembered all the times when we went to East Bay Deli.

"I don't know about you walkin' that far. How about I run and pick something up for us?" Jax walked to the kitchen to get the menu. Why we always looked at the menu was beyond me. We both could recite the menu by now and probably half of the prices as well.

"No," I simply stated as I walked over and grabbed my purse off the dining room table.

"No?"

"Nope, I'm walking. You can come with or stay here. Up to you," I said as I reached for the front doorknob.

"Slow down there speed racer, I'm comin'."

We walked, or waddled, depending on to whom you were referring, down the street, got lunch, then returned to the condo. While we were eating our lunch at the deli, Jane called to let me know she'd be over about 2:00 to pick me up. Once we got back, I packed a few more outfits while Jaxon sat on the bed, still griping.

He carried my bag down to the front door just before 2:00 p.m. I was nearly on the verge of tears at the thought of leaving him again. This was going to suck, but I needed to get everything sorted out and make a clear decision.

"All right babe, I'm gonna go. Can I call you later? Ya know, just to check on you?" Jax stood in front of me and tucked a stray curl behind my ear.

"Of course you can." I looked down and leaned forward until the top of my head was placed squarely on his taut chest. He circled his arms around my back and pulled me closer. He held my body tightly against his rippled physique.

"I hate that I have to let you go," he leaned down and murmured in my ear. "But I get it. I love you Leila. Please come back to me."

"I love you too Jaxon. And I want to, but I need to figure it all out first. I won't be any good to anyone until I do." I watched the tears drip off the end of my nose and drop to the top of his black Doc Martens.

He slid his calloused fingers under my chin, tipping it up to look at him. "I'll call you in a little while. Thanks for listenin' to me, babe. I love you."

He slipped his right hand along my jaw into my hair and pulled my lips to his. His kiss started off slow and sensual. My skin tingled from the tips of my toes to the top of my head. He groaned as I traced my tongue along his bottom lip, seeking entry. Tilting my head slightly, he opened his mouth, his tongue darting for mine. I grabbed at the sides of his cut, trying to pull him closer. Our tongues danced around each other and Jaxon sucked in my bottom lip.

By then the kiss was powerful, eager and starved as he nipped at my bottom lip. In that very second, I could feel his genuine regret, his passion and desire for me. I knew if I didn't pull away immediately, I would probably rip his clothes off right there in my foyer and fuck him on the hardwood floor until my knees were raw and splintered.

I pulled away, trying to catch my breath. "You should go," was all I could manage. I tried to take a small, discreet step back. I should've probably gone straight upstairs and changed my panties.

Sensing my arousal Jaxon stepped to me, grabbed my hand and placed it over his hard as a rock erection and murmured, "Tell me you aren't just as turned on as I am from that one kiss. Are you wet for me Lei?"

Oh God, my legs almost buckled. There was a serious chance I was going to have an orgasm just from his words. Heaven help me if he touched me. I'd be a puddle in less than fifteen seconds.

I groaned, breaking his wanton glare. "Ughhh Jax, you have to go. I can't do this."

He pressed his perfect lips against my forehead. "Bye sweetheart." He pulled the door shut behind him as he exited.

I'm so fuckin' screwed.

Chapter Twenty-Seven

~Leila~

Jane arrived shortly after Jaxon left. She couldn't wait to get home and show me her new purchases. She found a set of three beautiful photographs of the St. John's Lutheran Church over on Clifford Street in the Open Market. They almost looked like black and white photographs, featuring an old yet ornate, scrolling wrought iron fence, but the essence of the photos were these tall, vibrant red doors.

It was now about 4:00 and I needed a nap. I was exhausted. I climbed onto the bed, kicked off my sneakers and flicked the TV on and watched long enough to fall asleep.

*****

~Brody~

I finally left the office about 7:45, climbed into the Bentley and sped all the way home. I couldn't wait to see her. Having her at my house was everything I had ever wanted. Well, it was since I came to my damn senses.

I made the worst mistake of my entire life that night. I was so shocked by the news of her pregnancy that it sent me back to a time when I had let Jenifer get too close to me and she had claimed to be pregnant with my child. Of course it wasn't my child, hell, she wasn't even pregnant. I knew she was sleeping with other men at the time, but she insisted it was my child and could only have been my child. I knew then she was a gold digging whore. She was a special sort of stupid if she thought I was going to fall for that shit. She wanted to get married before she started showing, to "save appearances" as she put it.

Anyway, it was a year before, in the same penthouse in New York, standing in almost the same spot that Leila had stood, that Jenifer made her little declaration. I never told Leila any of this because I knew she hated Jenifer already, but tonight she needed to know the whole truth. She needed to know why I had flipped out the way I did and why I walked away.

It was a reason, though, not an excuse. There were no excuses for my atrocious behavior. I fucked up, royally. I had been trying over the last couple of months to make amends and win myself back into her good graces, but every time I got close, that dickhead Jaxon, would do something to screw it all up. He constantly goaded me into verbal sparring matches. So I pushed back. His stupid club would be having some significant real estate issues if he didn't chill the fuck out.

I pulled into the garage and killed the engine. I practically ran up the stairs to my bedroom. Opening the door, I heard the TV and expected to see her sitting propped up by a mountain of pillows watching some sappy show.

She was propped up in a shitload of pillows, but she was fast asleep. As I walked to the side of the bed and sat down, her lips slowly turned up into a tiny smile but faded quickly. She must have been dreaming. She was so amazingly beautiful, it took my breath away. She lay there, turned slightly on her left side, facing the door, her right hand atop her stomach, swollen with our daughter, while her left hand still had her phone resting loosely in it.

I sat there, watching her sleep for several minutes before I saw her belly twitch on the right side, just below her ribs. I could see a little bumping movement. Pulling back the soft gray cotton shirt, I sat in total astonishment as I watched our child move around inside of her mother's womb. I could see the little bump slide around, then disappear. Leaning down, I whispered quietly to her.

"Hi my sweet girl. Daddy can't wait to see you and hold you and love on you. We didn't have a great start and that's my fault. I was scared to let myself get close to someone again and have it turn out like last time. But this time you're real and you're all mine." I wiped a tear from my cheek.

"I promise you, right here and now, I am your daddy and I always will be. I promise baby girl I will not become my father. I could never hurt you like that. No matter what, I will never leave you until there is no air left in my lungs and my heart ceases to beat. I will love you fiercely, protect you always and support you endlessly."

As I finished my little speech, I felt her eyes on me. I looked up and realized she was indeed awake and listening to my rambling.

"How long have you been listenin'?" I secretly hoped she hadn't heard the whole spiel. I wanted to tell her about my father and the previous pregnancy scare, not have her overhear it.

*****

~Leila~

"Long enough. I'm sorry. Actually, I'm not sorry. I loved listening to you talk to her. You're gonna be such a good dad. I didn't mean to overhear the other stuff though. Why didn't you tell me before? I mean, about your dad? What did he do to you Brody?"

He sighed and I felt a hundred pounds of sorrow wash over him. "What he did to me wasn't nearly as bad as what he did to my mom. They always appeared to be the perfect couple. He was careful. He never let the mask slip in public." Brody hung his head as he continued. "He wasn't always an abusive asshole. My mom said he used to be caring and loving."

"What changed?"

"It was my fault that he hit her."

"Why would you think that?"

"She told me. He'd never hit her until I was a few months old. I had colic really bad and no matter what she did, I would cry all night. Over the years, it got worse. If I messed up or failed at something he would hit her. He never hit me, but he would tell me that she cried because of me."

Brody stood and paced the room. "When I was eight or nine, it was so bad I ran into their room and found her on the floor, bleeding, with him standing over her. I pushed him away and lay on top of her, you know, trying to protect her. That's the first time he told me that when I got married and my wife gave me a son that was such a horrible disappointment I would understand why he did what was necessary."

"Oh my God, Brody." My heart broke for the poor little boy who was killing himself every day at work trying to please a ghost.

"So when you told me you were pregnant, I kept hearing his voice in my head. Laughing at me, haunting me, telling me that I was going to follow in his footsteps. That I would be him."

He sat at the edge of the bed. "A few months before I met you, Jenifer tried to rope me in with a false pregnancy. When I lost it with her and threw her out, I thought I was justified based on her behavior. Back then I thought I was nothing like my father. But after that time I blew up at you on the patio in the middle of the night I wasn't so sure. And when you told me you were pregnant...well, we know how that went. I literally couldn't control myself. It was like an out of body experience."

For a few long moments I couldn't speak. What do you say to that? "Two things," I said as I leaned forward. "You are not your father. You don't want to be your father and I think you now know how to handle the emotional baggage he left you with. And if you need help getting a better handle on it, there are a few really great therapists I know that can help you get where you want to be."

He didn't look thrilled at the suggestion, but, to his credit, he nodded his head. "And the other thing?"

"You're going to make a great father, Brody. I have no doubt about that."

At my words, he looked at me with disbelief then turned to stare at his knee. "I never thought I'd hear you say that. I've screwed up so badly that I didn't think you'd ever believe I'd be a good father." He shook his head. "And Lei, what I told you was an explanation, not an excuse. There's no excuse for the way I treated you." He looked up at me, his beautiful blue eyes shining with unshed tears.

"I know I've said it before, but I'm so sorry babe. There are so many things I wish I had done differently. So many things I'm sorry for about that night. For screaming at you, throwing the bottle and scaring you. God, I hated the way you looked at me, but most of all for letting you walk away and not stopping you. God, watching you walk through the lobby, crying, it nearly killed me. I wanted to run after you, but I was so fucked up. I couldn't get out of my own head long enough to see I was letting the best thing that had ever happened to me just walk away. Jesus Lei, if I could go back and…"

He stopped. I sat there waiting, praying he would finish what he was about to say. "If you could go back?"

"If I could go back to that night in the penthouse, I would have said that I love you. That even though we weren't expecting this, I would take care of you and we'd be a family. I would've told you that I was terrified of being a dad and screwing up, but that with you as her mom, she'd be perfect. I should've told you that before you, my life was futile and monotonous, and after you came along, it was vivacious and complete. You fulfilled me in such a way I finally realized how empty I was before I walked into that waiting room and saw your gorgeous face. I would've made love to you all over that penthouse."

He turned and looked at me as if I were the answer to all his prayers. That look melted all of my defenses away and in that moment, I want nothing more than for him to kiss me.

"I should have done this." As if he were reading my mind, he reached over and brushed his hand along my jawline, then around to circle my neck and pull me to him. His mouth found mine. Gently sucking on my bottom lip he traced it lightly with his tongue. My body took over, and instinctively, I wrapped my arms around his wide lats, pulling him closer.

A deep groan resonated in his chest as I tilted my head and deepened the kiss. Feeling his warm tongue meet mine, my legs shuddered. His tongue expertly tantalized and tangled with mine. The sensation shot directly between my legs. I could feel his passion and hunger as he lifted me to him, pressing my swollen breasts to his tight washboard abs.

I moaned into his mouth as he laid me down and stood over me watching, waiting for a sign as to what to do. Then, without any warning or indication, he crawled over me. His mouth captured mine, then moved to my neck with warm, wet kisses from my ear to my collarbone. His tongue traced back up to my ear as he nibbled my earlobe. I tipped my head back and ran my fingers through his dark, unruly locks. And just as my inner lioness started to purr her approval, he stopped and all but leapt off of me.

"Fuck Lei, I shouldn't've done that." He looked so torn.

"What?" I said incredulously, sitting up on my elbows. "You shouldn't have kissed me?"

"Baby, it's not fair to you. I knew better, but I just couldn't help myself. I have wanted to do that since that night. That night that I destroyed everything." He looked at me with such guilt. "But Lei, you're still wearing Jaxon's ring. I want nothing more than to make love to you right now, but when we make love, and we will," he said cockily, "you won't be wearing his ring. You'll be mine, in my bed, in my heart and in my life. Forever."

Good one. Open the floodgates to my heart, and my panties. Then, right on cue, the rushing river of regret and guilt followed right behind.

And with the world's worst timing, in strolled Damon, Brody's best friend. "Knock, knock. S'up kids?"

I groaned and climbed out of bed to leave the room.

Brody cleared his throat and grabbed my hand before I got too far. "D can you give us just a few minutes? We were just in the middle of something."

Damon chuckled quietly. "From the look in your eyes and looks of her hair, you might need more than a few minutes B."

"Oh my God." I rolled my eyes at his crassness. "I'm going downstairs Brody. You know, to feed our child. We can finish our conversation later."

"Wait babe, don't go. Let's finish this now, I still have something I need to say to you," he pleaded and almost won, but then Damon's big mouth started flapping again.

"Oh, yeah, congratulations Leila. I hadn't seen you since this dumb fucker here screwed you over." He tossed his head in Brody's direction.

"Thanks D, I almost forgot" He flipped Damon the finger.

"And on that note, I'm going to eat. You boys have fun."

I exited the room and made my way downstairs. Jane was sitting at the table, reading on her tablet as I padded quietly on the hardwood floors into the kitchen. I had hoped to just grab a quick bite without disturbing her.

"Oh my sweet girl, you should know by now you can't sneak past me." I smiled, her words reminding me of something my mother would have said. She got up from the table and walked over to me.

"What can I make you? There is stuff for salads or there's leftovers from the other night."

"Actually, I really just want a glass of milk and ice cream." I shrugged.

"Well, I guess it's a good thing Brody had me stop yesterday and get some, huh?"

"Ooh, what did you get?"

"Butter crunch. He said that was your favorite this month." She grinned as she walked over and opened the mammoth refrigerator. She pulled out the milk and poured a glass. Then she pulled out the ice cream and, sure enough, there was my craving of the day.

"He's so sweet to remember." I smiled.

"What am I sweet to remember?" Brody came around the corner with Damon following.

"Who said I was referring to you Mr. Cocky?" I waggled my head, sitting on a barstool.

Brody walked up behind me and began massaging my shoulders lightly. "Let's just say I have my ways. Besides, your eyes light up when you talk about me."

Both Jane and I laughed. "Wow, if your head gets any bigger you're gonna have to trade your cars for convertibles."

As I took a sip of my milk he leaned forward and whispered into my ear, "From what I remember, you like my big head."

As I choked on my milk, he chuckled and walked to the refrigerator. Clearing my throat, I asked, "So what are you and Damon gettin' into tonight?"

"I came by to see if B wanted to get a drink and hang out for a little." Damon came over and sat next to me at the raised counter.

Brody started shaking his head and I could see he was going to decline, but he needed to get out and I needed some time to think. I needed to figure out what the hell I was going to do.

"I think that sounds like a great idea Damon. He needs to go out and relax." I turned my attention to Brody. "You do. You need to go hang out with the boys and get away from all of this craziness. Other than going to work, you've been stuck with me for a week."

He pursed his lips and cocked his head. "I'm not stuck with you Leila. This is where I've wanted to be. And if things weren't crazy at work, I would've blown that off too."

"Well, I'm telling you to go out for a drink. It's only one drink and you'll be back here in a few hours. Besides, I'm gonna eat my ice cream, take a bath and get in bed."

"Yeah, listen to her B. It's just a few drinks and we'll be back before you know it," Damon added. "Unless you're afraid of losing a few games of pool."

Brody threw his head back and laughed. "Shit, that was good." He pretended to wipe a tear from his face. "You, beat me, in pool? Nah bro, I don't think so."

He looked over to me and I nodded toward Damon, silently telling him to go.

"All right D-bag, let me grab my coat, but two drinks and one game of pool, then right back here," Brody declared.

"Deal. I'll drive." Damon turned to me. "Lei, thanks for the assist. Take care and don't pop that kid out before we get back." He smiled his million megawatt smile.

"I'll see what I can do, but I make no promises," I teased back.

Brody's eyes came damn close to bugging out of his head. "I'll have my phone. If you start having contractions again, call me. I'll come straight home."

"Relax, I'm not gonna—arrgghhh," I screamed out, hunching forward and clutched my tummy.

"Holy fuckin' shit man!" Damon jumped off his barstool and away from me like I just spontaneously caught on fire.

Brody sprinted to my side. "Contraction?"

I straighten with a huge smile stretched across my face. "Nah, just messin' with ya. Go have fun, I'm fine."

"Jesus Christ Leila. Don't do that. You freaked me the fuck out," he admonished as I grinned like the Cheshire cat. "Why are you still smiling? It's not funny damn it."

I struggled not to burst out laughing. Finally, when he left the kitchen, Jane and I lost it; we laughed 'til we cried.

"You do know I can still hear y'all up here, right?" Brody scolded us from the top of the stairs. This just made us cackle louder.

"Oh God, I have to stop, I can't breathe," Jane huffed with a bright red face.

"You?" I giggled. "I think I might actually pee in my pants. I better go to the bathroom before I do." When I came back from the bathroom Brody and Damon were standing around by the garage door.

"Jesus woman, what were you doing in there?" Brody taunted.

"Well, gee, let's see if I can explain this again." I planted my hand on my round tummy. "I'm almost nine months pregnant and my bladder is officially the size of a walnut"—I tapped my index finger on my lips—"because you knocked me up. So now I pee every twenty minutes. Oh, and because you knocked me up, I'm as big as a house or as big as your ego, which coincidentally are about the same size. So, if you must know, it can sometimes be difficult for me to pull my pants up."

"I think it's time you boys go and leave us girls alone to relax," Jane piped up.

Brody came over and rubbed my belly. "Bye my sweet girls." He looked down at me. "I'll have my cell, but I won't be late."

"Go, we'll be just fine. Stop stressing." I pushed him toward Damon. "Help me out Damon."

"Come on dude, before you actually hand over your balls willingly," Damon said, ragging on Brody. He earned himself a swift, stiff right jab to the shoulder. "Damn, man. Fuckin' with ya. Jesus."

"All right fucker, let's roll. Lei." He looked over his shoulder with hooded eyes. "We will finish our conversation when I get home."

I tried so hard not to smile as I shook my head. The not smiling? Epic fail. I was in a ton of trouble. I needed to figure this shit out and fast.

Chapter Twenty-Eight

~Leila~

Jane and I sat in the family room on the sofa watching TV as Ruger gnawed on a thick bone on the floor. It was around 10:00 p.m. when I decided to call it a night. As I started to leave Jane stopped me, taking my hand in her well-manicured fingers.

"If you're still awake when Brody gets home, I do wish you would speak with him dear. He's trying so hard to do right by you both. Please just hear him out. He's not been the same since you left." Jane frowned.

"What do ya mean?"

"The first month after you left here, he did nothing but go to work, come home, and drink that nasty scotch until he passed out. Then he'd wake up the next morning, usually in the study at the desk. He'd take a shower, then repeat the process again."

"Oh," I squeaked out softly. I wasn't sure what else to say.

Jane continued. "Around November it started to get better. He didn't seem as angry. He started talking to me again. When I say talking I mean he would give me more than the yes or no answers he had been during the first month.

"He told me everything that happened in New York. I tried to help him, but he wouldn't listen to anyone. The good Lord above could've come down himself and Brody would've just shrugged it off."

"I appreciate what you're trying to do Jane. I do. But I just don't know if I can trust him with my heart again." My throat constricted as I spoke.

"Oh Leila, I know he messed up something horrible baby, but I genuinely believe everyone deserves a second chance."

"That's the problem Jane. If I give him a second chance, then it stands to reason that Jaxon should get one too." I sighed and slouched back into the couch. "I don't know what to do. I mean, if it was just me, that'd be one thing. But I have this tiny human growing inside of me to think about, and I want better for her than what I had." I rubbed my belly as the peanut turned over.

"My dad walked out on my mom and left her alone with two kids. Now I have two men, who claimed to love me, and they both walked out on me. Granted, they both came back, but what's to stop them from doing it again. I don't want my daughter feeling like it's her fault."

"I'm sure your momma told you on more than one occasion, his leaving wasn't your fault, but if not, I'm saying it now. That was not your fault. You can't punish either of them for what your dad did honey, they're not the same men." She leaned back and tucked her feet under her on the soft, gray suede couch. "I don't know Jaxon. I don't know anything about how you feel about him or how he treats you. For those reasons alone, I can't help you make this decision. And I wouldn't anyway. That is for you to decide. Just be true to yourself and follow your heart. Love never fails."

I leaned over and wrapped Jane up in my arms and whispered, "Thank you."

"Anytime, sweet girl. Brody's not the only one here who loves you." She pulled away and held my face between her hands. "Regardless of what you decide, I will always be there for you. Now go, get some sleep and I will see you at breakfast tomorrow."

"G'night Jane."

"Sweet dreams honey." She picked up her tablet and cleared our glasses. Shortly after I climbed in bed, I heard her tell Ruger to go to bed. A minute later a cold wet nose nudged my arm.

"Come on, big dog, hop up here for a little since B's not here to holler at us." I patted the bed and he hopped up. He curled up in the crook of my legs. I picked up my tablet from the bedside table and noticed my indicator light was flashing on my phone. Two missed calls, one from Barb and one from Jaxon.

I called Jax back first, and he answered on the third ring. The noise in the background was so loud I wondered how he would even be able to hear me.

"Hey babe." His voice made me shiver.

"Hey Jax. You busy? I just wanted to call you back, but if you're busy you can call me tomorrow."

"Nah, I'm good. You wanna talk?" he asked.

As I got ready to say yes, I heard a woman's voice. "Hey Remi you wanna another beer babe?"

"Well, I was gonna say yeah, but it sounds like you're a little busy. I'll letcha go. Call me when you're done with your lap dance."

"Wait!" he yelled into the phone. "It's not what you're thinkin' Lei. I swear."

"Yeah, that's what you said last time." I was about to hang up when he stopped me.

"I'm sitting at the bar with Viper and Mark. It was the bartender babe. Hand to God. You can ask my brothers," he insisted.

"No, I know they'd say anything you wanted them to. Seriously, just do whatever it is you're doing. It's none of my business Jax. Call me tomorrow and we'll talk then. Good night."

"Leila just wait a min—" He tried to stop me before I hung up. Unfortunately for him, I wasn't in the mood.

"Think I'll just read for a while Ru. I guess I need to get used to you being the one who cuddles with me at night again, huh buddy?" Ruger opened his eyes slightly, sighed and curled back down into the bed.

My phone chimed as a text came in from Jaxon. He told me he'd try to call me tomorrow but that he had some club business to handle and he'd be on the road for the next week or so. I sent him a text back, with all of the hostility and passive aggression I could muster.

Well if you can pull yourself away from your ever more important club business, then by all means call. If not, I get it. The club comes first. Be safe.

It wasn't long before he replied.

Babe pls dont b like that. u know its business, I cant say no. I promise I WILL call u 2moro I love u Lei

I was tired and cranky at this point.

U can say no, u just choose not 2. Just like when I was n the hosp u chose 2 walk away. not me YOU. u cld say no but u wont. the club will always come 1st w/u. & I dont know if I can accept that

I didn't wait for a reply this time. I set the phone on the bedside table and opened my tablet to forget it all for a while and just read.

I heard the buzz of the phone vibrating on the bedside table. Even though I told myself I wasn't going to look, I looked.

Leila u come 1st. I'll expln evrythng when we talk. I cldnt hv said no, but this business is almst done. And 4 the record u & OUR daughter will always come 1st. I cnt say anymore rght now but I WILL expln. Evrythng ive done, ive done for us. Pls wait & let me expln 2moro. I love you. pls remember that.

I read and reread his text. It felt cryptic. Everything he's done, he's done for us. What the hell does that mean? I lay there trying to understand his message. Before too long, I was out cold.

*****

~Jaxon~

Feeling her slipping away, I decided I needed to try to explain what was going on without giving her too many specifics. I was stressing about her reaction. It was entirely possible she'd walk away when she found out the truth. When she found out what I had been doing all this time.

Looking down at the text she sent, I ordered another beer. Viper just shook his head. "Damn man, never thought I'd see the day when you were so fuckin' pussy whipped."

"Fuck off V. Maybe if Barb would let you get close to something other than her fuckin' pussy you'd get it."

"Nah. Don't need it. Don't want it. Only thing she wants is my dick, and I'm good with that. Ain't got time for any-fuckin'-thing else."

"You got no clue man. When you finally get it, and I mean really get it, you won't care who thinks you're pussy whipped or thinks you've handed over your nuts. The only thing that will matter is her."

"That's never happenin' man. Never," Viper said with a chuckle.

Finishing my beer, I dragged myself from the bar to my room here at the compound. It was a small barebones room with only a bed and dresser. Attached to the room was a small bathroom with a stand-up shower, sink and toilet, more than enough for me when I decided to crash here.

Entering the bathroom, I reached in and turned on the hot water, stripped down and stepped past the clear shower curtain into the steamy water. Standing there in the three-by-three-foot area, I let the water cascade over my face. The stress of the last few weeks hung from my shoulders like forty-five pound plates. Once I could tell her the truth, it would lighten the burden. The worst part was not knowing if telling her the truth will endanger her or our relationship.

Drying off, I pulled on a pair of athletic shorts from the top dresser drawer, checked my phone one last time and climbed into bed. I tossed and turned most of the night before I finally found sleep.

*****

~Leila~

The clock read 12:49 a.m. when I woke up and Brody was climbing into his bed with me. I started to protest, but then he tucked in behind me. Under the comforter this time. I was wearing a thin, spaghetti strapped tank and pajama pants. Jaxon's pajama pants to be exact. From what I could feel, Brody only had on boxer briefs. He wrapped his arm around me and pulled me back against him, nuzzling into the crook of my neck. When he started to babble incoherently, I could smell the alcohol on him.

"God Lei, I miss you so fuckin' much it hurts. I know I said I needed you to be sure, but I just want to hold you and never let you go. I can't think straight 'cause you're all I think about. I know I'm an asshole and I don't deserve you, but for tonight can we just pretend I didn't fuck up. Just for a few hours let me hold you," he pleaded.

I was no closer to a decision than I was yesterday. I tried to figure it out, but I was so torn. I loved Jaxon, but some part of me might still love Brody. If I let myself be here in this moment with Brody I knew the remorse would eat me alive. I wasn't sure if things were completely done with Jaxon and I still wore the flawless diamond engagement ring he gave me on Valentine's Day. I could see the hurt and pain on Jaxon's face if I'd have to tell him about such an intimate moment with Brody.

Ugh. What do I do?

Just then I heard Jane's voice in my head. *Follow your heart. Love never fails.*

If I could quiet the raging, sex-starved lioness in my panties, I might just be able to hear my heart.

"Baby?" Brody was waiting for an answer. Only I didn't have one. I wanted so badly to just enjoy the moment and just feel. Not think. Not decide. Just hold onto him and give into my desires, but all I could think about was Jaxon's text. *Pls wait.* I had to put a stop to all of this and figure this out because it wasn't fair to Brody or Jaxon.

"Brody, you're drunk. I don't think this is a good idea," I tried to reason with him. "You need to go get some sleep. Please."

And by doing that I was making a decision. The fact of the matter was that they both screwed up, royally. They've both apologized and swore to fix it. Brody had pushed everything and everyone aside when I needed him. When we needed him, he stepped up. But Jaxon rearranged his whole life for me just a few short months ago. He built us a home. A nursery. I wasn't sure if I could handle the club business bullshit. It was always super-secret squirrel shit with him, which required a massive level of trust.

But if I can get past Brody's fuck-up, then I should be able to get over Jaxon's. Right?

While I was waging war in my own head, Brody was still lying half-naked behind me. "You want me to go?"

His hurt rang out loud and clear. I knew after he kissed me things would get confused and fucked up. I didn't want to hurt him, but I needed to be honest.

"Brody you've been drinking and we need to all sit down and talk. I can't keep doing this. It's stressing me out and I can't take it. Please, can we just talk in the morning?" I begged.

He was quiet for a minute. "Yeah, all right." He sighed loudly and rolled out of the bed. "We gotta get this shit figured out Lei 'cause this"—he motioned between us—"this shit is fuckin' me up." Then he left.

Chapter Twenty-Nine

~Leila~

It was Monday morning just after 8:00 a.m. I assumed Brody had already left for work, so I started getting myself ready for my day. After finishing in the bathroom, I walked into Brody's closet, where he insisted I put my clothes. The dresses Brody bought me late last summer still hung delicately from the velvet hangers. The dazzling Jimmy Choos sat below. He never replaced his clothes in the space he cleaned out for me. I pulled a pair of maternity jeans off the hanger and grabbed a fitted white cowl-neck sweater. I was sitting on the upholstered chair in the closet struggling to reach my feet to put socks on when I heard him.

"You want some help with that?"

I looked up and there he stood. As sexy as the day was long, in his black Dolce & Gabbana suit, crisp white shirt and charcoal tie.

"No. I can do this," I said, looking back down. I tried to lean further toward my foot. I was infuriated that I couldn't even reach my own feet anymore. "Ya know what, this is bullshit. I don't need socks anyway. I'm gonna wear my flip-flops."

I gave up and threw the socks on the floor in a tizzy. I got my fat ass up off the chair and retrieved my flip-flops.

"It's okay to ask for help or accept it when it's offered." He looked on annoyed. "Jane has breakfast ready."

"Yeah, all right. I'll be there in a minute." I said and glared at him.

He shook his head and muttered something on his way out of the closet. I thought about asking what his problem was, but thought better of it. I needed to eat before I got into with him about last night.

After breakfast Brody left for the office. We barely spoke all morning. Around noon, my phone rang.

"You want me to grab that for you sweetie?" Jane popped up from the couch next to me in the living room, where we were listening to music and chatting.

She was already halfway there. "Could you please so it doesn't go to voicemail."

"Hello?" she said and walked back toward me.

"Of course dear, she's right here. Everything is fine. She was just on the couch. You know, she doesn't move too quickly these days." Holding out the phone, she said, "It's Jaxon honey."

"Thanks Jane." I took the phone as I tried to get off the couch. My feet were tucked under me so I was having some difficulties.

"You stay there, I was gonna take Ruger out to the barn to check on the horses." Jane turned, whistled and exited through the French doors onto the veranda.

"Hey," I spoke softly.

"Hi baby. You okay?" His rough voice, shot straight to my core.

"Yeah, better now." I settled back down into supple leather. "Where are you?"

"It's best you not know right now. I know I said I'd explain and I will, but first you need to know that I meant what I said. Baby, you come first, but there was shit going down that I had no control over. Heavy shit, but this bullshit's almost over. I can't go into specifics. All I can tell you is that we think someone within the club is trying to use our connections to run their own shit. That's all I can say and I shouldn't've said that much, but I owed you some sort of explanation. Once it's settled things'll go back to normal. I'll be home more." He sounded sincere.

"Jaxon, I get something's going down, but I needed you. Fighting or not, I was scared and I *needed* you more than anyone else. I really want to be able to forgive you, but in order to do that you need to be here. Fighting for me. For us."

"Babe, if you can just hang in there for a little while longer I will be. We're so close. And then I'll be home and we can get this shit figured out."

My pregnancy-hormone-haze brain to mouth filter stopped working. Because before I knew it, I blurted out, "Brody is still in love with me and wants me to move back in here with him permanently. He wants us to move in here. Me and the baby."

Oh goodie. That was smart Leila. Antagonize the poor man while he's in God only knows what sort of danger.

"Okay," he gritted out. "I pretty much knew that since he waltzed his preppy ass back into our life Lei. Did you figure this out all on your own or did he tell you?"

Wait one fucking minute...who in the hell was I on the phone with? My Jaxon would have flipped his shit.

"Uhh, um, well, he sort of said it yesterday. He also wants all of us to sit down and hash this out." I stumbled over my words still reeling from his reaction. Or lack thereof.

"Good, I told you I do too. But before we do that, you need to sit down with him and tell him straight up that you're mine."

"Am I? Yours?" I asked sincerely. Honestly, I didn't know the answer to that question anymore.

"What?" he asked in disbelief. "What did you just ask me?"

"I asked if I was still yours. I've seen you, what, maybe twice in the last five weeks. Talked to you maybe a handful of times." I was starting to get upset. "That doesn't seem like any sort of relationship to me. For God's sake, you didn't even come to the hospital that night. Club or not, I begged you." I couldn't help it, I sobbed. "In voicemail after voicemail, I pleaded. For the last five weeks we haven't been together. So yeah, I am asking you for a serious answer. Am I still yours? Because for the last month I haven't thought you were mine. You certainly haven't acted like it."

"You. Are. Mine. I don't care if I don't see or talk to you for a week, two hundred days, three years or two decades. You will always be mine. No amount of time or distance will ever change that Leila. Does that answer your question?"

I thanked God we are on the phone. He was seething.

"It answers the question." Yep. Brain to mouth was broken. I poked the angry, snarling bear. "But you should know, since you haven't communicated that prior to now, I thought we were over."

"What does that mean Leila? You're telling me something without saying it?" He was quiet for a minute, then the bear lashed out. *I think he may have ESP.*

"Son of a motherfuckincocksuckin' bitch. You fucked him?" he roared through the phone. So much so I had to pull the phone back.

"You let that piece of shit, no good motherfucker touch *my* fuckin' pussy? Because that is *mine!*"

"Shut up Jax!" I yelled back, but he was still cussin' and muttering things about killing Brody slowly. "Please just listen."

"I swear to Christ Leila." But he finally stopped.

"No. I did not sleep with him, fuck him or let him touch me like you are thinkin' Jaxon." *Okay, here goes nothing.* "But he did kiss me."

The line was silent. It was so quiet I pulled the phone back to see if the call was still connected. I pressed the phone back to my ear. "Are you there?"

I heard a long sigh. "Yeah. Did ya kiss him back? How many times he kiss you? When did it start?" He was eerily calm now.

Well, fuck me. Why did he have to ask all this shit?

"Yes. One time. Yesterday," I answered quickly in the hopes to skim over the yes.

Silence.

"Jaxon?"

"Yeah babe?" he rasped, one syllable at a time.

"Why does everything always seem to be so hard? Why can't we just have a normal relationship like we used to?" I asked.

"I don't know Leila. I want, more than anything, for us to be good." He paused. I felt a but coming on. "But we aren't right now. And I'm not sure how to fix what I've broken. What we've broken."

He was right. He didn't do this alone. My situation with Brody was a big part of our issue. He was the main problem for our fights. Well, that and the club.

"But I want to baby. More than I want my next breath. I don't wanna come home one more time and walk through our house and not see you there. I don't want to go to sleep in our bedroom alone." He stopped for a minute. "Come home. To me. Let me fix this."

"I want to Jaxon. I do, but you're not there. You're never there anymore." I fought the tears. "If I thought you'd be there and not turn around and ride out for the club, I would come home. But right now I need someone with me at all times. Someone to take care of me in case something happens or I start having contractions again. And you can't do that."

"But he can," he says abrasively.

"Jane can, and she lives here. Yes, Brody is helping to take care of me, but, honestly, it's mostly Jane. She's become like a second mom to me Jax, and I really need that," I explained.

"'Cept that she's probably telling you that you belong to him."

I knitted my brow together. "Actually, her exact words were, 'Just be true to yourself and follow your heart. Love never fails.' She's really wonderful Jax. I can't wait for you to meet her because she's gonna be in our lives, like a grandma to this little girl."

"Listen babe, I hate to say it, but—"

"No, please don't say it," I begged.

"I gotta go baby. I don't wanna but I gotta. I've ignored three calls and a shitload of texts. Prez is probably flippin'. I'll try to call you back later tonight. I'm gonna get this shit wrapped up and come and get you. I love you Leila."

Well, that did it. My resolve shattered and I cried.

"Baby please don't cry. You're killing me here. I'll see you soon. I promise. Later babe."

"Bye Jax. I love you too. Please be careful." I wiped tears away with the sleeve of my sweater.

After ending the call I sat and reflected on how I felt, knowing he wanted me back and knowing that's what I wanted too. As I sat there glowing, basking in the knowledge that somehow, some way Jax and I would find our way back to each other, my daughter rolled and dragged her tiny foot across my tummy.

Looking down, I realized that if I decided to forgive Jaxon and take him back, I was going to have to break it to Brody, my little girl's father. He had changed so much over the past several months. He had become the doting, expectant father.

He opened up to me and became the man that I once fell in love with. He was charming, charismatic, funny and sweet. He was everything I ever thought I wanted in a husband and father. The thought of hurting him gave me a physical pain in my chest and made me nauseous. I felt my heart breaking at just the thought of possibly telling him I was going back to Jaxon.

That kiss we shared was mind blowing and made me think of all of the things we could have been.

Sitting there watching my stomach stretch in different direction, I wondered how to choose between the man who stole my heart and the one who imprinted himself on my soul. I couldn't help but think of Brody and how we had made this tiny miracle, together. It was in that moment I realized that I still loved him, despite what I told Jaxon.

I needed Drew. Whenever I was in turmoil Drew was my go-to. This would be the most important, life altering decision of my life. I needed to vent and he was the only one who would truly understand my issues trusting Brody or Jaxon again.

I never would have believed I could be in love with two people at the same time. Two very different people.

But, sitting here, I realized I was.

And I hated myself for it.

LEILA, JAXON, AND BRODY'S STORY CONTINUES IN

TORN,

COMING FALL 2015!

ABOUT THE AUTHOR

A.F. Crowell's love of books did not start until her husband forced her to watch *Twilight* one weekend when they were snowed in. From there her love only grew. Contemporary romance, paranormal, YA, and dystopian are her preferred reads, but she also loves Patricia Cornwell novels. *Pushed* is her debut and the first book in the Torn Series. It will be followed by *Pulled*, book two, and *Torn*, book three.

Crowell lives in Charleston, SC, with her husband and also her two boys, who at seven and eleven share her love of reading. The family has two dogs, Diesel, a German Shepherd rescue, and Dez, a black Labrador Retriever.

For more information on release dates and upcoming work, please visit:
www.facebook.com/authorafcrowell
twitter.com/AuthorAFCrowell
boroughspublishinggroup.com/authors/af-crowell

Did you enjoy this book? Drop us a line and say so! We love to hear from readers, and so do our authors. To connect, visit www.boroughspublishinggroup.com online, send comments directly to info@boroughspublishinggroup.com, or friend us on Facebook and Twitter. And be sure to check back regularly for contests and new releases in your favorite subgenres of romance!

Are you an aspiring writer? Check out www.boroughspublishinggroup.com/submit and see if we can help you make your dreams come true.